WAR'S
TROPHIES
A Vietnam Novel

By Henry Morant

DEDICATION

To Lyndon Johnson, Richard Nixon and Henry Kissinger, without whose folly this tale would not have been possible. And to two real pathfinders, Jacquelin Singh and Don Berry. Additional thanks to BBQ, ADW and DA for their eagle eyes. And let's not forget two great children and a great son-in-law.

DISCLAIMER

Prologue – The Black Virgin Winds Up The Charm, 1966

The first human to be framed in Jeremy Hall's M-16 rifle gun sight slipped through the barely opened louvered door cautiously, shyly. First a hand on the door. Then a face for a look about. Then the full figure.

The figure came directly at him.

Not a sly barefoot sapper wearing only shorts and a satchel charge who stayed low and picked his way professionally through the night that was brightly illuminated by a full moon, a real hunter's moon. Nor a careless guerrilla on a jungle path. That's what Hall was in Vietnam to shoot, what he wanted to shoot.

This was a shy figure walking primly from a house.

Having decided to slip into the night, the figure walked smartly to get its business finished and return.

It was now beyond the intermediate shadow thrown by a large mango tree and 30 yards from the dirt berm behind which Hall waited. Its middle was thrust out and its arms swung way out rapidly. Like a Vietnamese woman.

A small Vietnamese woman.

A girl!

Dressed only in shiny black pajama bottoms. Her black hair shoulder length.

Hall pulled his head back from the rear sight and looked to his right.

Captain Wozniak lay behind the same berm about 10 yards away. The Backatya Boy Buu was another 10 yards beyond Wozniak.

Hall looked left. Backatya Boy Hau waited. Backatya Boys Nguyen and Ky had been dispatched to set up the ambush on the small village's main path.

"My ace in the hole. Always have that ace in the hole," Hall had heard Wozniak grunt as the two Backatya Boys slithered away in the mud a klick or two outside Ap Thuy Tu.

Now Hall, Wozniak, Buu and Hau waited on line behind the same berm, the boundary where the rice fields ended and the village began. Nguyen and Ky were to be in position by 0222 hours,

1

Wozniak had ordered.

The last time Hall looked at his watch -- just before the figure had slipped from its door -- it was 2:15 a.m.—only lifers thought in military time!

Hall framed the figure's chest in the gun sight. Then he pushed the barrel lower in the berm's dirt. Night shooting could be tricky. Always aim low at night, they said in training at Benning.

The girl continued her brisk walk directly at him.

She gave no sign of seeing him or Wozniak's gang. She clearly wasn't armed, meant him no harm. Maybe she was 10.

She stood before the berm. She still didn't see the gunmen in the mud. Hall watched her hands reach for the waistband of her pants.

She was going to pee right there. Maybe on his gun barrel. She spotted something!

Maybe the motionless gun barrel. Maybe him. The child's mouth opened in alarm. One hand pointed at him as she began her spin towards the house.

Hall was over the berm and on her before she could scream. He had his left hand over her mouth, his right arm around her waist. He hoisted her back to his original position behind the berm. He pinned her below him, his left hand still over her mouth.

Now he felt panic's immobility. The fingers on her face felt her pulse race. Otherwise she was motionless and made no effort to bite or struggle.

What was he going to do?

He looked at Wozniak. But the captain's gaze alternated between the house and his watch. The ambush should be in place and Wozniak clearly was ready to move.

Hall held the child silently in the mud beneath him until Wozniak finally looked over. He did his "round'em up and move'em out" gesture with his hand over his right shoulder. Hall shook his head violently.

Wozniak crawled to him. "Well, lootenant. You finally got with the program."

"What are we going to do with her?" Hall asked.

The News Room, 1986

Reporter Shiloh Weeks, her figure framed through the large window by the 76-story black Columbia Center -- better known in Seattle as the Dark Tower -- turned to fix him with a malignant stare as she surprised the assembled editors with, "There's one more thing. The killer put a clothes-pin on the judge's nose."

Hall's hands tried to grip the arms of his leather chair but they couldn't arrest the revulsion that made him shudder as he heard Shiloh announce that Stephan Wozniak had left for him -- and him alone – his horrible calling card.

He fought for breath and control. It was Hall's meeting so he had the head of the table to himself. He braced his chest against it and spread his arms and held on to the edge with his hands.

At the window behind him he heard Francis Van Gelder, the editorial page editor, braying, "A clothes-pin! Don't be absurd. How ridiculous! Now I've heard everything!" The braying meant Van Gelder would be opening the window and taking a long pull on his Black Russian and exhaling the foul smoke in a cold wind that would carry past Hall. He braced for it.

There was general babble from the editors arrayed around Hall's meeting table.

After the smoky draft passed, Hall looked up at Weeks, who remained at the window. She ignored everyone but him. They all had missed his reaction to the news about the clothes-pin. Not Shiloh Weeks. She rarely missed anything.

Hall looked away, surprised at himself. All through the meeting he had known a message from Wozniak was coming. He knew because he had checked. Wozniak just had been released from Leavenworth.

And already the clothes-pin was found on the nose of U.S. District Court Judge Mary Kanawha.

Such a mysterious murder of so prominent a jurist was, of course, the main business at Hall's morning story conference. Hall had little to say. He had selected pros -- to the extent the publisher let him -- who knew the news business. More importantly, he had

—

much bigger problems on his mind. He could barely concentrate on Mary's murder, no matter how important she once was to him.

Hall found himself listening off and on until Shiloh dropped her bombshell. Mentally, he drifted in and out of the meeting, mostly stared at the Dark Tower. It was a relatively new building. He had viewed construction of the shiny black building with all its concave angles gradually rise to block his view of Puget Sound with a sense of foreboding, knowing Wozniak's prison term had to be winding down.

As he sat through years of meetings and watched its construction, he couldn't help but wonder if the rising black structure wouldn't bring some horror that would parallel the horror that took place at the base of the Nui Ba Den -- the Black Virgin-- all those years ago in Vietnam.

Wozniak's clothes-pin marker confirmed he was bringing his horror to Seattle.

He tuned back into the story conference, moving uncomfortably in his leather chair. He hoisted one buttock and then the other to pull the Penney's pin-stripe trousers loose but found little give. He spread the busy Bill Blass tie as best he could over his belly and pulled uncomfortably at his tight size 40 calfskin belt.

"Armageddon," the art director was saying. "We have color of the gurney being pushed into the coroner's van. Wild-eyed FBI agents with Uzis protecting the body, a small group of sullen street skinheads in the frame. It's great. It's like civilization is about to unravel."

Hall rubbed his forehead. "Tell me again what the story says."

City Editor Anne Fisher looked surprised.

"Shiloh went all through . . . ."

"Run through it once more," replied Hall, the executive editor of the paper.

"It appears Judge Kanawha stayed late in her chambers to finish some work. Law clerks and staff were gone. It's unclear what happened between about 7 p.m. and 2 a.m. Around 2 a.m. is when the judge's husband called the cops. She was in her chambers. Murdered. We don't know details," Fisher replied.

"What work have we done so far?"

"We had a reporter -- Shiloh -- and a photographer at the courthouse at 4 a.m. Exclusive. Shiloh called the photog at home.

Then she got some good quotes and color at the scene. We've told you about the photo."

"How did we manage to have someone up and around to hear about this in the middle of the night?"

"I'm not sure how Shiloh got on it," said Fisher, clearly annoyed her boss was distracting her with that kind of question.

"Go ahead, Shiloh. Tell Jeremy how you found out about this. I'm sure we're all very interested." It was Van Gelder at his window.

Hall looked back at Shiloh, still at the door. She was beautiful even if she had been rousted early in the morning and hadn't had time to put on full war paint. No rouge on her cheeks, no blue eyelids, nothing. And her dark hair, usually worn elegantly, was pulled back in a plain pony tail. Hall never before had seen her wear the same outfit two days in a row. But she was.

He watched the flowered skirt as she swung gracefully into one of the lesser chairs at the table. He waited as she crossed her legs, smiled around the room and turned her eyes squarely to his.

She stared. And then. "I was with someone. He got a call."

"It sounds as if someone is giving new meaning to the term 'in bed with the police'," came Van Gelder's braying from the window. "Are we going to have to march you in front of the ethics board, Ms. Weeks?"

"Tell us the rest again," snapped Fisher, trying to keep the meeting focused on business. Her tough business-first attitude again made Hall glad he had hired her.

"Blow the God-damned smoke out the window," snarled Hall at Van Gelder.

"Whooops. . .," Van Gelder, slyly….

Fisher interrupted quickly and decisively. "Finish, Shiloh."

Weeks sat forward in her chair and flipped open her notebook with a flick of her wrist. She began, "The judge was in her chambers late. Someone defeated a number of electronic security systems -- alarms and cameras -- and slipped by two middle-age General Administration guards. The cops are talking about some kind of phantom. Anyway, the perp got in, did the judge and left just as mysteriously as he or she got in. No suspects, no clues -- unless the clothes-pin is one -- no motive, no nothing."

"What happened to Mary?" Hall asked, quietly.

"It's early yet. But it appears the judge had only one mark. A

—

5

bruise over the heart," she replied.

A smoky, cold draft struck Hall as Van Gelder asked, "Pardon me, but is anyone asking one elementary question? Perhaps this is just a heart attack or stroke. She struck something when she fell. That wouldn't explain the clothes-pin, but she was a flaming liberal -- who knows what primitive rites liberal federal judges celebrate when they are alone?"

Weeks still was watching him. "Oh, it's murder, all right. Of course they're not sure yet, but it appears it was done with a single blow to the chest. 'A very elegantly placed punch or karate strike' -- that's how one source at the scene put it. They are waiting for the coroner to tell them more."

"Karate experts punch, you know. Most people think they strike with the sides of their hands, but most of it is punching," volunteered Van Gelder from his window.

Fisher jumped in fast to prevent any further deterioration. "Shiloh, it sounds like no one started looking for the judge until fairly late. Why is that?"

"Um, I understand the judge often stayed out late for various social interests," said Weeks.

"A whiff of scandal?" asked Van Gelder, his interest piquing.

"The FBI and cops are looking into it," Weeks replied.

Hall looked beyond Weeks at the Dark Tower. "Anything else?" he asked after a pause.

"That's about it. I've got an appointment for lunch that should yield the latest. I better go. I've got a lot to do," Weeks replied.

Hall didn't know if Weeks looked at him as she left. He couldn't take his eyes off the black building as the editors, under Fisher's direction, began a general discussion of the assignments that would have to be made to cover the story for tomorrow's paper.

"Assign Ed Caldwell to find out what Mary did at night," Hall interrupted, speaking slowly, absentmindedly.

He sensed Fisher now was glaring at him. But Hall was preoccupied with the black structure before him. And with the arrival of Stephan Wozniak.

—

6

Black Virgin, 1966

"What the hell do you think we're going to do with her?" Wozniak asked matter-of-factly. The moonlight caught the familiar twinkle in his eyes.

The captain drew his Gerber stabbing knife and stuck it in the mud near Hall's right shoulder.

"Make sure I get that back," whispered Wozniak, beginning his crawl to his original position.

"You want me to kill her?" Hall demanded, almost shouting. That stopped Wozniak flat.

He twisted back his head. His eyes still twinkled, but there was no merriment. Just the wide brightness of the owl, hawk or cat.

"Shut up or I'll kill you too," Wozniak whispered. *"Now do it. Accomplish your mission and we'll get to our rendezvous."*

"I'm not killing her," declared Hall flatly, finally.

"I don't have time to discuss this with you, lootenant," came the captain's low reply. *"I'll tell you this just once. This is an intelligence mission. Mission is everything and surprise is the only friend we have. We're not losing that over some kid. No one can know an allied unit was in this ville tonight. No one. I can't emphasize that enough. Now, you've got a direct order, you snot-nosed little fuck. Are you going to jeopardize my mission on me? I truly hope you are."*

Hall's eyes tried to follow the crawling captain. But they stopped at the dagger. The handle was a rough, almost abrasive, non-slip metal. The small hand guard was just large enough to stop the handle from being buried in flesh during a hard, deep thrust. The bright metal blade was long and thin. There was enough moonlight to see Wozniak kept both sides razor sharp.

Hall pulled the girl's head to the left to ensure she couldn't see the knife, which was only inches from her face. He looked up, breathing deeply.

Ahead was the house. Apparently the family was rich. The house with the four louvered doors was larger than others he saw on the approach and it had a tile roof. The large mango tree framed one *side of it.*

The overwhelming image was the huge, black shape of Nui Ba Den. The Black Virgin. A black basalt mountain rising thousands of feet from the central Vietnam rice paddies. It was as if the house before him was in the belly of the black mountain.

Hall looked around. Mostly there was open paddy and Wozniak and his Backatya Boys. At 10 o'clock was a long hedgerow. It could conceal a North Vietnamese Army platoon. He looked for a Popular Forces camp. Such a camp probably would have an American adviser. No sign of one. He would never make it running even if the Popular Forces had a fortified camp in the village. There was too much open field between the berm and the rest of the village. And Backatya Boys Nguyen and Ky waited in ambush somewhere in the village.

Then release the girl and shoot Wozniak and his goons.

He was in the middle and Hall knew he never could shoot all three.

Wozniak would kill him before he fired a shot.

Could he just release the girl and refuse a direct order? For certain he would never get to put the issue before a courts martial board. For certain the girl would not get three feet from the berm.

The girl. She was quiet, making no effort to struggle or escape. Her racing pulse betrayed her calm. Hall could feel her beating heart through his heavy flak vest.

Hall twisted his wrist at the girl's head so he could look at his watch. The radium glow showed 2:22. Wozniak's departure time. Hall looked at Wozniak. Wozniak pointed at his watch, then at the house. Then the captain aimed his rifle at him.

Hall wrapped his fingers of his right hand around the knife handle. His left hand tightened over the girl's small face. She stirred slightly but still did not struggle.

He shifted more of his weight to her. "Struggle, damn it!. Fight! Bite! Scream!" Hall felt the sweat flow down his dirty face. It washed salty grit into his mouth. He was confused, he knew terror.

His left hand closed around the girl's mouth and nose. There. Now she was struggling. His hand took the knife to her back, about three ribs up from her abdomen.

Tears joined the sweat on his face. He was choking. The girl too had become desperate. The knife point now had enough pressure behind it to break skin. Almost involuntarily, Hall arched his back

—

and his hand positioned the knife handle so it was beneath the thick flak vest. The vest made him only vaguely aware the weapon was there . . . .

All Hall could think, could hear, were Wozniak's words: "This is an intelligence mission . . . ." Mission was everything. You were expected to slaughter your men, yourself, everyone around you . . . children . . . in the name of mission. That's what the army said.

To hell with the mission. To hell with the army.

Wozniak had said more. He had said, "No one can know an allied unit was in this ville tonight." The words reverberated through his skull. "No one can know . . . No one can know . . . ."

There was more. Hall grasped for it. He couldn't think, couldn't remember.

"Surprise is the only friend we have." That's what Wozniak said. Without surprise, they had nothing. They wouldn't survive. He wouldn't survive without surprise. Wozniak knew . . . .

The girl was fighting. Hall could feel her mouth working. Was it trying to bite? Or just trying to grab a gulp of air?

"Oh God," he whimpered into her ear. Just relax now. Relax and maintain the surprise they had to have. Their friend.

He let his weight go. He relaxed and peace came. At first he felt the hilt resist the flak jacket but then the resistance was gone and he didn't have to arch his back so much.

But his hand, which still grasped the knife handle between the girl and his flak jacket, felt wet. Something warm was on his hand. He pulled back in horror. . . .

Executive Office, 1986

"Jeremy. What is it about Mary Kanawha's life you don't want us to know?" asked Shiloh Weeks.

She was sitting in one of the leather chairs in his spacious office. Hall sat behind his large, glass desk. The curtains were pulled. His office also had a view of the Dark Tower.

"Lucky for us you were staying up with a friend," Hall replied, sensing the lameness in his voice.

"What happened to you in there?" she demanded.

"Oh nothing, just Van Gelder's usual shit. . . ," he began.

"It wasn't that. Was there something between you and Kanawha?" Weeks demanded, her voice hard.

"Hardly knew the woman. Knew she was very lovely. And very bright."

"There is more than that. Why did you assign Ed Caldwell to cover the social aspects of her life?" Shiloh spit the word "social."

"Look, Shiloh. You've got a major story to work on. You've got the best part of it. But you'll need help. Fisher has the capitol folks doing the political part of her story, the court guys on her legal career and who covets her bench. Someone needs to look into the social stuff. You yourself said she spent a lot of nights out . . ."

"Jeremy, she could have picked up her God-damned killer catting around. She might have brought the killer into the building. Whoever hoisted her black robe for her could be the most important angle to this story!" protested Shiloh.

"Ed needs a big story. He knows the pressure is building on him. He'll come through this time. Let's move on. You'll be busy with the feds. I'll have the cop reporter find out what he can and feed you. Maybe have someone from the back-of-the-book do a sidebar on her home life, you know, some stuff from the tea party and cocktail circuits?"

Shiloh tacked. "Something is very wrong, Jeremy. I want to help you." She spoke gently.

"Help me by getting a Pulitzer prize on this. It's been years since we've had one. One more on my watch and Van Gelder will be

---

shuffling columns and editorial cartoons on the editorial page until they retire his ass out of here. Go get it. It sounds like you have the right sources and there's no question about the talent."

"I'll do my best. Just one thing."

"What's that, Shiloh?"

"Keep Caldwell out of my way." She rose and marched to the door. She left without looking back.

Hall turned his chair and faced the curtain that blocked the black building.

Black Virgin Resolved, 1966

*Instantly Hall rolled away from the girl, unwilling to look.
He jumped to his feet. Wozniak and the Backatya Boys saw the move
as the signal to hit the house and they rose, crouched and advanced.*

*Hall cried. He couldn't look at the girl. He felt his knees give
out after stumbling a few feet toward the house.*

*Then a hand had his flak vest collar and he was pulled to his
feet.*

*"Get your ass in gear, lootenant. We've still got that mission
to accomplish." The voice was Wozniak's. The hand propelled him
toward the house.*

*But Hall no longer cared about the mission. Or anything
else. He wanted the house or the hedgerow to explode in automatic
weapons fire. He stumbled in the rear as Wozniak and his Backatya
Boys spread out so each could enter the house through a different
opening.*

*Approaching the house, Hall could see he had been right
about the tree. It was a mango. He looked up into its high branches.
Fat mangos were visible. They looked dark. But they probably were
green and red and orange and yellow. Why, with a fine knife like
Wozniak's he could make a shallow, surgical cut around the fruit
and peel back the yellow-green-red-orange skin to reveal the sweet,
stringy yellow fruit. It was all in the cutting. The sharpness of the
knife was key. . . . Make a series of cuts and peel it back and there
was the fruit. No fuss, no mess. It must be wonderful to have such a
tree and so many mangos. And the sharp knife. So much cutting.*

*And there, in the moonlight, Hall saw a large garden. The
rows of cabbage, leeks, other stalks and leaves, all the vegetables in
straight rows, orderly, loved. And beyond the lovely garden, an
enclosure.*

A bunker? No, a pen.

*He could see small shapes lined up against the irregular
wooden fence. Noses or something stuck through. Ducks or geese,
maybe. No, they were pigs. The pigs were alert, watching, interested.
They made subdued pig noises.*

This time it wasn't their turn. No one came to lift one of the piglets by a leg from the sty and flop it down before the other piglets and hold its stomach with a bare foot and then hold back its head and pull a shiny, sharp Gerber knife across its throat.

It was the people's turn this time. Hall turned his head away from the pen and let his eyes linger on the garden before turning them towards the house. He was almost under the roof's overhang and at one of the four louvered doors. The wonderful tree and garden and the grateful piglets were gone and the horror truly was back.

Maybe the farmer. . . . Not the farmer. Hall made himself confront it. Maybe the father and mother and brothers and sisters of the girl -- were gone . . . . or waiting with their AK-47's. Hall hoped they waited armed, fury in their eyes.

But there were no blessed gunshots. Hall walked through one of the doorways. The shadows showed the Backatya Boys using their rifle butts to crush the heads of the sleeping.

Wozniak suddenly seized his arm and whirled him around. The captain pushed him to the open door through which the girl had exited minutes earlier and hissed, "You're lookout. Keep watch out there."

Hall lay down but saw nothing. He buried his head in his arm. Behind him the thumping ended and he could hear only quiet noises, as though Wozniak and Buu and Hau were searching the house. Outside the house he heard the sounds of a peaceful night. Bugs flying. Crickets chirping. Hall looked toward the paddies, still hoping he would see a large number of enemy soldiers. He wouldn't fire a shot, would give no warning. His own execution would be a blessing. He visualized himself kneeling, the muzzle of the SKS with the folded bayonet against the back of his neck. . . . But there was just the still, peaceful moonlit night.

Hall's eyes shifted to the doorway. On the left side was a small alter at about the height of his face. Placed on it were a variety of dried flowers, a foot-tall elongated white Buddha statue— the slim Vietnamese Buddha with legs crossed, soles facing up, fingers that were intertwined but now were broken, as the icon had been smashed in half. The glass over a yellowed photograph in a simple frame was broken. There was enough light to see the photograph was of a girl. Possibly a relative of the one behind the . . . who left the house and came to the berm. Possibly it was she . . . .

PAY ATTENTION!...now only broken mirrored glass surrounded the rimmed the frame.

Having no interest in what occurred outside if the VC weren't going to come, Hall concentrated on the mirror. Despite the poor light in the house, he just could see Wozniak and his Backatya Boys in its reflection. They were searching for something. Buu seemed to be directing the search. They were methodical. They missed nothing, not even the sleeping benches or the corpses on them.

Wozniak came to the alter and cleared the statues and flowers and picture with a slash of his rifle butt. The mirrored glass shattered when it struck the rough wooden floor. Ignoring Hall, Wozniak pulled apart the wooden alter. Finding nothing, Wozniak moved on.

Silently, Hall's left hand released his rifle and righted the broken picture frame. Enough glass remained to see much of the room. He also saw his own right hand in the reflection. It still held Wozniak's slender knife. His hand released it as if it was on fire. His body shuddered and he closed his eyes.

When he reopened them, he saw in the reflection that Wozniak and the Backatya Boys were concentrated around what appeared to be a primitive kitchen. The men moved pots and other implements. Buu used the barrel of his rifle to scrape the floor. Embers jumped. It was some kind of cooking pit. Buu used his boot to move greater quantities of ash. Then Buu was on his knees digging with his hands. Red embers still jumped around the bare hands.

There was a low whistle. Wozniak reached down. Wozniak pulled a small metal box from the cooking hole and took it to one of the sleeping benches to open. It appeared in the reflection to be a candy tin.

Wozniak pulled out papers and examined them. He tossed them aside. Then he pulled out a wad of paper. The wad drew grunts of pleasure and surprise from the Vietnamese. Wozniak pulled something from his breast pocket and a pin-point of light illuminated the wad.

Money.

Hall watched Wozniak count it and divide it into five piles, including one each apparently for Nguyen and Ky for their ambush service.

Slowly, Hall's dazed and unwilling mind accepted what his

eyes saw.

This was no intelligence mission.
This was an armed robbery.
"No one can know an allied unit was in this ville tonight."
That's what Wozniak said.
Before all the killings.
Before the little girl had come outside to pee.
Before he had pulled her behind the berm . . . .

Carefully, Hall's finger moved the switch above the M-16's trigger from semi-automatic to automatic. He began his turn. He would spray the room. After that, who cared?

Suddenly the house shook. Then the earth itself. Then a loud, prolonged rumble arrived.

"B-52's. Only a few klicks away. Let's didi mau. Hurry, now!" Wozniak was shouting.

The captain and his Backatya Boys raced past him. Hall jumped to his feet, pausing only long enough to pick up Wozniak's dagger. He stuck the weapon in his jungle boot and covered the handle with his filthy pant leg.

Wozniak and his Backatya Boys ran toward the moonlit hulk of the Black Virgin. Hall followed. Behind him were shouts in Vietnamese. Then bursts of automatic weapons fire. Nguyen and Ky, Wozniak's aces in the hole, were having their turn.

Hall sprinted for the Black Virgin.

Lunch, 1986

Shiloh Weeks pressed her body against Lt. Jerry Buck's side and moved the fingertips of her right hand lightly over his belly where a roll of fat was spreading over a foundation of hard muscle. She took a handful of the roll and momentarily was tempted to dig in her long red nails. Instead, she moved in as close as she could get to him.

"Come on, lieutenant, you got what you want. Now give." Then she caught herself. She was going to stick with the tease for now. But she didn't have much time. She'd have to get tough if Buck didn't start talking soon. Lunch had gone on too long already and it had been all sex so far.

"Where'd you learn all that?" asked Buck, attempting to turn towards her.

"Journalism School," she answered, truthfully. She pushed him on his back again with her massage hand.

"I said give. I've got a big story to write today and I've already spent too much time screwing with you."

Weeks felt Buck's muscles relax. The bastard was going to press against her -- and say nothing -- until it was time to go home to the frau or back to the office. If she let him.

"That's it," said Weeks, trying to pull away. But Buck's weight caused a deep dip in the weak springs of the motel's cheap mattress. The dip was like a black hole in space that pulled uncomfortably on her back while the policeman was on top of her. Later it had tried to suck in both their bodies as they lay panting.

So Weeks rose, retrieved her notebook and pen from her purse and walked like a whore to the room's only chair. She noticed it was badly stained but she slid her naked bottom into it. Still slow and sexy like a whore. Buck couldn't take his eyes off her. But he had all he was going to get. Weeks knew how to play games too. Now she was all business.

"Jerry, what do you hear? The coroner has scheduled a news conference for tomorrow afternoon. I'm not waiting until then."

"It was a murder this morning and it still is," said the cop,

16

sighing. He rose and walked to his camel hair sports jacket he had draped over the Magnavox TV set.

Weeks watched the tall cop walk. His thighs under his ass brushed against each other. The love handles hung over his hips. The man was big, but no longer an athlete. Red hair grew fairly thick high on his back. The red hair on his head was beginning to thin.

He fished through his jacket.

"Like what you see, huh?" he asked over his shoulder.

Weeks did not reply.

He took a Marlboro from his pack and lighter from his pants pocket and returned to the bed where he lit up.

Big mistake, thought Weeks. She hated screwing men who smelled like cigarettes. Especially middle-aged men who thought they were hot shit. Buck was never going to get a very long ride on this train anyway.

"Still killed with a punch?"

"Appears that way. Coroner said most blunt instruments would have made some kind of abrasion. There wasn't any."

"What killed her? Plenty of boxers get hit over the heart and they don't die for at least a few years. Usually the brain goes first," said Weeks, annoyed at herself for the long question containing editorial comment. Just business now, stupid.

"You remember, don't you, that this is federal territory. The coroner is reporting to them. You know the feds. They suck everything in and don't let shit out. I'm just telling you what little is on the grapevine."

"You'll have to do. For now. I don't know any Feebbii's like I know you," said Weeks. And that oversight was going to be corrected very soon, she added to herself.

"So how does a punch in the chest kill someone?"

"The scuttlebutt is the punch was delivered by an expert. Maximum force concentrated in one area. Thousands of pounds of pressure per square inch. The sternum shattered. The heart, well, it just exploded," said the lieutenant as he flicked ashes in the thick yellow and tan shag carpeting.

"How about she just tripped and fell. Maybe struck her chest on her desk. A sharp corner of a cabinet or something."

"Someone who knew what he was doing punched her in the chest," said the lieutenant.

"Suspects?"

17

"Zip."

"Come on, lieutenant. She's a judge. She sentences people all the time. There's got to be suspects up the kazoo. Drug lords, gang bosses, Mafia, who knows how many people she has pissed off."

"Most of those kinds of people leave messages the plain folks can understand. A .22 to the back of the head I could understand. One through the mouth I could understand. This one doesn't seem to mean anything."

"Nothing taken, no files rifled or anything?"

"Nothing unusual, I hear. So far as the secretaries and law clerks can find."

"What about the clothes-pin. What does that mean?" asked Weeks.

"Who knows? The only thing I get out of it is that someone thinks something stinks, and used a clothes-pin since Kanawha wasn't in any condition to hold her own nose," replied the cop.

"Anyone professional use clothes-pins as calling cards?"

"Not that the computer knows about. And ours is tied into the national net, the same one the FBI will be searching. Maybe someone young just breaking in. But . . ." the cop was going to try to slide away from the point if she let him.

"But what, Jerry?" demanded Weeks.

"It's just speculation but I don't think it is fresh talent." The cop stopped for a drag before squashing out the smoke on the headboard. He flicked what was left of the cigarette across the room.

"Give, lieutenant."

"Today's talent lacks sophistication. There was class to this one. Kids and punks today think a drive-by with an ejaculation from their Uzi or a sawed-off is a big deal. They don't take the time to learn how to do someone by hand. Even the mob has had to import pizza men from Sicily to get any style. Someone with a sense of craftsmanship, pride in their work. Besides, there isn't anyone around here smart enough I've run into who could break into the federal courthouse the way this phantom did and do a kill. There are good second story guys, but they are not killers. Unless they are cornered and this perp wasn't cornered."

"Was she having an affair?"

"She knew a lot of people, knows what greases political wheels. It's an angle being checked out."

"If she was married and fooling around there has to be a

cuckold raging somewhere. How about the hubbie?" asked Weeks.

"First one they looked at. Solid alibi. Playing poker with the crème de la crème. Besides, he's more interested in his Irish Mist than his hard-charging lady judge. Got all the money he needs. No big insurance policies naming her big winner. Just nothing there."

"Well, Kanawha was a politico too. She knew a lot of lawyers and others with fancy suits and reeking cologne. Lots of motivation there. Humiliated some hotshot in the courtroom, a decision that cost someone a lot of money -- maybe a developer who couldn't get a permit and build a taller building than the Dark Tower. Maybe we're not talking criminals here at all. Maybe this is personal. Involving some kind of YMCA kung fu heart throb. Or a wanna-be or used-to-be. You know, a jilted lover. A political opponent with a grudge," suggested Weeks.

"That's probably the best shot. Someone who doesn't go around killing people for a living. But someone who once had some training and maybe works out. Has the bucks to bribe a couple of old fart guards, or maybe even knew the guards because he was a regular at the courthouse. We don't think the guards are lying, though. More likely we are looking for an ex-Marine or ranger or something. I understand the FBI is putting a lot of assets in that end of it. But your typical swinging young cock yuppie from the Y karate class probably couldn't have gotten in and out without a trace. And had the intestinal fortitude to remain silent," replied Buck.

"So why was she out at night a lot?"

"Oh, charity events. Political fundraisers, that kind of thing."

"Charity and fundraisers sound like good cover to me. What was she really doing?"

"Is that all you reporters do? Screw someone and expect to be handed all the answers? Why don't you go do some poking around yourself? You might be surprised at what you'd find. You may not have to look all that far," said the cop.

"What does that mean?" She paused to think.

Then she demanded: "You looking at someone at the paper or something? Maybe someone who covers the courthouse and knows it and its guards. Or someone who has covered it?"

"I got crimes to solve, bad guys to put away, city councilmen to suck up to," said the lieutenant as he got up. The bed kept the indentation where his weight had been. The cop went to his clothes on the TV and dressed.

19

"Not so fast, lieutenant. I want to know how the paper is connected to this," said Weeks.

"I didn't say it was. I told you to look around the yuppie crowd and there are a damn lot of them at the paper. And I told you I've got work to do. Why don't you get dressed? You look like a tramp."

But Weeks was staring at the drawn shades on the window. She remembered how Hall reacted when she mentioned the clothespin. How distracted he had been in the story conference. Spent most of the meeting looking out the window, his mind far, far away. How he had assigned that incompetent junkie Ed Caldwell to look into Kanawha's night-time activities.

"He used to cover the courts. And he was in Vietnam. He told me. He was an intelligence officer who did a lot of weird stuff," she muttered.

"Who was in Vietnam doing weird stuff?" asked the cop as he yanked his tie against his Adam's apple like a hangman setting the knot on a convict's neck.

"None of your business," Weeks responded. "And what did you call me, you shithead?"

Village of Thuy Tu, 1966

So which cop was Shiloh shacked with when the call came in? God, what a bitch she was. And Mary? Why did he always get involved with the bitches?

Was Shiloh doing it just to hurt him? Or had she merely seduced a cop to drop him into her bag of contacts and sources?

A bag that no doubt would be very useful as she pursued the Mary Kanawha story. His beautiful bloodhound was on a real blood scent this time.

If only he could tell her the real story about Stephan Wozniak. But to tell her, or anyone else, would mean telling the real story about himself. Stephan Wozniak was unfinished business. His unfinished business.

"Here Shiloh, here's the real story you'll never know. Or print," Hall said softly to himself, as he pulled back the heavy white drapes.

The reflective black walls of the Dark Tower were dreary in a gray rain. Despite the drizzle, two window washers hung from its side, valiantly scrubbing its black glass.

Little good scrubbing the Dark Tower would do. There was only one way to deal with the horror it represented to him.

What did he know about Stephan Wozniak? What could he remember? He would have to know everything he could about Wozniak to . . . what? . . . to find and kill the clever, highly trained professional killer. Killing Wozniak was the only way out for him.

He had to remember everything. . . . Old images formed as Hall studied the black building that was so like the Black Virgin so long ago in Vietnam. . . .

Wozniak had been a complete unknown to Hall during his first few weeks at the 303rd Special Services Battalion's base camp hidden on the Vietnam coast.

Then came the day the colonel ordered Hall into the field for seasoning. And there was no better way to get it than a mission with Captain Wozniak and his Backatya Boys, the colonel had said.

The next thing Hall knew was that after a long chopper flight

---

21

over a bombed, pock-marked country, he and the little group joined a mechanized infantry platoon waiting at a fire support base in III Corps...between Saigon and Cambodia. And then he was sitting in a speeding armored personnel carrier.

"Why are we going to Ap Thuy Tu?" Lieutenant Hall shouted at the terrain map before him. Smoke from Captain Wozniak's cigarette and trapped bluish fumes from the APC's diesel engine made it hard to see the handful of black boxes and dotted lines representing the hootches and trails of the village amid the browns and greens and reds of the terrain map. From what he could see through his tortured red eyes, it looked like any other village in Vietnam's rich agricultural regions in the southern provinces of South Vietnam.

Since it wasn't in one of the notorious free-fire VC strongholds, such as the Iron Triangle, Khe Sanh, Ho Bo Woods, Quang Tri or Central Highlands, Ap Thuy Tu was supposed to be pacified. That meant it surely had a few Viet Cong guerrillas plus a platoon of theoretically pro-government Popular Forces living in a fortified camp in or near the village. Hall was green but he was pretty sure the wall of concertina wire and tanglefoot and claymore mine booby traps would hold a few VC among the Popular Force irregulars—who wouldn't hedge his bet in such a war as this? Proof enough: they were being carried to a point near the village in a platoon of APCs with 50 caliber machine guns on their turrets.

"Did you hear me, captain?" shouted Hall, looking up from the map.

The captain didn't answer but Hall was sure he had heard, despite the roar of the engines and the jabber on the radio.

Wozniak was sitting back and smoking, holding the cigarette as though he was in a country club, not an armored fighting vehicle whose tread at any minute could strike a primitive mine fashioned from an unexploded USAF 250-pound bomb.

Wozniak was grinning and staring at Hall. His eyes twinkled even in the gloom of the bouncing APC.

Wozniak spoke only when he was ready. Despite the twinkle, his voice was hard as he said, "You're here, lootenant, because the colonel said I had to take you. I don't want you here. In fact, you piss me off."

"What's our mission? I've got to know what is going on in case something happens to you," Hall shouted.

"Nothing's gonna happen to me. I'd worry about myself if I was you. Just stay out of my way and do exactly as I say. Remember, this is an intelligence mission. Things aren't always what they seem. And the only rules are the ones I make." Wozniak gave his reply in what seemed a normal conversational tone that transcended the engine roar and the radio chatter.

Hall looked to Wozniak's eyes for a clue as to what the guy was about. They twinkled. In madness? The only thing for sure was this captain was enjoying himself in this tense, smoky hell.

Wozniak had remained a mystery in the brief time Hall had been in the intelligence battalion. Maybe the guy had been in Vietnam too long and liked it too much. Liked playing soldier so much he made a personal army. He recruited from the Chieu Hoi -- VC turncoats -- who came the 303rd's way. Hall didn't like the way Wozniak had armed the Viet Cong turncoats with automatic weapons and had given them the run of the compound. Wozniak called his group of six former VC the Backatya Boys. They seemed to come and go at will. Often they disappeared with Wozniak outside the American compound sitting in the midst of a South Vietnamese Army airborne brigade base camp for days at a time.

If Wozniak was going to sit and grin at him, Hall stared back, studying the strange man. Long blond hair was visible at the base of his green jungle hat. Wozniak rolled up the sides so it looked like a small cowboy hat, as did many GI's. The cowboy look was augmented by a white silk flare parachute cloth around his neck which made him look GI dandy. The rest of his outfit included a green tee shirt visible at the neck of his green jungle fatigue blouse. Like many intelligence officers and enlisted men, he wore neither branch nor rank insignia on his collars. Instead the initials "US" had been sewn on each collar. The sleeves were rolled high to display surprisingly slim arms. He also wore green jungle fatigue pants. Unlike most rear echelon motherfucker soldiers, he hadn't bothered to have the bagginess tailored out. The green and black jungle boots were scuffed and muddy. Around his waist Wozniak wore a web belt with a canteen, a stabbing knife and a .45 automatic. Bandoleers of M-16 clips crossed his thin chest. Unlike Hall, the captain wore neither flak vest nor helmet. Wozniak held a scuffed M-16 between his knees.

Hall shifted his eyes to the Backatya Boy Buu, the most evil-looking Vietnamese he ever had seen. A large scar descended from the middle of his forehead, across his nose and cheek and disappeared beneath his left ear. While Wozniak's eyes always sparkled with a merry twinkle, Buu's eyes always were unblinkingly serpent-like, although with Americans he wore an ear-to-ear grin. The bully displayed no grin around other Vietnamese -- any Vietnamese.

He appeared to be the Backatya Boy closest to Wozniak, although in camp the captain seemed to treat all of them more like children than friends. Buu wore a tailored Vietnamese army uniform with no indication of rank. His green jungle hat was worn cowboy style, apparently in imitation of Wozniak. He wore bandoleers of extra clips and used the white silk of a parachute flare as a rifle strap for his AK-47. One end was tied around the barrel, the other end was around the stock. Buu, like many Vietnamese, wore it so the rifle hung across his chest.

"Time, captain," shouted the young armor lieutenant who had pulled his head through the hatch from behind the .50 caliber machine gun set at the top of the APC. The enlisted driver kept up speed as he peered through the narrow slit that served as a windshield. The armor lieutenant was off the small stool on which he had been standing behind his machinegun and sat by Wozniak. He and Wozniak pointed at a bouncing map used to bring them to their location, wherever it was. Wozniak nodded and rose into a crouch.

Pausing briefly only to grin at Hall, Wozniak opened the heavy armored doors at the rear of the vehicle and jumped. Buu followed immediately.

The vehicle must have been traveling at 20 miles an hour. Hall was tempted to pull the doors closed and leave Wozniak in the mud.

Even if reason screamed in outrage, Hall knew the army's rules demanded he jump. And he didn't want to be separated from the mission's leader.

So he jumped into the rooster tails of mud spewing from the APC's tracks.

He should have landed in a run to compensate for the moving vehicle as Wozniak and Buu had. But he didn't.

His feet slipped from under him in the deep mud. The tumble to his stomach knocked the wind from him just as his face was buried in the mud. He drew in a mouthful as his lungs struggled for air. At the same time he felt chunks of mud thrown up by the APC's tracks *rake his back.*

Even the fear couldn't stop the coughing fit that began as Hall fought for air.

Immediately someone was on his back, pushing his face deep into the mud.

Hall struggled desperately to remove the weight.

"Shut it up, little fuck," hissed a voice in his left ear.

Hall tried to twist around and hook an arm of his assailant to flip him.

But the assailant had wrapped his leg around Hall's in a judo lock and the voice's free hand had him in a powerful half-Nelson. The assailant with the hissing voice pushed Hall's head deeper. And he couldn't move.

Hall released his hold on the gun and went limp. He was blacking out, perhaps dying. It didn't seem so bad. The convulsions had stopped.

As death's fog gathered, in his mind's eye he saw:

A tan dog creeping. No, not a dog. Nor a wolf. Something not as big. A coyote, a skinny coyote, loping, dodging, alert, looking for something. If there was a way, the coyote would find it. The coyote sniffed, ran on, ears erect. Then it dropped to stalk, its lips curled to show long canine teeth . . . . it crept close . . . . . ready . . . .

Hall was only half conscious of the hand that jerked back his head by the front of his helmet. The strap dug sharply into his neck. He gasped for air and then opened his eyes to see Wozniak kneeling beside him. Wozniak was slapping him although Hall felt nothing.

"Don't go choke in that mud, lootenant, If you're gonna die today, I want the pleasure of killing you myself. Now shut up. The Cong scouts follow these APC's watching for surr-ep-titious insertions like the one we just made. This is an intelligence operation. We are trying to sneak up on these folks, boy. We don't want every VC in the country knowing we are here," Wozniak hissed.

Then Wozniak's fingers were in Hall's mouth, roughly pulling out remnants of the mud. Hall shook his head, coughing and spitting. Then he noticed Buu was kneeling nearby. The Vietnamese's eyes were transfixed on Hall's watch.

"Now get with the program!" ordered Wozniak as he gave Hall a rough shove. "Stay down."

Hall nodded.

They were now arranged in a rough fighting circle. The only

Americans were Wozniak and Hall. There were four Vietnamese, all Wozniak Backatya Boys. While Buu had ridden in Wozniak's APC, the other three, Ky, Nguyen and Hau, had ridden in another armored vehicle.

Hall was one spoke in the fighting circle. The realization scared the hell out of him. All he needed now was for VC scouts to hit his sector.

He snapped a round into the chamber, grateful his M-16 was not ready to fire when he tumbled from the APC. An accidental shot at the beginning of the mission and Wozniak surely would have killed him on the spot.

No VC scouts appeared so Hall relaxed a little and looked around. They had jumped into the middle of a rice paddy. Wozniak and Buu had taken positions that offered some shelter behind dirt berms. He and the other Backatya Boys lay in deep mud. Seeing nothing except paddy, Hall cleaned the rifle as well as he could. Then he used one hand and rolling movements of his body to dig a shallow depression in the mud.

Where he waited in the worst hell he could imagine. He didn't know where he was and didn't know why he was there. He was surrounded by cutthroats more enemy than friend who were threatening to kill him, if only for his watch. But he didn't dare move.

Not even when he felt something move off his web belt and on to his kidney under his loose jungle jacket. There were plenty of snakes in Vietnam. If this was a snake, it was nightcrawler size. Hall remained motionless as it inched its way up his spine. Soon it was on a part of his back he couldn't reach even if he dared to try. Hall looked at Wozniak. He was on his back, apparently oblivious. His head was resting on the berm. His eyes closed and he was smoking. So was Buu. Hall scanned as large a zone as he could without turning or raising his head. Nothing was visible in the paddy. But who knew what watched from the tree line about the distance of two football fields away?

Hall had no idea what might be behind him in the Backatya Boys' zones. His focus returned to the thing on his back. It had stopped. He felt a slight discomfort in the area the nightcrawler waited. It didn't feel like fangs entering his skin. He had given the animal no excuse to bite. God, he wanted to roll over quickly and crush it with his weight.

But Hall didn't dare. He waited in the mud for Wozniak to

26

move.

The hours passed. He became conscious of the sweltering heat. Mosquitoes dined. Hall covered his face and back of his trigger hand in mud then buried his free hand in it.

Hall, his body encased in the heavy helmet and flak jacket, was sweating heavily. Rivulets of sweat gradually removed much of the mud from his face, providing the insects new opportunities. He caked on more mud and dug himself deeper.

The thing on his back seemed to find what it sought as the hours passed. And he felt no paralyzing venom, he wasn't losing feeling anywhere in his body.

Wozniak finally crawled over at about 2200 hours as dusk descended.

"We can go now, lootenant," he hissed. "Here are the rules. Do what I say. If we set up a fast ambush, stick with Buu. We already have our drill. If we are ambushed, attack the shooters. Only a chump tries anything else. They'll have claymores covering all the escape routes. If you can't keep up for any reason -- any reason at all -- I'll kill you."

"The mission, captain, why are we here?" snarled Hall.

"I told you. It's an intelligence operation. You have to have a need to know," said Wozniak, his eyes twinkling at his joke.

"Sir, you're nuts."

"I've heard that. Got any leeches you want off before I put out my smoke?"

"Something's on my back," Hall replied, suddenly grateful Wozniak was there.

"That won't bother you. I thought you might have one close to your ear. They always end up crawling in your ear. Those dudes will suck out your brain, you know," chortled the captain. He turned around to Buu and made a gesture with a crooked finger at Hall's ear. Buu replied with a quiet laugh.

"So when did the leeches get yours?" hissed Hall as the captain crawled away. Hall heard him laugh.

Then Wozniak made a cowboy "round'em up and move'em out" gesture over his head with one hand.

Hall looked in the direction Wozniak had pointed. That's when he saw the monster mountain for the first time. The Black Virgin rose from the flat plain. He couldn't believe he hadn't noticed it when they choppered into the area. The black mountain looked as though it was something living and evil that had risen suddenly from the dark mud. But it was just a mountain. A large, black basalt mountain fully visible in the fading daylight.

"That's where we are going," said Wozniak.

Hall knew little about it. An American communications base was at the top. Monkeys, monks and VC lived on its steep slopes. At least that's what a 4ᵗʰ Infantry trooper who had fought at Tay Ninh said when they mounted their APC's for their infiltration.

Then they were on the march through the paddy. Single file. Hau, the Backatya Boy who had defected from one of the area's VC squads, was on point. At least he was supposed to be. From what Hall could see from his position, the Backatya Boy didn't act like he was watching for trip wires and ambushes.

The man had his rifle slung across his chest, a cigarette dangled from his mouth and he walked at a fairly fast clip, apparently indifferent to danger.

Wozniak followed Hau. Buu brought up the rear. They had placed Hall, as the weakest link, in the middle with Nguyen.

Despite the danger, the lulling pace of the march and the peace of the beautiful, cool night and the fact that Hau was walking on the berms instead of through the mud relaxed Hall. He began to hope he might survive this mission after all. He noticed small things, like the way calm water in the paddies sparkled as they reflected the light of the full moon that seemed to hang right above the small group.

Occasionally the moonlight was augmented by powerful flares that floated gently from the sky. Once, far to the southeast, wonderful waving red lines were drawn against the black background of the sky. Hall had been in country long enough to know that someone closer to the beautiful red lines was in stark terror of them. They were the tracer rounds spewing from the Gatling guns of a Spooky gunship. Something like 600 rounds per minute scorched the ground.

All the time Hau kept his small party heading for the heart of the Black Virgin. It loomed like an overbearing monster, growing larger.

Suddenly Hau, and then the rest of the group, like dominos falling in a row, jumped into the mud beside the berm.

Hall scanned the darkness. He saw the problem. Someone was coming their way, following the berms above the mud.

Hall watched. Soon he could see it was a figure in dark pants, a white shirt and peasant's conical hat. The figure was walking generally in their direction, but probably would pass on a parallel berm. Like Hau, the figure did not seem particularly alert for danger.

Then Hall caught a movement to his right. Wozniak was on the move. He was snaking through the mud on an interception course.

Fearful of raising his head too high and giving away the group, Hall lost sight of the captain. The figure continued walking, framed in the outline of the Black Virgin. Suddenly, the figure dropped.

Hall heard a quiet whistle. Buu gestured for him to move forward. The Vietnamese seemed to feel there was no need for stealth, so Hall walked upright in a line with them. Buu directed them into a fighting circle around Wozniak and his victim.

Hall was close enough to see Wozniak was searching the person.

"Finding anything?" whispered Hall, tired of the third-string role Wozniak and the Backatya Boys had assigned him.

Wozniak grinned.

Hau crawled over to the captain and checked the victim's face. He muttered something to Wozniak.

"That will make you feel good, lootenant. My boy Hau here says this little lady is a big VCI – that's Viet Cong Infrastructure for you green assholes -- poohbah," grinned Wozniak.

"You killed her?" Hall hissed at him.

"Bear shit anywhere he wants?" chortled Wozniak.

"If she's important we should have taken her alive. We're in the information business, remember, captain?"

Wozniak looked at Hall. Then he picked up the dead woman's head and turned it towards him as though it was part of a ventriloquist's dummy.

"Here that, VC poohbah? The lootenant says you should still be alive. What a rotten deal for you. Cheez. Life stinks, doesn't it, pal?"

Hall watched Wozniak reach into his pocket and pull out a clothes-pin. He pinched the clothes-pin on the dead woman's nose and dropped her head into the mud.

"No doubt about it, life just stinks. You just hold on to that

pin. It's all yours, lady," laughed Wozniak.

Story Conference, 1986

Could he have been wrong?

Stephan Wozniak was out of prison. He knew that. But maybe he was not in Seattle. Maybe a crazy, pathetic kook named Harry in an act of incredible statistical improbability killed an important woman and stuck a clothes-pin on her nose?

Just a coincidence?

How had Wozniak killed the woman on the Vietnamese berm? Could have been a punch in the chest. He just didn't know.

Maybe it was a coincidence. Maybe Wozniak never put it all together why those Backatya Boys who had been at Ap Thuy Tu died. Maybe he doesn't even know why he was caught and went to prison for so many years. Unlikely. Much too unlikely. So what kind of game was Wozniak playing?

The pain originating in Jeremy Hall's head linked about midway up his spine with nausea spun from the acid churning in his stomach. He didn't remember feeling this bad before -- *except at Ap Thuy Tu* -- he knew he should turn the story conference over to Fisher. But he took two large gulps of the foul, tepid tea before him and grinned at the editors around the table.

"It's just too bad our phantom didn't jump on our time," he said.

"He means, Shiloh," came Van Gelder's voice from the window, "Too bad you didn't overhear another serendipitous telephone call in the middle of the night. And I must say, Jeremy, you're looking awfully chipper for someone who can't be sleeping well if you are awake for the night owl television news."

Weeks glared at the editorial page director.

"Children, please," intervened Hall. "Yes, Francis, I do feel great."

"What time did the police find the body?" asked Fisher.

"About 1 a.m. KUTY must have had someone monitoring the police radio and a crew sitting around on its collective thumb. They were live by 2 a.m. That's pretty good response, considering the original cop chatter would have been coded and then they would

---

31

have switched to telephones," replied Hall.

"What did the TV report say?" asked Fisher, who was ready to take notes and nodded towards Weeks so she would do the same.

"Basically the guy who killed Kanawha committed suicide. He was some kind of paramilitary nut. Wore camo fatigues. The police lieutenant on the scene told the TV crew the guy's closet was an arsenal. Guns, lots of military stuff. And there was no evidence of foul play. Just a murdering nut who couldn't take it and jumped. End of story."

"You haven't said what tied this guy to the Kanawha murder," Weeks commented, hostile.

"I said he was a sick, paramilitary nut. No doubt he was good with his hands. He punched her," said the executive editor.

"That doesn't tie it in yet," persisted Weeks.

Hall smiled broadly around the room. "I'm sorry. Yes, there was one other thing. He had a clothes-pin in his pocket."

"And," he continued, pausing and leaning forward to underline his point, "There was a package of clothes-pins in his room. Same type as the one found with Judge Kanawha. Two were missing from the package. Obviously one that was in his pocket, the other was on the judge's nose. Cop on the television news said they were all the same brand. It's all tied up very neatly. It's just too bad about this. We're way behind television but that's not unusual for breaking news."

As he ended his sentence Hall picked up the paper that had just been distributed that very morning. It featured Weeks's story reporting that law enforcement still was looking for clues in the Kanawha murder. Still no motive or suspects, although the story reported unidentified law enforcement officials saying the search was concentrating on possible social or legal acquaintances with special training in military or martial arts backgrounds.

The story concluded with details from the coroner's press conference.

"At least Shiloh scooped everyone on the cause of death," smiled the executive editor. "Shiloh, of course you'll do the wrap-up story on this whole sordid thing for tomorrow. You know, the usual, find out all you can about this suicide, Harry somebody, and whatever other loose ends there are."

He turned to Fisher. "And you can assign Ed Caldwell back to whatever he was doing. And now, let's get away from the crime stuff and talk about some real journalism."

"Excuse me," said Weeks, as she rose from her chair.

Hall watched her. She was so lovely, especially when she had the time to get up early and work on the hair, the full red lips, the rest of her face. He recalled so many mornings at the out-of-the-way bed-and-breakfasts when she would be up at the dressing table by 5 and he would lay in bed and pretend to be asleep, watching her careful drill. The result was always the perfect Nordstrom model. He thought he caught a whiff of Poison perfume as she walked towards the door. He remembered their first embrace when that perfume had removed all doubts about her intentions and he had risked the potentially career-shattering charges of sexual harassment with the first kiss. The scent of the perfume, her soft hair, the way she moved her hips and thighs into his had overwhelmed fidelity's pitiful last line of defense. . . .

"Sure, Shiloh, another great job. Case closed. Super job," said Hall. The reporter left without acknowledging the compliments.

After she was gone the editors at the table turned their attention back to Hall. And he finally gave his attention to them.

"Now. For tomorrow. As I said, we probably won't be able to depend upon the police blotter for the top of the fold," said Hall amiably.

"Thank goodness," said Van Gelder. "Although after a suitable mourning period for our dearly departed pinko judge I plan to launch a full editorial campaign urging our senators to seize this opportunity to bring a dose of solid, conservative common sense to the bench here. Take Kanawha's decisions *utterly* depriving persons of their constitutional rights to be compensated for government seizure of development rights of their property in those open space cases. My God! Where did the woman get that nonsense . . . ?"

"Thank you, Francis," interrupted Hall. "Do what you must. Anne, please tell us what else you are working on. I'll tell you one thing, though, I want to see -- what's that slug on the sleight-of-hand non-reduction of state workers story instead of the real lay-offs the governor promised? Ghosts? I want Ghosts resurrected. I want it across A-1. This is major public policy and this state Legislature is not going to play these kinds of tax games any more. If they are going to cut expenses by laying off people, let's take the bull by the tail and face up to it. If they aren't going to do it, we're not going to let them play games. These state employees are people too. They

---

33

don't need to have this stress if it is just political posturing."

"Thank you," began Fisher as she walked to the conference room's blackboard. She discussed a number of stories that had been listed by their slug names. As was her fashion, she made a strong personal case for or against each story, discussing in detail its proposed placement in the paper and its length.

Hall found he wasn't able to follow closely. Beneath his smiles his stomach and head pounded like alternating pistons. And God, he was tired. He tried the tea. Dreadful as usual. He forced down a large swallow. But the lids of his eyes demanded the right to drop. He just couldn't arrest their descent. So he sat forward and rubbed them as he listened to Fisher. He rubbed them until his eyes hurt.

"Jeremy, what do you think?"

Hall's eyes snapped open at the sound of his name. He looked around the table and shook his head. "Sounds good. Sounds very, very good. Just make sure you give Ghosts the position it deserves."

The expressions of the editors around the table told him that wasn't the answer they expected. But he ignored them and rubbed his eyes again.

The contagion of his heavy eyelids spread to his whole head. He could not hold it up. He stretched his neck and arms behind him. He just had to keep moving to stay awake. When he wasn't stretching he was working his butt into the chair. Or rubbing his neck. Or turning his head in circles.

With difficulty he tuned back into the meeting. He heard no talking. Maybe the meeting was over and he was in his office. He could just get up and tell Harriet no calls, no interruptions. Then go to the big couch and finally get some real sleep. Then maybe he would awaken and Shiloh would be there again, and her hair would be soft, and he would draw her slim, perfumed body to him and . . . .

Hall opened his eyes. He was still at the conference table. The staff was staring at him.

"Okay, is that it?" he asked, flashing a forced smile.

Some of the editors exchanged glances, he noticed.

"So we've got the basics of the next edition shipshape? We'll meet again at 3 p.m. to deal with the breaking stuff. Any questions? Remember, I want to see Ghosts on the top of page 1 tomorrow." Hall pushed back his chair to rise.

"We have one more to talk about," said Fisher. "It's one of

those ugly ones we always have a hard time with. It's a real tragedy but it is a crime story, Jeremy. We know how you feel about keeping crime off the front page."

Hall felt the heavy weight of his exhaustion descend again. All he wanted was to get to his couch.

"Tell you what, Anne, you know I trust your judgment. Just do what you think . . . ."

"It's a kid," said Fisher. "A minority. Prominent family. The community is in an uproar. There are many more dimensions than just your routine druggie or drive-by gang murder."

"All right, Anne, if you insist, tell me about it," replied Hall, hoping his irritation was obvious.

"Simmer down, Jeremy. The woman simply is trying to put out this newspaper for you," exclaimed Van Gelder. The shot was delivered in a cloud of Black Russian smoke and cold air.

Hall was too tired and too disappointed that the meeting was dragging on to fight with Van Gelder. So he looked at his watch and waited for Fisher to start. She appeared to be waiting to see if Van Gelder had another salvo.

Or maybe she was deliberately prolonging this agony. Fisher was a good, tough editor. But she damn well better watch her political games. Hall glared at her and then at his watch.

Finally, Fisher began. "Little girl killed in her back yard. In a fine Magnolia neighborhood. The family is wealthy. The neighborhood is in an uproar. Our switchboard has gotten hundreds of calls. I'd hate to be the dispatcher at the police station or the mayor's secretary. And it's not just the immediate neighborhood, the whole Vietnamese community . . . "

Vietnamese.

The word struck Hall in the stomach like an armored personnel carrier smashing a hedgerow at 40 miles per hour.

"How little?" he snapped.

"About 10 or 11," replied Fisher, looking at some notes. "No, she was 9."

"Ha . . . how . . . was she killed?" Hall spluttered. He was looking at Fisher but all he could seem to see was the black building through the window. He saw the little men on the side washing and cleaning it, but the Dark Tower stayed black, stayed in his face. No matter how hard the little men on their platforms cleaned. . . .

"Knifed. In the back. No motive. No reason," Fisher was

35

saying.

"No reason! No reason in hell!" Hall heard himself screaming.

* * * *

One of the editors in the room later told Shiloh Weeks that Hall's strange words came out in a voice that sounded like a primeval shriek.

Suspect, 1986

"No one will know!" insisted Shiloh Weeks.

"It's an evidence scene. I could lose my badge. Anyway, the clothes-pins are gone. To an FBI evidence room. And I can't -- repeat CAN'T -- get you into that!" replied Jerry Buck.

"You owe me a lot more than this. I want to see the apartment for myself."

Buck took a draw on his Marlboro and exhaled the smoke. Weeks rolled down the Taurus' window and turned to the chilly night air to take her next breath. She waited, face out the window.

"All right. But I have to make sure everyone has cleared out first. Wait here," he caved. He opened the driver's door. She watched him flick aside almost a whole cigarette before entering the door of the seedy Second Avenue apartment. That pissed her off. He'd smoke around her but wouldn't take the Goddamned cigarette into a rathole apartment!

She looked at the pavement where the body was found and then up at the fifth floor window from which the fat guy named Harry had jumped.

"Damn!" she spat. She'd had such a great start on the Kanawha story. And now it was all over. Buck said the FBI was sure this Harry guy had done her.

Well, she couldn't believe it. There was a big fat loose end -- the way her boss reacted in the story conference to the bit about the clothes-pin. That little tidbit almost knocked him off the chair. A loose end she would hold to herself -- or sell very dearly.

She looked back to the doorway, no sign of Buck. He had said all the FBI guys were gone, they'd gone through Harry's room and taken everything that conceivably could be evidence. She still wanted to see this guy Harry's room. See what vibes it gave her, what her instinct said.

Right now, her instinct said this was all wrong. Nothing to explain Jeremy's reaction in the newsroom -- except two things.

One: Jeremy cheated with two women, the judge and her. That hurt. How would that bitch of a wife of his like that? She really

---

37

hated the idea Jeremy was cheating on her as well as his wife. . . .
Maybe he got back together with Kanawha after she was done with
him?

That would explain why he assigned that junkie Ed Caldwell
to look into Kanawha's nightlife. Self-protection.

But Caldwell's assignment also would explain possibility
number two.

Two: It was a very ugly thought. It was one born in the motel
room with Buck as he philosophized about Kanawha's possible
killer. It was hard to believe because she had come to know her boss
pretty well during the year they had their affair.

And that insistent, itchy, ugly thought was that Jeremy Hall
might be a murderer. Things fit . . . .

Buck opened the door.

"Let's do it if we're going to. I don't like this one bit. . . ."

"Put on your big boy panties. I told you, it's all off the record.
I won't write boo about it. I've got to see this guy Harry's room,"
Weeks replied.

"BAAAAAAANNNNNNNNNGGGGGG," reverberated the
detective's car door after she slammed it for emphasis. A couple of
passing bums stopped at the sudden noise but shuffled on when they
saw the unmarked but official-looking white Ford and the obvious
cop.

"This place is filthy," warned Buck as he led the way up
trash-strewn steps. The litter led to a hallway that smelled of cooked
lard and ripe garbage and piss and -- beyond that Weeks had
difficulty separating the smells. A variety of loud television channels
competed with a crying baby somewhere up the poorly lit stairs.

"Which was his?" she asked, stopping at a row of old, ornate
metal mail boxes. The slits of several contained paper. No letters,
just junk mail, Weeks noticed. Grocery circulars and more ads mixed
with wet old newspaper and fast food wrappings at the base of the
row of boxes. A couple of the boxes had names -- Carlton and
Johnson -- printed on fading paper in name slits below the slots.

Buck's knuckle tapped box 5D. Nothing protruded.

She followed the wheezing cop toward the blaring TV's and
crying child.

"You got to knock off those smokes," she told him as he
gasped for breath in front of 5D.

"Huuuuuuhhhh, huh," Buck wheezed, pausing and gasping

hard to get oxygen to his lungs.

"Second trip," he managed to slobber. As she waited, Weeks studied the shreds of plastic yellow tape around the door. She read the letters "Crime scen . . ." on one piece. Several of the yellow pieces bore letters that probably read "FBI" before the vandals got to them.

"Open it."

Buck took several deep breaths. Then he unlocked the door and pushed it back.

Weeks recoiled from the peeling old blue linoleum that smelled like very recent urine and cooked cabbage, cats and possums, poverty and hopelessness. Following Buck she tiptoed past the old black and white TV with the busted rabbit ears. Past the sagging, stained, worn green sofa which apparently served as Harry's bed.

The door to the room's only closet was open. Someone, probably FBI agents, had pried off two padlocks. Weeks went to see what was so important that the closet needed two heavy locks and hasps.

In contrast to his filthy, infested apartment, this Harry had kept his closet gleaming. Weeks turned on the light. No doubt about it. There was no dust. Nothing out of place. Laundered, cardboard-starched military fatigues hung with West Point precision on the rack. Everything went in clean. Clean and oiled where the guns were concerned.

At least the outlines of guns drawn on the low shelf showed dry traces of brownish oil. Harry apparently had given each weapon a marked place on the shelf. He had had pistols and short rifles or shotguns, judging from the outlines.

Weeks shifted her attention to the wall of the closet to the left of the door. Newspaper and magazine articles covered it. The clips were lined up like soldiers in military formations. A leader, then ranks of clips.

There were phalanxes of stories about wars and fighting around the world.

Then stories where maximum police force was used. Bombs in Philadelphia. Armored cars with battering rams in Texas. SWAT teams from several states.

Finally, a formation of clips about police and FBI sniper teams.

At the side of the formation of clips, as though they were marching before it in review, was a small, yellowed U.S. Department of Defense paper titled "Standing Orders, Rogers Rangers." Standing order number 17 was underlined. It read, "If somebody's trailing you, make a circle, come back onto your own tracks, and ambush the folks that aim to ambush you."

The closet window was blacked out.

Weeks examined the starched clothes again. Three sets of army fatigues and a set of dress greens. They were the uniforms of an enlisted person, probably a private.

Then a blue marshal's uniform from Troy, a small eastern Oregon town.

Security guard uniforms from three different companies.

Four sets of hunter's green and black camouflage outfits.

"This guy really was a kook, wasn't he?" Weeks mused aloud.

"Certified."

"FBI got the guns?"

"Of course. You ready to go?" asked Buck.

"Tell me about the clothes-pins."

"The package -- made by Forster -- all hardwood, top quality, made in Maine -- was on the couch. Pack had 48 in it. Came with 50. Two were missing," said the policeman.

"A Forster's was on the judge's nose?"

"Roger that."

"If one was on the judge, where was the second one?" asked Weeks.

"In Harry's pocket. On the sidewalk."

"Like he was leaving to kill someone else. Only when he attempted to fly there -- just like he flew into the federal courthouse like a damn phantom -- he dropped like a rock, right?"

"Don't be a smartass. The guy was a kook. You saw his closet. The clothes-pins make it pretty clear. Same brand as on the judge."

"I'm not so sure," replied Weeks. "And you shouldn't be either."

Dead Meat, 1986

"Let's cut to the chase, Shiloh, something is on your mind. I know you didn't bring me here to get shit-faced with the likes of an old man like me," said Francis Van Gelder.

He lit a Black Russian and placed his arms behind his head. The chair was pushed back from the table. He was sitting on his spine, his long, lanky legs comfortably crossed. His coat was open, revealing his expensive red and white stripped shirt covering his cadaverous chest.

"I certainly don't view you as an old man . . . " began Weeks, who sat across the table from him, her fingers lightly massaging the sides of her Scotch glass.

"The chase," interrupted the editorial page editor.

"I think Jeremy killed Judge Kanawha."

To her surprise, Van Gelder's only reaction was to raise the hand holding the Black Russian to his mouth and take a long drag. To her further surprise, the editor did not envelop her in the exhaled smoke. The smoke went out the side of his mouth. He studied her face while he took another pull.

"Pretty strong stuff, Ms. Weeks," he said at last. "Shall we talk about it?"

"Please," said Weeks.

"What shall we talk about first? Why you think so? Or why you are telling me? Or what you want from me?"

"Why I think so," she replied. "You were there when I mentioned the clothes-pin on Judge Kanawha's nose. Jeremy almost fell off his chair."

"Didn't notice a thing and I was right behind him, Shiloh. Even if you are right, 'tis hardly the stuff of which an indictment is made," said the editor.

"You were there when Jeremy shrieked as Anne told the story conference about the murder of the little Vietnamese girl."

"It was a horrible thing, Shiloh. Sometimes I want to shriek at what I hear in there, although it generally has to do with the antics of liberals in Congress and on the bench. You still won't get an

---

41

indictment from a grand jury. Nor me."

"Francis, Jeremy didn't just shriek. He called something, I was told. Something like, 'There is no reason in hell'. Francis, he knows something about that too. It was not a normal response."

"Let's just call it a reaction to something horrible, unspeakable. Editors are human too, you know. Let's look at the rest of the evidence, if you have any. And waiter, bring us two more," called Van Gelder.

The editor no longer was lounging with languid indifference. Van Gelder was sitting forward, toward her. He was speaking to her quietly, conspiratorially. And he had ceased smoking his blasted cigarettes.

"What is the importance of the girl? Are you suggesting he killed her, too? Are you saying Jeremy is some kind of child molester as well as a murderer? I flat don't buy that t'all."

There was more than just a physical shift in Van Gelder's position. Clearly he wasn't ready to buy the little girl. But there was something about the way he accepted her reference to Mary Kanawha's death. To Van Gelder, it was not fantastic that Hall somehow could be involved.

In other words, Van Gelder knew something.

The waiter brought fresh drinks. "Pour vous," he said. Then he whisked away the empties with a professional flourish.

"Please signal when ready," said the waiter in a heavy European accent.

The waiter also pulled out a silver lighter to get Van Gelder started on his next Black Russian. The editor waved him away.

The editor really was interested.

"I don't know. I think there may be some connection to the little girl," she gambled.

"Let's hear why," Van Gelder replied.

"Francis. You know Jeremy was in Vietnam. Things happened there. I don't know what exactly, but I think they were horrible, troubling things."

"Again, why the girl as well as the judge?"

"He was an intelligence officer. He lived in a gray, Machiavellian world. Spooks. Termination with extreme prejudice. Fuck'em if they can't take a joke. All that kind of stuff."

"Shiloh, how do you know he didn't spend the war drawing maps during the day in an air-conditioned building and his nights in a Saigon brothel?"

Weeks hesitated. Then she said, "He wasn't in Saigon. He was in a front-line, hush-hush unit. Maybe the Phoenix Program. I don't know. Whenever I asked he would only say, 'Rest assured, a good time was had by all'."

"Past tense, Shiloh. Why the past tense?"

Weeks ignored the question.

"He's got souvenirs. A Chinese pistol. A K-54 or something. He once told me -- he tells me -- only enemy officers and big shots had them. You don't get that stuff in Saigon brothels."

Van Gelder took a sip of his Chivas.

"All right, let's concede he was some kind of spook. An assassin even. That's not good enough to link him to the girl. Or the judge. Are you suggesting some kind of post-Vietnam Stress Syndrome -- or whatever it is called -- here?"

Weeks continued. "Under his handkerchiefs in a drawer he's got a very long, sharp, skinny knife. A stabbing knife."

"So?"

"It's just a knife. It's dirty. He never cleans it. It . . . it looks like it has dried blood on it."

"Any more beads you want to put on this string," asked Van Gelder, "before you tell me why you know what Jeremy has in his hanky drawer?"

Weeks glared.

"Francis, we had an affair. A long one. Sometimes, when his wife was away, we stayed at his condo. It's over now. Okay?"

"Not prying," said Van Gelder, holding his long, nicotine-stained fingers in front of him like a wall.

"Because we slept together, I know Jeremy's sleep is fitful, full of nightmares. Violent nightmares where he thrashes and fights with something. He shouts in another language, maybe Vietnamese words. He wakes in a sweat. There were times he was so violent I had to pin him down, wake him up and get him interested in . . . well, other things to calm him down. When we had sex after a nightmare you can't imagine the passion, how he would cling. . . ."

Weeks hesitated then continued, "Usually his love-making was very methodical, slow, taking his time. He enjoyed himself and made it good for me. But he was violent after the nightmares. Violent like he was another person."

Van Gelder said nothing and sipped his drink, apparently

—

43

waiting for her to continue.

"So, Francis, I know from personal experience Jeremy steps out of his marriage to sleep around. You have known Jeremy longer than anyone here. You were a reporter with him. What can you tell me about his relationship with Judge Kanawha?"

"The police solved that crime. Remember the man who jumped out the window?" asked Van Gelder.

Weeks shook her head vigorously. "I don't believe it. Not all the rank-and-file FBI agents do either. It doesn't wash. The fat guy Harry was just an easy way to close a nasty, explosive case."

"How do you know what the rank-and-file FBI think?"

Weeks looked away. "I hear things," she said to the floor.

Then returned to the offensive. "Some cops and FBI types think this Harry was some kind of gun nut. A dumb, fat slob who never did anything right. Who never could have gotten into a secure federal building and killed a judge like a karate expert. Harry was more your mass killer in the burger joint. The kind who climbs a tower and opens fire. There was no evidence at all the FBI found that he was into boxing or karate."

Weeks found the words just tumbled now. "But Jeremy. I don't know what he knows about fighting. But he has a sly way. It usually is covered with his liberal do-gooderism. High principles and right thinking. But there is something else there. I feel it. I've sensed it, seen it in the little tricks and games we have played. They were harmless games. But Jeremy always was so cunning, elaborate and diabolical. Pushed to the wall, I fear what Jeremy could -- would -- do."

"Want to tell me about them, Shiloh?" asked Van Gelder.

"Once . . . ." she began. "None of your business. Let me tell you something else. Jeremy makes jokes about the army. You know, 'army intelligence, a contradiction in terms,' that kind of thing. He told me he went to an intelligence school in the army and I think they taught him how to pick locks there.

"So maybe Jeremy can pick locks? Maybe break into a federal building?" asked Van Gelder.

"You bet. Something has happened to him, Francis. The clothes-pin bit. The shriek over the kid. And every time I see him in his office, he can't take his eyes off the Dark Tower -- the Columbia Center. He hates the building, maybe fears it. He is so distracted. The last straw was when he assigned that junkie idiot Caldwell to

---

44

look into Kanawha's background. He did that because he was going through the motions. He didn't want something about her found out. That's why I have come to you, Francis. What was there between them? Was he sleeping with her, too?"

Van Gelder made a slight movement with his hand. No more than the motion a millionaire makes at the auction to buy a Van Gogh. It was all the smart-ass, French-spouting waiter needed. Weeks watched the waiter step to the bar and hold up two fingers. The barkeeper, a large man in a white shirt, black bowtie and black vest with an enormous handlebar moustache and slicked back hair parted down the middle, reached for the Chivas bottle. Weeks thought the bartender walked right out of the British Raj of a Kipling novel, a strange contrast to the slick French waiter.

Van Gelder waited patiently for the Chivas to arrive.

Then he asked. "Shiloh. If Jeremy was your lover, why are you pursuing him like a wolfhound?"

"We broke it off. He's no one special now. Except a suspect. Just like any other suspect. And I am a reporter going for a story. Going for truth. That's my job."

"That isn't the whole story, Shiloh. I don't even think it is the lead. Does Anne Fisher's appointment as city editor have anything to do with it? I have to tell you I thought Jeremy was quite righteous on that one. Shiloh, you are a natural reporter, a fighter pilot, a Texas Ranger. Fisher is an anchor, a plodder, a librarian. Go with what you are good at. Don't aspire to stodginess."

Weeks's voice was cold. "The lead of THIS story -- is that ace reporter Shiloh Weeks leaves dinky, wet Northwest city to become investigative reporter for The New York Times.

"The second paragraph of the story is that the newspaper also announced that Francis Van Gelder, long-time editorial page editor, was appointed executive editor. He replaces Jeremy Hall, who is enjoying an extended vacation at Western State Hospital due to a serious case of Post-Traumatic Stress Disorder. End of story," Weeks said, her eyes defying Van Gelder to push it further.

Van Gelder watched her as he took an extra long sip of the amber drink. Then another, shorter sip. Maybe for courage.

He leaned close to her across the cold marble of the small table top. He was close enough for Weeks to smell, and be repelled by, his strong smoker's breath. She moved her head closer to him, flinching slightly.

"You're right, of course, Shiloh. Once Jeremy and Kanawha knew each other fairly well. What I am about to tell you is confidential. Off the record. It never comes back to me. Never. I'll deny it before a grand jury. In fact, open your purse. I want to make sure you don't have a tape recorder."

Weeks did as he demanded.

"Agreed. It never comes back to you," she said.

More Dead Meat, 1986

"Mary Kanawha was a pretty young thing just out of law school," Van Gelder began.

"She had been a secretary -- for a bank, I think -- developed some hustle and went to school at night. Graduated with okay grades. But no patron, no major contacts -- no summer internship to open the door to a prestigious job after passing the bar. She had to keep working at her secretary's job through school, you understand. She hung out a shingle after graduation. Not much happened. She was an ambitious woman finding it hard to make the breakthrough she needed."

He paused, probably to let the shit about ambitious women needing a breakthrough sink in. Weeks gave Van Gelder the evil eye and her lips moved ever so slightly, forming the words, "Fuck you."

"To make ends meet, and to develop a professional record and make contacts, Ms. Kanawha was relegated to taking overflow cases from the public defender's office. You know, the minor drug dealers, wife beaters, petty welfare fraud. Whatever the staff guys didn't want they'd throw her way. Unfulfilling, nasty work with clients who basically didn't know where or who they were."

"More importantly, it wasn't the forum to meet, and impress, the heavy horses from the top law firms. She needed big civil or high-profile criminal cases to do that. And no one was hiring her for them. None of the big law firms were interested, although I gather she did date a few senior partners in that phase."

"So, what did she do?" asked Weeks.

"What every two-bit lawyer who doesn't get the hand-up does, of course," replied Van Gelder. He stopped to attend to the drinks.

"You hungry?" he asked. "I understand they have a delightful steak tartare in the restaurant here."

"Thanks, no. And thanks for not suggesting oysters," said Weeks.

"Don't worry. Not interested in . . . ." began the lanky editor. He stopped to sip the new Scotch that had been placed on a fresh

47

paper napkin before him.

"... Hall's leftovers?" Weeks said, finishing Van Gelder's sentence.

"Something like that," grinned the editorial page editor.

"Why don't we get back to the life and times of Judge Kanawha?" Weeks wanted to knee the man and walk out. Instead, she smiled indulgently.

"Sure."

"What does every two-bit lawyer without a hand-up do?" she asked.

"Why, turn to politics, of course."

"Which means turning to the press as well, doesn't it?" asked Weeks.

"Of course. And in Ms. Kanawha's case, the press was Jeremy Hall."

"Because?"

"Jeremy was receptive to the turn of a lovely lawyer's ankle. At that time Jeremy had been the court reporter for a while. Many lawyers still believed it was beneath them to advertise then. That left them in a dilemma: How to get their names known in a positive way?"

"And how to slip your enemy the perfumed ice pick and walk away whistling Dixie?"

"As it has ever been. The answer in both cases was the press. Get your name printed winning cases and so on. Sic the press on uncomplimentary stories about your enemy. Elementary."

"Of course," said Weeks.

"All that gave Jeremy quite a lot of power. Treat him right and you were quoted by name in the cases you won. Cross him and you were a non-person. Relegated to the status of 'One defense attorney said. . . .' or 'Prosecutors argued.' Piss him off a lot and your name only appeared in association with cases you lost."

"How did Jeremy use the power?"

"Properly -- from a reporter's point of view -- for the most part," replied Van Gelder. "He dealt in information. Give him information and voila, your name was in the paper. Fail to return his phone call and you were the man -- or woman -- who never was."

Weeks crossed her legs so her foot brushed Van Gelder's leg.

"For the most part, you said. But for a pretty lady named Mary Kanawha, there was an exception," she asked.

"That was obvious, But there was more. Much of this must be conjecture," said Van Gelder. "What occurs between a reporter and his source is fairly private. But let's say I was an interested bystander. So I noted the timing of things, how they flowed, the curious coincidences."

"I understand," said Weeks. "Tell me about them."

"Sure you wouldn't like a little dinner? I'm starved. This could take awhile, you know. And I've reached my limit on Scotch. But a nice Merlot? Well, I'd be quite partial to that," said Van Gelder.

"Why not?" asked Weeks.

They rose and walked across the bar to the restaurant. It had a provincial French decor. Heavy chairs. Large fire place with heavy iron cooking instruments. Large, barred wine cabinet with iron wolf and bull faces that looked like an ornate mobile prison cell from the Inquisition. Baskets of broken baguettes on each table.

"Bonjour," said the maitre d'. He ushered Van Gelder, with Weeks following in his wake, immediately through a small crowd of people waiting to get to a table. Van Gelder's table turned out to be a prime one next to a window. A waiter appeared.

Weeks waited patiently as Van Gelder ordered the steak tartare and wine for two. Generous salads appeared at their places.

"We were talking about curious coincidences," Weeks said.

"Yes. Well, as I recall, the public defender's office assigned to Ms. Kanawha a pathetic wretch who was a minor figure in a major racketeering case of the period. While the client was minor, the assignment gave her access to all the government's files through pre-trial discovery. In other words, the U.S. prosecutor's big racketeering case was laid bare before her while still in the investigative phase.

"As you might expect, the feds simply squeezed her client, she recommended he take the deal they offered and I think he was used to play a role involving a medium size fish before a surveillance camera. Suddenly, before anything was public, Jeremy started breaking some wonderful stories about the investigation. The feds were furious. The revelations forced them to call in undercover agents and close things down before they wrapped up the really big fish."

"But it wasn't justice for the really big fish that interested Kanawha, was it?" asked Weeks.

"Shortly before the whole story was broken by Jeremy, Ms.

Kanawha had filed for a municipal court judge's seat. The incumbent had been on the bench there for some 25 years. Knew who should get the breaks, who to hammer. He was invincible. About the third day after he broke the racketeering story, Jeremy did a major front-pager implicating the incumbent in the racketeering scandal."

"Was he a crook?" asked Weeks.

"Possibly. The story implied he was. I believe it said he was a fishing companion of some of the bad guys, co-signed loans with them, that kind of innuendo. Maybe there was something about the propriety of gifts the judge and one of the hoods exchanged. Perhaps a fishing rod or boat parts or something. My impression is that it was all minor stuff, no wads of cash stuffed in tin boxes or anything like that," said Van Gelder.

The wine appeared. Van Gelder smelled the cork that had been laid before him like a holy relic.

"It has had time to breathe?" he asked the waiter.

"Certainment!" the man replied.

Van Gelder took a sip from the small quantity the waiter poured in the glass.

"Bien," he announced. The waiter smiled and poured the purple-red Merlot into their glasses. The waiter withdrew and reappeared with two plates of raw meat garnished with a striking display of thinly sliced carrots, beets and a radish. The vegetables were topped with a rose as purple as oxygenated blood from the lungs.

Van Gelder cut a small, almost delicate piece of meat and popped it in his mouth.

"Eat up. The steak will give you strength."

Weeks also cut a small piece of the raw meat. She chewed it daintily. She could taste the paprika. The hot cayenne. A delightful mustard.

"The chef prefers to prepare everything in the kitchen. I'm afraid he doesn't trust the customers to do the mixing," said Van Gelder.

Whatever the chef did worked. The raw meat was surprisingly good. She followed the meat with a sip of the Merlot. It was full bodied, rich. Also very good.

"So. What happened?" she asked.

"The shoo-in candidate was dog meat. Jeremy wrote a very complimentary pre-election profile of Mary so of course Kanawha achieved her breakthrough. She was elected to the bench. Jeremy had his big breakthrough too. He soon was promoted to the city desk and designated golden-haired boy. Number One Boy," Van Gelder said, not bothering to hide the sarcasm.

"What happened to the incumbent who lost?" asked Weeks.

"Gone. Went and opened a restaurant on the coast somewhere. Somewhere very obscure, last I heard."

"Francis. I cut to the chase when you asked me. Now cut to the chase for me. Jeremy and the judge have history. But I haven't heard anything that would cause Jeremy to kill her so many years later. Any curious coincidences that might bear on that?"

"Ah, Shiloh. You do want to push me out on that limb. Tell me, how do you read the politics at the paper?"

"Politics?" she asked. She paused for more meat and wine. Then resumed. "If there was an opening . . . . There isn't anyone else possible but you for the move to the executive editor's chair. Everyone else is either too old or too new. Fisher has the brains but she is too new and probably too female."

"How about new blood?" asked Van Gelder. "Your antenna pick up any chance the publisher would look outside?"

"Never has before. He promotes from within and I'm not picking up anything different. What's the matter, do I detect a lack of self confidence?" she asked.

Van Gelder shook his head and sipped his Merlot. "The slope will get a lot steeper and slicker now, Shiloh. You understand that?"

"Just tell me where I ought to look. I'm the reporter. I'll check it out, nail down what is true, what isn't."

"Then go back with me all those years. Jeremy was the young reporter. Just out of the service, product of a state college. . . ." Van Gelder adjusted the lapels of his expensive jacket to underline his point.

". . . He had a lot of potential and was no dummy, I'll grant you that. As I told you, he played those lawyers like a Stradivarius, not that it's a particularly difficult trick. But there was also a raw quality about him. He was a troubled young man. Erratic. He couldn't decide something about himself. His search for something distracted him from his writing, which suffered. He almost didn't make probation, I recall."

Van Gelder drank a dollop of the dark red wine. He poured the last of the Merlot into Weeks's glass.

51

Then he resumed. "It was my feeling this unholy alliance between press and bar provided more than professional advantage to each."

"Why the feeling?" asked Weeks.

"Remember, I never hid under the bed, Shiloh. But I watched them once at a company party. Oh yes, Jeremy brought his lovely barrister. Jeremy had a couple of glasses of the good stuff -- Chivas, as I recall. He became quiet and despondent. No fun at all. I noticed Mary Kanawha led him to a side table. Away from the people and the noise. They had a long and intimate conversation -- there was this beautiful lawyer patting his hand and arm. Once he reached out and put his hand on her shoulder. She reached up and placed her hand on his arm. They stared into each others' eyes for a long time without saying anything, although I believe they were communicating. They must have been fairly open about their relationship around the courthouse. Some of the old courthouse buffalos and bailiffs still gossip about the romance between the beautiful young lawyer and hard-charging reporter. "

"Just fucking beautiful. Really moving," said Weeks. "What happened then?"

"Jeremy broke his scandal series. Kanawha was elected to the bench. And then Mary Kanawha married the first of the law firm partners who have been her husbands. Jeremy was promoted off the court beat," said Van Gelder.

"You think she dumped him for a pair of striped pants?" asked Weeks.

"Who knows? The line between love and hate is very passionate and thin. Did they meet again? Ask Jeremy. I can tell you Jeremy certainly retained a deep contempt for the bar. At first he just frequently referred to lawyers as whores and paid gunfighters. In later years he has loosened up. Still loves a good lawyer joke, though. What do you call 1,000 lawyers at the bottom of the sea? A good start. What's the difference between a bottom-dwelling, muck-eating, slimy sturgeon and a lawyer? The sturgeon is a fish. Ha, ha."

"How did he meet his wife, Beth?"

"Jeremy got married shortly after Mary dumped him. Beth was a pretty, not very bright but a very ambitious administrative assistant at the court house. I think Beth picked up Jeremy on the rebound and slam-dunked him, if that is the appropriate trite basketball phrase. Maybe it was all sex—and a handy permanent source in the courthouse. Stupid marriage, stupid woman. If you ask me. I wasn't too surprised to hear Jeremy's eye wandered . . . ."

Weeks ignored Van Gelder's insinuation.

"Boiling down your curious coincidences, Francis, I'm gleaning two things. One: If I'm right, and Jeremy did things in Vietnam he doesn't put on his resume, Kanawha may have known about them. Two: she may have wrung out his little heart and then dumped him as soon he helped her make the big time."

"A small, but fair, pile of bones," agreed Van Gelder.

Weeks drank half her glass of the purple wine. She wiped her lips and noted the bloody ruby the combination of purple and red lipstick produced on the napkin.

"So, where do your excavations take you next, Shiloh?" asked Van Gelder, making the slight movement with his hand that would fetch the second bottle of Merlot.

Weeks thought a few minutes.

Then she replied, "If Mary Kanawha had something on our paragon of liberalism and human dignity, perhaps I'd better find out what it was. I guess I'd better look up some of the Vietnam counseling organizations. If Jeremy had a problem after Vietnam, maybe those old farts know what it is. I'll also call the army. I doubt it will say anything."

"Counselors aren't supposed to tell reporters that kind of private thing, Shiloh," scolded Van Gelder.

"They're just men. And as Jeremy says, just sick, lame and lazy men at that." Weeks took the last bite of her meat.

Van Gelder grinned at her as she ate. "I told you the steak tartare was excellent here," he said.

"I didn't think I would like bloody, raw meat. But I did," admitted Weeks.

"It's delicious," agreed Van Gelder.

"Francis. You should know something, especially if something has snapped in Jeremy's head."

"What's that, Shiloh?"

"I told you Jeremy had troubled times when he slept. Mary Kanawha's murder has given me some insight into some of the raving I sweated through with him."

"Do tell."

"I believe he was troubled because he killed people who were supposed to be on his side in Vietnam. Francis, I think he turned on

—
53

his *own* people. And *killed* them!"

Police Death, 1966

"VC bad, Chivas good. You drink," Lieutenant Jeremy Hall urged, pouring the whiskey into the clear plastic cup the Backatya Boy and ex-VC fighter Nguyen held before him.

It was hard to pour because Nguyen already was drunk from drinking beer during the canteen movie and he giggled as many Vietnamese did when they drank.

Hall was only drinking a little. Just enough to take the edge off murder. But he wanted Nguyen very, very drunk.

"Numba one," Nguyen giggled before taking a big drink.

"Numba one," agreed Hall, grinning and holding up his own glass in a toast.

Nguyen grinned and replied, *"VC no good. Numba 10."*

The other Americans drinking in the hootch laughed.

Nguyen grinned foolishly in return.

"VC no good. Numba 10," laughed Hall, lifting his glass again. *"Cheeevass."*

The other Americans dressed in civvy bermudas and green tee shirts lifted their glasses. The Dead jammed on a small tape recorder in the background.

Nguyen babbled on with his new friends. Hall knew Wozniak was gone -- who knew where? Nguyen was left alone in the Backatya Boy tent. Hall took a chance and invited him to join the Americans at the nightly movie and drinking session.

"VC no good," Nguyen declared loudly when the English talk drifted away from the pidgin babble about the VC.

Hall roared with laughter and shook Nguyen's hand each time he did so. And poured him more of the cheap PX Chivas.

"VC -- no good. VC numba 10. G.I.'s numba one. Cheeevas numba one," shouted Nguyen.

"American G.I.'s numba one, Nguyen numba one," agreed one of the lieutenants from the enemy Order of Battle section. *"Now Nguyen sleep. Kill beaucoup VC tomorrow."*

"Kill beaucoup VC. VC no good," chortled Nguyen loudly, lifting his glass in toast and following it by taking a long drink of the

Chivas.

The lieutenant pushed him towards the door. "VC no good. We kill VC tomorrow. You sleep now."

"Cheeevasss," giggled Nguyen.

"Chivas tomorrow," said the lieutenant.

"Cheevvass numba one," giggled Nguyen as he was pushed into the night.

Hall picked up his M-16 and coaxed in a clip.

"Going for a walk," he mumbled. The other officers looked too drunk to hear or care. The drinking was a routine. In a few hours the rockets that sounded like speeding trains and screaming mortar rounds would slam into the compound. They all drank to suppress fear so sleep could come.

It was cool and Hall could see the beautiful white stars. No moon. Somewhere howitzers fired, disrupting the night with their booming. But the firing was far off and it was friendly fire. He liked the booming.

The officers lived in one of a line of sandbag-protected hootches. There were doors at each end. Nguyen had exited the door that led to a wooden walkway used in the monsoon season when the compound flooded. On the other side of the walkway where Nguyen stumbled was a series of deep bunkers, designed to provide quick protection when the fusillade of incoming arrived.

Once outside, Hall moved stealthily through the sandbagged buildings to the walkway. Nguyen sat giggling on the walkway. The Backatya Boy seemed confused. Well, he never before had been invited into the hootch used by the American officers.

Hall slipped into one of the bunkers Nguyen would have to pass to return to the tent in which Wozniak's Boys lived. The entrance to the black structure was L-shaped to prevent shrapnel from entering.

Hall moved down and through the L-shaped entrance and waited in the dark.

In minutes he heard giggling. Then a heavy thump. He peeked out. Nguyen had fallen and lay giggling on the wooden walk.

"VC numba 10. VC no good," he laughed.

"Cheevas," Hall whispered from the bunker.

The giggling stopped.

"Cheevass," repeated Hall. Then, "Cheevass numba one."

"VC no good. Kill VC. Cheevasss numba one," Nguyen

whispered back to the night.

"Cheevass," whispered Hall.

"Give Nguyen Cheevasss?" Nguyen asked as he entered the narrow entrance. Hall waited in the blackness as the drunken Vietnamese stumbled around the right-angled entrance and down the crude wooden stairs.

Then he swung the butt of the rifle where the booze smell was the strongest.

Hall cuffed the unconscious Vietnamese's hands behind his back and cut away his uniform.

Hall removed the POW tag from his short's pocket and wired it to Nguyen's arm. Then he dragged the unconscious Nguyen to a jeep and drove him to the MP's POW compound. He returned to the headquarters hootch to complete his preparations.

In the morning he drove back to the compound.

Several prisoners, steel wires just above their elbows to secure their arms behind them, squatted in neat rows just inside the barbed wire gate. Nguyen lay in a heap, unconscious. Dressed only in red shorts, he looked like the Viet Cong fighter he once was.

Hall took a newly arrived prisoner to the adjacent interrogation hut and forced him to squat facing the wall in a corner. Then he watched the squatting PW's through a small, rough window in the plywood wall.

After a half hour or so, Nguyen moved. But he seemed unable to get up. His face remained in the dirt. Hall watched him vomit.

Finally, despite the handcuffs, Nguyen was able to struggle to a sitting position. He looked around stupidly, not comprehending where he was.

He looked over his shoulder at his tag. Then pulled his hands to one side of his back and looked down to study the handcuffs for several minutes.

Nguyen looked at the other squatting prisoners. None of them acknowledged him.

For several minutes he shut his eyes and grimaced, apparently fighting back many pains.

Then he struggled to a standing position and approached one of the MPs lounging at the gate.

From his position in the interrogation hut, Hall watched Nguyen whisper.

The tall MP looked at Nguyen. "Chieu Hoi?" he asked

loudly, sealing Nguyen's fate with the prisoners. "Too late to chieu hoi. Way too late to give up, Charley," said the soldier.

The other MPs laughed.

"Go back to your pals," said the first soldier. He gave Nguyen a rough shove with his boot that dropped Nguyen to the deck.

"No VC. VC no good. I Chieu Hoi," Nguyen pleaded, on his knees and unable to get up.

"Beat it," the soldier said.

"No VC. Chieu Hoi. Dai Uy Woz-nee-ak," he blubbered.

Wozniak's name was enough for one of the MPs to bend over and examine the tag on Nguyen's arm.

"Says he's a VC political officer," the soldier told the others.

Another MP said, "He's the one that the intelligence guy dropped off late last night. Must be a bad dude, looks like the spooks really worked him over."

An MP kicked Nguyen.

"No VC, No VC," Nguyen wailed. An MP threatened him with his boot and the others laughed.

Nguyen collapsed by the gate and wept.

Soon a deuce-and-a-half with several Vietnamese MPs arrived and they called out names listed on a paper on a clipboard. One-by-one, each of the squatting prisoners rose and shuffled to the truck. The Vietnamese soldiers tossed them in the back like cord wood.

Nguyen's name was not called. The truck filled and left.

After a time Nguyen shifted to a squatting position and hung his head. And waited.

Finally a jeep containing three National Policemen in white uniforms arrived.

Nguyen was on his feet as soon as he lifted his head and saw them. He went back to the MPs at the gate.

"Chieu Hoi. Dai Uy Woz-nee-ak. Keet Carson," Nguyen pleaded with the Americans.

"Beat it, Charley," said one.

"No VC. No VC," Nguyen blubbered.

But the MPs had turned their attention to the men in the white uniforms, what American GI's called White Mice.

Mice who did the heavy political work.

After a brief conversation, one of the White Mice walked to

Nguyen and examined the tag on his arm.

"Nguyen Van Pham," the policeman said to his two companions.

Nguyen stopped crying and softly spoke to the policeman in Vietnamese. Several times he said "Dai Uy Woz-nee-ak."

It was against all regulations and good sense to leave the compound, but Hall decided to follow the White Mice as he listened to Nguyen invoke the name of Captain Wozniak.

One of the White Mice shouted at Nguyen and pointed at the jeep. Nguyen collapsed.

Two of the policemen pulled him by his arms to his feet. The third slapped him hard across the face.

Nguyen protested again and the policeman slapped him again.

Then Nguyen was thrown in the back seat of the jeep. One policeman with a carbine sat next to him. The two others took the front seats. Hall watched the jeep drive for the 303rd's main gate.

Hall drove his own jeep to his hootch for his rifle, helmet and flak jacket and continued over the oil-covered dirt roads to the main gate.

"MI. Intelligence documents for ARVN HQ," he told MPs at the gate, referring to the nearby headquarters of a Vietnamese army airborne brigade in whose midst the 303rd had been placed for security – and ostensibly for concealment, but that was absurd in Vietnam.

"Alone sir?" a burly MP asked, very skeptical.

"I'll be all right," Hall replied, pulling his helmet low on his head.

"Haul ass, sir. Don't stop for nothing, and don't turn your back on them gooks down there" advised the MP.

It was a short drive through the ARVN base to the Vietnamese Army gate.

The ARVN troopers clearly couldn't care less if he left the base. But Hall thought he heard one of the Vietnamese in a sand bag pillbox mutter, "dinky dau". Maybe he was crazy. But he left the security of the bases.

Hall drove fast on the narrow highway built high on crushed rock above the paddy that lay on both sides of the road.

He didn't have to go more than about five miles. He stopped about a hundred yards behind a jeep stopped in the middle of the road. *Two White Mice stood on the shoulder pointing and laughing.*

The third was aiming a carbine.

Hall turned to the field to find the policeman's target.

Far to the right, several people in conical hats were bent over, apparently planting rice shoots in the mud. They did not look up.

Then Hall saw the target. A man in red shorts, hands behind him, slogged through deep mud.

The carbine cracked. The man in red staggered, recovered, continued to slog at an even slower pace.

Crack!

The figure in the shorts was face down in the mud. His right leg still pushed.

The leg stopped pushing after the carbine fired again.

Icy Death, 1966

The trickiest part came now. Hall had to prime the trap and get away from the refrigerator without blowing up himself.

It had taken him an hour to set up the claymore mine and run most of the wire. The mine itself was wired securely at belly button level amid Budweiser and Pepsi cans on a shelf in the fridge. The mine's business end faced the door. Wire linked the mine to the electric wires serving the fridge's internal light socket.

He wiped the sweat cascading from his face and went to the canteen door. No one was around. The troops would be at work or out on missions. The biggest danger was the canteen manager or the Backatya Boy Hau himself would arrive early. No Backatya Boys, ARVN translators or American troopers were allowed in the canteen until 6 p.m.

Hall returned to the fridge. He closed its door. All was ready, except for the two pieces of stripped copper wire that would complete the circuit from the power to the claymore's charge. One piece, about six or seven inches long, protruded from the bottom of the fridge in the front just where the door first would pull away when next it was opened. Another wire, of similar length, protruded from the bottom of the fridge's door. Hall had left two to three inches of insulated section with which he could work behind each of the six-inch sections of stripped wire.

The two pieces of wire faced each other.

Lying on his back and working at an uncomfortable angle over his head, Hall formed an inch-wide loop with the stripped wire sticking from the base of the fridge. Then he bent the loop to form a right angle.

Then the hard part.

Don't be a fool! It can't explode -- yet!

Maybe so. But Hall was soaked by sweat. His OD tee-shirt was now a dark, dripping green. He carefully pushed the stripped end from the door through the small loop. He couldn't avoid the thought: a touch was all that was needed to detonate the claymore mine.

61

Hall's hand began shaking. Sweat clouded his eyes. He didn't dare wipe the burning salt water away. He paused, holding the male end in the middle of the loop.

Was someone on the floor right in front of an exploding claymore mine safe? Of course not. Even if the hundreds of small ball bearings missed, the concussion would get him.

Hall couldn't stand it. He couldn't see. This was his first booby trap. So there might be some risk. Static electricity or something. Still, he had to get that sweat! He slowly pivoted his head first to the right and then to the left to wipe his forehead as well as he could on his bare arms.

Now. Finish!

Hall's right hand continued to push the straight wire through the small loop.

There!

The stripped piece of wire from the fridge's door was through the loop so that stripped pieces of wire couldn't quite touch.

Hall stood up and used the front of his tee-shirt to wipe his face from soaked to damp. He looked at his watch. He reckoned he had about half an hour.

But little left to do.

Hall returned to the wires at the base of the fridge. He fashioned a second loop with the male piece that ran from the door through the first loop.

He now had two interlocking loops of exposed wire around each other's short insulated section.

The next person who opened the fridge door would pull the two loops together, completing the electrical circuit.

Which should detonate the claymore.

Wiping more sweat from his face, Hall checked the wires once more to make sure stripped sections were not touching. He looked around to make sure he had not left strips of insulation or his needle nose pliers at the fridge's base.

Hall went to the back of the fridge and, cringing despite himself, plugged it in. He waited. The back blast of a claymore was as deadly as its murderous ball bearings. There was the sound of the fridge's motor starting -- but no explosion.

He listened. The generator behind the canteen also was humming. The generator would be kept in good running condition no matter what because it kept the beer cold.

—
62

Hall left the canteen, taking a circuitous route along the walls that would not expose him to the front of the fridge.

Then he was outside in the hot Vietnamese sun. Hall immediately sought the protection of the sandbagged wall of a nearby bunker.

He waited. He saw no one.

He wanted to return to his desk, just be done with it.

But he had to make sure Hau was the next person to enter the building. Killing Hau would be nothing. Having to dismantle the trap terrified him.

For three days now Hau had left the Backatya Boy tent at 1 p.m. in the heat of the brightest sun on foraging missions, stealing whatever he could find.

He went through different hootches on each of the days. But he always took a swing through the empty canteen and came out loaded with cold beer.

Perhaps Wozniak was back in the compound. Hau didn't go pilfering when Wozniak was around. But Hall hadn't seen the captain in three days . . . .

"Afternoon, sir. Sure is hot." said a voice.

Hall looked up. It was Burchard. A buck sergeant who was in Vietnam as a prisoner interrogator. He had proven much more proficient at pilfering at a grand scale so he had been made canteen manager. So his skills could be used to procure uncounted pallets of cold beer and soda and the newest old movies. Burchard was staring at his soaked shirt.

"Afternoon," replied Hall. "What's up?" The question was stupid and inappropriate. Even suspicious. Just like his shirt. Officers didn't get so sweaty unless they were playing volleyball or fighting. He didn't like being surprised this way.

"Got a delivery due. Gotta hang around till it comes," Burchard said with a wave, continuing to walk towards the canteen.

"Wait!"

"Sir?" Burchard asked, stopping at the canteen's screen door.

Hall looked at his watch. 1:10 p.m. Hau could arrive at any moment.

"It came," Hall said.

"My delivery?"

"Yes. I told the drivers they came to the wrong place."

63

"Sir?" demanded Burchard, clearly angry. "Why did you do that?"

"The driver said the load was for the 303. But I looked at the bill of lading. It was supposed to go to one of the Marine units at Danang," Hall lied, gambling big.

"Jesus, sir. That could have been one of the loads we were expecting. There are often last minute changes . . . ." Burchard began, then stopped, apparently realizing he didn't want to explain to an officer how a supply shipment destined for Danang was showing up at an army unit in central Vietnam.

"Maybe you can tell them about the mistake out at supply -- maybe it is not too late," Hall suggested.

"Right, sir," said Burchard, moving into a double time away from the canteen.

Hall again swept his face with his wet shirt. And waited.

In 20 minutes a nonchalant Hau showed up.

The Backatya Boy walked boldly to the canteen and pushed open the screen door. Hall supposed he would play dumb gook if anyone challenged him.

Hall slipped away and was at his desk in a fresh shirt talking to one of the warrant officers when the nearby explosion sent everyone to the deck.

* * * *

The colonel assigned Hall to conduct the investigation into the booby trap at the canteen that killed the Backatya Boy Hau.

When Hall attempted to interview Wozniak about the incident, the captain just laughed and told him he would take care of his Backatya Boys.

Hall watched while Wozniak and his Boys launched their own informal investigation to find the VC sapper among the hootch maids, sand bag fillers, ARVN interpreters, mess hall workers, laundry women and other Vietnamese with access to the compound.

Hall carefully followed the book. Neither investigation -- despite the innovative and brutal efforts used by Wozniak -- produced a clear suspect.

Hall found a couple of Vietnamese with family ties to known

64

members of the local VC infrastructure. They were banned from the compound.

The scuttlebutt was the Backatya Boys killed a pretty hootch maid who had had a falling out with Buu.

Wozniak told Hall he sanctioned the slaying because it would be good for the Backatya Boys' morale and send a warning message-- admittedly blurred -- to the rest of the Vietnamese civilian employees.

Burchard procured a new Marine fridge within three days, as long as it took for the Vietnamese laborers to repair two walls and the roof of the canteen and add more sandbag layers around the sides.

High Death, 1966

The rough gray metal floor was slick with vomit and the Backatya Boy and former VC fighter Ky's legs sloshed across it with the bucking and plunging of the chopper. He stayed aboard only because of his grip on a short piece of nylon strap hanging from the wall of the passenger compartment.

Hall grasped the aluminum bar on the back metal wall and looked around the Huey one more time.

The pilots in their wasp-face helmets and goggles were preoccupied with surviving the battle. The co-pilot had stuck his carbine through a slot in the front on the side of the Huey's windshield and was popping rounds at the Cambodian jungle below. The rapid M-60 machine-gun bursts said the crewmen on either side of the chopper also were scared and busy. The crew had good reason to be concerned. Something big, probably a .50 caliber, was firing amid the small arms from the jungle below. The crew gunners, stationed starboard and port behind the open sides of the chopper, fired their M-60s like crazy men.

Hall wasn't going to get a better chance to commit his third murder.

He saw no reason not to take the chance.

But he might not have much time. They all could die soon.

He waited to see which way the chopper would lurch next.

Suddenly, the boy prisoner, who was clinging to Sergeant Lieu's leg, screamed and turned and another stream of vomit arched towards Ky, who was on the back side of the helicopter's passenger compartment next to him.

Ky had enough presence of mind to scream in Vietnamese at the boy.

Hall had the presence of mind to kick first at Ky's left hand, which had second position on the small nylon strap. The right hand was doing the real work of keeping Ky in the chopper. The real work of Ky's left hand was to hold an M-16 by the flash suppressor at the end of the barrel.

Hall kicked hard, moving as though he was shifting positions.

"Hiiiiyyyyyyy!" screamed Ky through the din. He released the rifle. The Huey was in a steep roll to the left, so the passengers virtually were suspended at a 60 degree angle. The rifle disappeared instantly through the port opening. As with most Hueys used in Vietnam, both side doors on the passenger compartment had been removed.

Hall looked at Sergeant Lieu, an interpreter from the South Vietnamese Army, and the boy clinging to him. Both whimpered, their faces pushed into the filth of the metal floor.

Ky's eyes were focused on Hall. They were wide with surprise and disbelief. His face presented a target Hall could not miss. This time there was no point in pretending he was shifting positions.

He kicked the heel of his right green and black jungle boot hard at Ky's face. Most of Ky's scream was lost in the thumpa-thumpa-thumpa of the helicopter blades and extended bursts from the port-side M-60.

Fury replaced disbelief in Ky's face. And he was still holding on to his strap.

Hall's heel smashed into Ky's nose. A stream of blood joined the vomit on the metal floor.

Ky clung to his nylon strap.

Hall's heel went up a foot or so into the air and came down hard on Ky's hands.

Another scream somewhere in the cacophony of the engine, blades and machine guns.

Ky's right hand clung to his strap. But his left fist pounded Hall's calves. He screamed in Vietnamese.

Hall kicked his mouth. More blood flowed from Ky's broken face.

Ky's left fist withdrew so Hall kicked at Ky's remaining hand on the strap. After the second kick the right hand pulled away, but the left hand quickly took its place on the strap.

Again, the boot. And again.

Ky's hands clearly were too damaged to hold the strap any longer. He released it as the helicopter leveled. Ky rolled two or three feet across the helicopter's metal floor to the forward end and wrapped his arms around the boy's waist. Lieu and the boy had no interest in the on-going murder. They continued to wail.

Ky kicked at the wall dividing the passenger compartment

67

from the pilots, apparently attempting to get their attention.

As the chopper leveled again, Hall rolled across the filth, grabbing Lieu's shoulders.

He now focused on Ky's head.

The Backatya Boy took three kicks before sliding along the boy's legs towards the opening behind him. Hall followed, shinnying down Lieu's body to remain in range.

Again, the boot. And again.

Ky's head recoiled with each kick. In obvious desperation, he looked at the doorless hole yawning behind him. His legs already hung in space over green jungle.

Hall cocked his leg at the knee. Ky grimaced in pain and wrapped his arms tighter around the boy's legs. Hall saw he even tried to grip with his broken hands.

"Thunk." The boot went for the right hand and struck the prisoner's leg. The pitch of the boy's whimper did not change.

Hall kicked again, going for Ky's head.

Ky's head snapped back. He moved further out the door. Only his head and shoulders remained in the chopper. His arms remained wrapped around the boy's legs.

Hall sidled closer.

After shaking his head, Ky looked at Hall. Rage and fear seemed to be gone. The eyes in the broken, bloody face seemed bewildered. Uncomprehending.

Hall kicked at the eyes.

Ky's head snapped back. When he recovered, he slid further through the opening. Now he was at the prisoner's ankles, still holding as best he could with his arms, his useless hands held away from the legs.

Again he was looking at Hall. This time there was desperation, pleading in the broken face.

Hall pulled the Nikon with the long telephoto lens from around his neck and held it by the strap like a mace ready for the next strike.

The eyes glanced quickly at the camera that swung heavily in the dancing helicopter. Then they linked back up with Hall's. The fearsome little ex-VC assassin had become truly fearful.

Hall paused, remembering the eyes of the little girl when she first saw him and pointed and turned . . . .

He visualized the closed eyes of those villagers sleeping on

68

their platforms . . . . the half-awake eyes of the villagers who ran out to escape the B-52's. . . .

Hall gestured with his chin for Ky to go.

Ky looked behind him and then down.

Hope appeared in his bloody face. He paused and then released the boy's legs just before the chopper pitched suddenly to port. The prisoner, Hall and Lieu now were suspended at what seemed like a 90 degree angle.

Almost vertical, Hall saw what had given Ky hope. It was the chopper strut. Ky's broken hands grabbed for it as he fell towards the jungle. But the strut was no longer below him as he fell from the open chopper because of its sudden, radical change in position.

Hall used a sudden starboard turn as his opportunity to roll back to the aluminum bar.

The co-pilot pulled his carbine back into the chopper and the chopper went into a steep climb. It leveled off hundreds of feet above the jungle and the Cambodian village and the racket from the .50 caliber machine-gun in the village ceased.

Hall pulled himself to the edge and looked down. The pilots were following the winding brown river to the east. Twenty minutes and they would be in Vietnamese airspace again.

And then the secret mission would be over and American and South Vietnamese authorities again would acknowledge they existed. And look for them if they went down in the jungle.

Stalking Wozniak, 1966

*The Stones' "I Can't Get No Satisfaction" song had been
over for minutes and the expensive, garish juke box hadn't yet found
the next selection. Odds are it would be played again. It had been
played many times already.*

*The men in the black cowboy hats and yellow scarves
couldn't let go of the words about the failure to find satisfaction.*

*They sang it, only it came out in raucous, desperate, toneless
holler.*

*Hall stood in the dark shadows of a bunker watching,
waiting.*

*The chopper troop's canteen was only about twenty feet
away.*

*It was heavily fortified for the first three or four feet from the
ground by sand-filled 50 gallon fuel drums and sand bags. From the
top of the sand bags to the roof there were only support posts and
screens.*

*Through which Hall could see the long, expensive polished
wood and brass bar. Rows of liquor bottles. Several refrigerators. A
buck naked, pretty Vietnamese woman moving on the bar at one end
under a jerry-rigged spotlight. She danced in a distracted way,
movement unrelated to the music's beat, unable to attract much
attention. Every once in a while a trooper in a black cowboy hat led
her from the hootch into the shadows and pulled down his fly as she
knelt.*

*They weren't really cowboy hats. These hard men were the
chopper crews who considered themselves hard-riding cavalry. The
black hats and yellow scarves were residue of the uniforms worn at
Little Big Horn. In addition to the hats and scarves, the revelers
mostly wore cut off fatigue pants and OD tee shirts.*

*Amid this collection of black cowboy hats there was one
green jungle hat, rolled on the sides to look cowboy, over the blond
hair.*

*Captain Stephan Wozniak was partying with the pilots,
holding up a lot of money, buying a lot of drinks.*

Wozniak spent a lot of free time buying drinks for the chopper pilots. But then, he was a man who wanted a lot of special favors from them. Special insertions and presumably, reliable, fast extractions and some special delivery work. And a lot of suppressing machine-gun fire as he and his Backatya Boys pursued their private war for grins and riches.

Wozniak's private war could end this night.

It was a long walk back to the MI compound with many ambush sites. This night Hall finally brought the .45 after days of studying Wozniak's movements.

Hall focused on the captain. Wozniak didn't join with the black-hatted soldiers crying out for sat - is - fac - tion. Maybe he knew how to get it.

Nor did he drink much. He seemed to be just sipping as he ordered more and more rounds for his pilot friends.

He would not be dealing with a drunken, shit-faced Backatya Boy if he went for Wozniak.

But Wozniak had to die. There was no doubt he was enemy. As much an enemy as the VC sapper and double agent. More evil than any sapper or double agent.

Hall's reconnaissance of recent days revealed Wozniak spent a lot of his off-duty hours with cavalrymen. And he took a variety of routes when he returned to the MI compound.

The ambush would be tricky.

The Rolling Stones resumed, with the airmen in loud support.

Hall heard Wozniak's voice rise above the song.

He was offering to buy a last round.

"Any more you chickenhawks want me to rent you more beer, now's the time," he shouted.

He had a lot of takers and Hall watched him hand a bunch of scrip to a G.I. behind the big bar.

"Keep it," Wozniak said, waving off folding funny money change.

He moved slowly towards the door, stopping to slap several troopers on the back and shake hands. Hall moved back along the bunker's walls and deeper into the shadows, his hand moving for the pistol in his fatigue shirt.

Behind him was the doorway to the bunker.

It was from the doorway that he heard the quiet, respectful words, "Trung Uy."

Hall stopped, unsure if the Backatya Boy Buu intended to kill him. Should he turn and fire? Turn and smile?

Hall eased his hand from his shirt and turned.

Buu did not appear to be armed. But only a portion of his body was visible in the bunker's doorway. One arm was hidden in the blackness of the bunker.

Buu smiled his evil grin. The contempt was clear on the Vietnamese's face.

"Good evening, Buu," he said as he walked past, waiting for the searing pain of a bullet in his back.

Bye Bye Buu, 1966

Only Buu, of the Vietnamese Backatya Boys at Ap Thuy Tu, remained alive.

Sitting on a lawn chair positioned among the sandbags at the top of a bunker, Hall pondered the affront.

He wore sun glasses and a jungle hat, brim pulled out wide and low over his eyes. He balanced a fast-warming beer on the green tee shirt covering his stomach.

The chair was positioned so it overlooked the Backatya Boys' tent. Hall often took the sun in that chair. No one paid any attention to him.

Buu lay on his side on his cot. It was the only cot in the shady part of the tent. Its sides were rolled up so the occupants could take advantage of any movement of the air. Hall watched Buu bully members of a new crop of Backatya Boys recruited from the ranks of Chieu Hoi into constantly changing places so his cot remained in the shade. Hung, the most recent acquisition of the Backatya Boys band, had to squat in the dirt to get any shade from the sweltering sun.

Buu clearly was bored. Hall watched him chatter at Hung, sometimes leaning over to give him a rough push on the shoulder. The shoves were accompanied by paroxysms of hyena laughter. Hung wouldn't play. He just moved miserably into the sun each time Buu shoved.

Then Buu spotted more interesting prey.

Professor Nha attempted to scurry by unnoticed.

"Hai," shouted Buu when he spotted the shy academic. The Backatya Boy unleashed a barrage of words in Vietnamese. The sharp words sounded like orders. Or insults.

Professor Nha lowered his eyes and shook his head. Buu extended a hand and gestured for Nha to come to the tent. Buu made the gesture with his fingers up. It was the way Vietnamese beckoned water buffalo and cattle. Humans were called with fingers facing down.

Professor Nha shook his head and went into a little short-stepped run to escape Buu's abuse.

73

Buu shouted in Vietnamese until Nha was out of sight. Then Buu laughed uproariously, shoving Hung until he joined in with a nervous laugh.

The next day Hall sat before Professor Nha's schoolboy-like desk when the small office in the ramshackle hootch was clear of Americans.

"Good morning, Dr. Nha. How are you today?" asked Hall.

Professor Nha giggled shyly.

"Trung uy. You know I did not receive my doctorate. This war, you know. And it is very difficult to find time to continue my studies at the university in Saigon. Still I am a professor. And I work for you. Your soldiers bring me too many documents. You must stop the war for a few months so that I may catch up. You must -- how do you say -- stand down?" Professor Nha giggled at the notion of stopping the war. Then he asked, "While we wait for the war to end, I have to ask why you attempt to flatter me by calling me 'doctor'?"

"Ah, this stupid war can't go on much longer," Hall replied, ignoring the question.

Professor Nha giggled. "This war will not end. You like our women, our drugs and murdering us too much to leave. Fuck us if we can't take a joke."

"Dr. Nha. When the Americans leave, what do you think will happen to the Backatya Boys?" persisted Hall.

Professor Nha twisted his mouth and looked down in a sign of contempt. "They are killers. They do not think one day beyond their bowls of American rice and cans of American beer. Their 30 pieces of silver, as your Christians say."

"But Buu is not like the rest. He thinks. And he is strong," said Hall.

"He is not like the rest in that way. But he is still a brute and a murderer," replied Professor Nha. He added, "He will probably become the president of our country when the Americans leave -- unless he kills everyone in his rise to power."

Hall lifted a sheath of papers from the Vietnamese scholar's desk and sifted through them. Many were letters and reports written on pages ripped from cahiers of the type used in Vietnamese schools or from cheap pads of paper. Some were clean, some crumpled, some dirty, some stained with dark blood. They had been collected from the enemy tunnels and bomb craters and bodies throughout much of South Vietnam.

"You see and read a lot of these, don't you?" asked Hall.

"That is my job. Translating the enemy documents," replied Professor Nha.

"And you have been doing it for many years, long before I arrived?"

"Five," replied Professor Nha.

"You've probably seen many letters written by common soldiers to their families? And learned how a VC officer would write an official report? And how a VC intelligence operative would report as well?"

"Yes, of course."

"For example. You are familiar with names of individual officers and agents? Know their units. Know what kinds of security measures they use, code words or whatever?"

"I think I know much about that. Of course they attempt to be clever and ah, secure. So probably I do not know everything."

"I suspect you know very much. You are very good. Your analysis is very good. These intelligence reports of the Viet Cong, they are all done by hand?" asked Hall.

"Mostly. The VC travel with the -- how you say -- few things they must have. Although the base camps in Laos and Cambodia have typewriters. Not new electric ones like yours. Old ones that do not work well," said Professor Nha.

"But a Viet Cong intelligence officer operating in your country, say in a tunnel, would not have a typewriter. He would write by hand, wouldn't he?"

"Uaaa. Yes."

"Professor Nha. Could you write such a letter?"

"One that would appear to have been written by a VC cadre?"

"Yes. But it would have to be very good. Experts would read it. They would have to believe it."

Professor Nha stared at the paper piles. He looked up.

"I could do that."

Hall believed Professor Nha's response was simple, clinical. It was a statement of fact that he could forge an enemy intelligence report.

"Dr. Nha. I have reason to believe the Backatya Boy Buu is a double agent. He is working against the interests of the Republic of Vietnam. But I cannot convince Captain Wozniak of this. I believe serious damage is being done to the allied cause. I want your help in getting Scout Buu removed from this unit. I believe he belongs at Con Son Island. There they will have the leisure to sort through the question. In a scientific manner."

"What are your scientific reasons?" asked Professor Nha, giggling, apparently at the reference to the methods of persuasion to which science would be applied to get to the desired truths at the notorious prison island.

"He has failed the lie detector test we require all Vietnamese who work for Americans in sensitive jobs to take with our CIA each year."

"I know of that. I have had to take the polygraph tests. I know those. I fail them too. They work on a very interesting principle . . . ."

Hall interrupted, "You are not at the university now, Dr. Nha. You are in a war. Do you believe the VC would stop at some ethical barrier?"

"That is not for me to say. I know that someone must draw the lines at ethical barriers. If no one did, can you imagine the world in which we would live? I am an academician, as you know. A man of learning," insisted the Vietnamese man.

"Dr. Nha. In order for persons of science and learned men like yourself to have any impact on this world, men like the Backatya Boy Buu must be defeated." Hall paused. Then he added, "Eliminated."

Professor Nha sat back and studied the hootch's tin roof. He picked up from the table and held between his eyes and the roof a black pen with the inscription in white lettering "U.S. Government."

Hall studied the translator's hands. He seemed to be holding the government pen up as if he were trying to see through it. Hall's eyes dropped to the man. He was a very thin, ugly man. His face was pock-marked, his teeth yellow. Despite the hot weather he wore a frayed and stained but pressed long sleeve shirt and tight-fitting pants. He was no match for Wozniak's de facto lieutenant, Buu, the killer with the scarred face and ubiquitous grin.

"You want me to write a document purporting to be that of a Viet Cong cadre that would implicate Buu as an agent of the Viet Cong?"

"Yes," replied Hall simply.

"What would you do with this document?"

"I would take it to the CIA."

"The Phoenix killers? The 303 kills many spies itself. Why do you need the Phoenix killers?"

"Because of Captain Wozniak, this is a CIA matter. It might end up with Phoenix. I wouldn't personally take it to them. I will take it to the CIA station chief."

"What do you think will happen?" asked the Vietnamese man.

"As I said, Buu may be taken to Con Son Island where the issue will be examined in a methodical way," replied Hall. "That is why the document must be very good."

"I don't think it will happen that way," Professor Nha replied.

"Tell me."

"Dai Uy Wozniak has close relations with the CIA. I believe they will give him the letter. They will let the dai uy resolve his own problems according to his own wishes. You know, the CIA knows, the 303 does as much of what you call dirty work as the Phoenix killers."

"As I said, that may not produce the solution we are looking for. We have tried to convince the captain of Scout Buu's unreliability," responded Hall softly.

"I can write a document the dai uy will believe," said Professor Nha flatly.

He picked a school cahier and pulled out a page. He studied the American pen against the roof again.

Hall rose silently and walked away as Professor Nha put the American-issue pen down in his breast pocket and began writing on the page with a cheap pen of the type sold on Vietnamese streets.

"Remember, I am a mister, not a doctor--yet," Professor Nha said softly to the paper as he labored. "I know you attempt to flatter me."

* * * *

"Dr. Nha, I have not seen the Backatya Boy Buu for many days," said Hall casually, picking up another of the captured documents from the pile. He read and waited.

The document was a cheap piece of newsprint propaganda, printed in Vietnamese on one side, English on the other.

The English headline read, "G.I.s IN THE 1st AIR CAVALRY DIVISION!"

The bullshit began, "Isn't it that the drumfire of fierce attack of the Liberation Armed Forces in the Quant-tri -- Tua Thien battlefield still resounds unto you? Is it that the scene of thousands of casualty of cavalrymen and 350 choppers shot down or destroyed there hasn't blurred out from your memory?"

Hall's eyes dropped through several paragraphs of similar babble to the end to see what the Viet Cong recommended the Air Cav troopers do.

"Demand the withdrawal of U.S. troops home, Let the Vietnamese people settle their own affairs! G.I.'s, don't die the worthless death of the last man in the last battle in Vietnam."

Hall tossed the paper to the worthless pile.

"Dr. Nha?"

"Buu is dead." Very clinical.

"Tell me."

"I know only what I hear from the Vietnamese on base. It is gossip. You must ask Dai Uy Wozniak."

"You know he will not tell."

"The dai uy is very angry. Very dangerous. I do not wish to talk about it."

"Let us walk."

Hall led the Vietnamese by the arm along the walkway that went to the pisser. The little Vietnamese man looked back several times.

Then he began, remaining scientific.

"Dai Uy Wozniak shot him."

"Tell me everything you know."

Professor Nha stopped and looked at him. "To make sure your ethical line is secure?"

"So evil is defeated."

"By more evil?"

"That is an interesting philosophical point that will keep many more generations of academics employed. Tell me about Buu's death."

Professor Nha resumed his walk.

"I am told the dai uy and the Backatya Boys went to the home of a Vietnamese family in a village. They waited outside the door while one of the gang made a signal. A man came out and the dai uy

---

78

*placed a wire around his head. They marched the man for many
kilometers away from the village. Then Dai Uy Wozniak shot him
and Buu as well."*

"The other Backatya Boys did not attack Wozniak?"

*"They were surprised Dai Uy Wozniak would kill his friend.
They did not attack the dai uy. They -- how do you say it -- emptied
many clips many times into Buu's body,"* said the scholar.

"To watch it jump," he added.

Now, Wozniak, 1966

The old Vietnamese man lay face down -- really face down, like someone drove his nose and eyes and forehead through the dirt floor. His arms and legs were spread.

He must have been dead before his face impacted. Because Hall had been waiting across the alley, hoping he passed for a drunk G.I. in civvies negotiating mouth to ear with a hooker. Despite the din of whores, hawkers and Honda bikes, Hall would have heard a live man scream when his face smashed into the ground.

If the old man still was alive, it was someone else's worry. Hall's only care was to see what brought Captain Stephan Wozniak to this dark stall on a crowded back Vung Tau alley after remaining alone in a hotel room for two full days and two nights.

It wasn't just that Wozniak finally had chosen to leave his lonely vigil for this strange stall in a sin city where all other G.I.'s came on three-day leaves to whore and drink and smoke and shoot up.

It was more that Wozniak had come in carrying a cheap cardboard briefcase and left an hour later carrying only an 18-inch high green and white ceramic elephant.

Hall found the briefcase stashed behind a row of ceramic elephants of various sizes and colors. The case was empty. Smelling it revealed nothing. It had no secret compartments.

Alert and holding a cocked .45, Hall carefully searched the stall, gambling Wozniak would return straight to his lonely hotel room. His own head would be driven through the floor if Wozniak returned.

It appeared Wozniak had brought something to the old man. And purchased or stolen an elephant. In one area of the floor, where the man apparently sat on a dirty cushion to work, there was a crude pick with a wooden handle and a small pile of white powder. And some fresh, moist white paste, some of which was on the tip of a small USAF-issue screwdriver.

It looked as if having killed the old man from behind, Wozniak had stashed his case, and slipped with the elephant into the

---
80

crowded, noisy alley.

It was the last thing he had chosen to do after a hard year of combat and ugly intelligence work in Vietnam: take a briefcase to an old man in a beach-front city where any sin was encouraged for cash. It was plausible Wozniak's idea of sinful pleasure was killing. But a helpless old man killed for a ceramic elephant?

The unit clerk had told Hall that Wozniak was history as far as the 303rd was concerned. He was going directly from Vung Tau to Tan Son Nhut Airport and stateside.

That meant Hall had only hours left to get Wozniak. But Wozniak had checked out of the hotel by the time Hall returned.

The bribed desk clerk said the tall American with the blond hair did have a large green elephant when the jeep took him to the landing strip for the Chinook lift to Tan Son Nhut. Hall had missed him by half an hour.

Tan Son Nhut -- a big, bustling place with lots of shooters. A hard place to pay a debt.

* * * *

Hall found Tan Son Nhut more warehouse than international-class airport. Most everyone was going, a very few high-ranking officers or civilians were arriving. New grunt arrivals were treated more like cattle and herded through other parts of the airport to the replacement depots. Far off on a runway, but close enough to see, Hall watched troops on a deuce-and-a-half throw heavy body bags to the ground and other troops carry them into the back of a large transport plane.

The combat survivors congested in the shabby main terminal were not going anyplace in a hurry. It was the old military hurry up and wait.

That meant some GI's slept on chairs, on the floor, on their gear. Many others huddled in excited groups, telling for the first time the exaggerated war stories they would embellish and retell for the rest of their lives. A few privileged or uncatchable Vietnamese ragamuffins trying to do a few last favors for cash also were added to the sweaty, anxious stew.

Hall stuck to the walls, stepping over the sleeping, slipping

---

81

behind the groups. He was in clean but disheveled jungle fatigues and wore his broad-brimmed jungle hat low on his face. The khaki and olive green mass that was Wozniak's camouflage also was his own. He rounded out his camouflage by carrying a duffel bag filled with laundry over his shoulder. The .45 was in his belt, covered by the long jungle fatigue shirt.

It was an impossible mish-mash of hundreds of GIs. Officers and enlisted men crammed together, standing in lines together, all dressed pretty much alike. There was no privilege here.

There was only one thing that would distinguish Wozniak in this mass of green and khaki. A large, green ceramic elephant.

Keeping his head and eyes low to conceal his face behind the hat brim, Hall searched for a stand-offish loner with the elephant at his feet. Probably a loner acting like a gunfighter in a strange bar -- standing or sitting with his back to a wall.

Hall moved left to right around the terminal's wall from the main door. He ended up back at the main entrance. No green elephant.

He moved through the center of the room toward the tarmac exit. That's where the MPs, Customs and Immigration guys had set up long tables. Inspectors combed the contents of all the duffel bags and souvenir boxes on the tables.

There were three inspection stations, so three long lines of jabbering troopers. All holding copies of their orders and kicking impatiently at their luggage as they inched towards the inspectors.

No green elephants were being nudged along in the first two lines.

But five people back in the line at the third station Hall spotted a flash of green behind a pair of high, well-polished jump boots.

Head down, Hall ambled closer, staying in crowds as much as possible.

The jump boots belonged to a tall, black E-4 wearing the shoulder patch of the 82nd Airborne.

The elephant appeared to belong to the man behind him.

Without looking up, Hall made a slow, meandering circle back to a spot at the wall and sat down on the duffel bag like one very bored trooper.

He counted back from the table.

Wozniak waited patiently fourth in line. He wore a frumpy, poorly ironed khaki uniform. The gold leaf insignias on his khaki garrison cap and collar showed he was no longer Captain Wozniak. He was now Major Wozniak. Above his left breast pocket he wore a highly coveted metal Combat Infantrymen's Badge. And a small ribbon with vertical blue and white stripes around a single red stripe—indicating he had received a Silver Star medal, a major award for gallantry in action.

He was very cool. Loose clothing. No sweat stains despite the humidity and temperature dancing in tandem at around 100.

Behind Wozniak a group of raucous, apparently drunk or high, infantry men whooped and laughed.

Wozniak ignored them, a beatific smile on his face showed him to be the patient officer willing to let a few heroes let off some well-deserved if disrespectful and disorderly steam. Above the beatific smile, Wozniak's eyes searched. Probably scanning the terminal for something -- anything -- out of place.

The man was good. Very good. He and his elephant -- probably he would say it was a present for a mythical darling son or daughter -- would breeze through the inspection with his souvenir.

Wozniak now was number 3.

He had to be unarmed. He couldn't get on a plane if he was packing.

But Wozniak would not be totally unprepared for a surprise.

Hall looked around for a bodyguard convoy or escort. Someone to come out of nowhere to the rescue if Wozniak needed it. As Buu had materialized in the dark.

There was no sign of a bodyguard convoy, but Hall doubted he or anyone else would spot one.

Hall also doubted Wozniak had one. He probably was carrying his stash and didn't trust his friends.

So go for him. Right Now.

Hall looked again. Even if Wozniak was unarmed, there were several MPs very close armed with M-16's as well as pistols.

Tan Son Nhut was a well-known VC sapper target and security forces were ready for any threats. And if the MPs or White Mice didn't get him, there were hundreds of combat-hardened veterans who didn't want anyone coming between them and a plane heading back to the world with American female stewardii and cold beer. For any reason.

The upshot was Hall would not get away if he made his move now.

And he could not leave Vietnam for months. Would he be able to track down Wozniak in the States?

And he didn't want Wozniak to leave Vietnam. Ever.

The airborne trooper was at the table. Wozniak was next.

"Hey, GI, you want grass? Smoka in batroom big bird you go home?"

A small Vietnamese boy, or girl, about eight, was whispering in his face.

Hall looked away from the elephant.

There were two kids, one set of eyes focused hopefully on him, the second scouting for the next chump if this one turned up sour.

He felt sweat meander in rivulets around the .45 pushing into his stomach.

"Didi mau. Go," Hall ordered.

The kids scrambled, next target already selected.

"Wait."

"We go batroom, sell numba one grass," said the kid.

"You want $50. U.S.?"

"You bet G.I. What kinna numba one kinky sex you want?"

"No sex. Twenty dollars now. Thirty dollars later. One hundred dollars later you do good job."

"Roger wilco, G.I."

Hall watched the kids tumble into a game of tag through the crowd of soldiers.

Wozniak was at the table. Hall watched a Customs guy point at the elephant. Wozniak said something, the corners of his mouth turning up like a wistful father talking about a child he had not seen for a year.

The Customs guy opened the front of Wozniak's duffel bag and reached in the top. He felt deeply in random places along its sides and then pushed in the bottom. Meanwhile an MP studied Wozniak's orders.

The Customs guy smiled at Wozniak and turned and gestured to the next soldier to move up. Wozniak pushed his relocked duffel bag across the table to a Vietnamese who was building a pile of duffel bags and suitcases on a baggage cart. Then Wozniak leaned down for his elephant.

Which is when a whirling dervish of playful small brown

———
84

arms and legs spun into the elephant.

Wozniak tried too late to intercept the children. The elephant fell several inches from his hands to the concrete floor and shattered as it hit.

The Customs men were looking at the cash and clear plastic bags containing something white, gotta be heroin.

An MP pushed the barrel of a .45 into the back of Wozniak's head. Another spread his arms over the table and kicked his legs apart. Another stood back, M-16 ready to fire. Cuffs came out. The crowd moved in.

Hall returned to the war.

He's Back, 1986

Executive editor Jeremy Hall closed his drapes slowly, allowing the heavy fabric to cover the sides of the black building outside his window. Until it was obliterated.

Even though the Dark Tower had been blocked out, he paused, feeling a chill. And he felt reluctant to turn his back on the building that seemed so intrusive in his life. And so symbolic.

He turned and sat at his desk, which meant he was facing the office door and his back was to the window.

Hall turned on the brass nautical lamp on the glass top of the desk. The light illuminated the area of his desk immediately before him. It barely illuminated his extensive notes which were in two piles. A heavy stone paperweight pinned each pile to the desk. Dark shadows cloaked the rest of the office.

Hall pulled one pile of papers and notebooks toward him. He had to be sure he was right. He knew he was. But he had to turn over all the rocks. He insisted his reporters turn over all the rocks, he could do nothing less himself. He never had.

The army pile:

The interviews with various army spokesmen, over the last few days, had produced the following information: Major Stephan Anthony Wozniak, Social Security Number 839-22-0019, had been arrested somewhere in the Saigon area of Vietnam on Sept. 15, 1966. The charges were multiple counts of drug and currency trafficking. Additional narcotics charges had been added when the defendant was returned to the United States. Off-the-record, a public affairs officer had confided the records showed the additional charges were based on the contents of a safe deposit box registered to Wozniak at a bank near Fort Meade, Maryland.

A general court martial convened at Fort Bragg had convicted the fallen and disgraced officer on all counts and sentenced him to 60 years in the federal prison at Leavenworth, Kansas.

"Sounds like they made an example of him," said the flack.

The prison pile:

Hall had just taken three days and flown to Leavenworth. Court martial records showed Inmate Stephan Anthony Wozniak had been released several weeks earlier. The rest of the official record was confidential, a prison spokesman said.

For more, Hall had returned to his reporting skills. He started with the president of the local correction officers union. He had played up his professional status as editor of a major newspaper and the comprehensive work on prison conditions upon which he claimed to be working. He promised he'd get into all the issues -- the plight of the guards who had to work with Black Muslims, White Aryans, motorcycle gangs, drug cartels, shanks, filth, intimidation, family threats, riots and the rest. The union president soon introduced him to outspoken union members. They were overworked, underpaid, unappreciated, in danger and eager to contribute to Hall's story about prison working conditions. They were impressed with the attention they were getting from the executive editor of the far away newspaper. Eventually, on background or off-the-record, they were willing to break the rules and discuss what they knew about one particular inmate, Stephan Wozniak, Inmate No. 936782.

The upshot was they basically were afraid of Wozniak. He was a quiet man who avoided the rackets, scams, sex and dope. He had few friends but many associates who were willing to play runner and look-out. In that sense, he was a con boss. But a subtle shot caller. He was suspected of killing one inmate, another tough con boss, upon his arrival in 1966. The other toughs got the message and left him alone. Looser rumors were that he had killed inmates as well, motives unclear. The snitches never were sure. Nothing was ever proved. No evidence existed. Nothing stuck.

Because nothing stuck, and because he never caused the administration any trouble, he was released shortly after doing a third of his time.

If there was anything outstanding about the man, it was this: Stephan Wozniak was a man with a cause. He wanted out as soon as possible. Maybe he wanted to go straight. Maybe a great job or an inheritance. Maybe there was a special woman. Maybe he had a score to settle on the outside.

Then the trail grew cold. Wozniak's overworked probation officer wasn't sure where Wozniak was and didn't seem to care. After all, he wasn't in for anything violent. Just currency and drug stuff. A hero field grade officer crucified to set an example. No enlisted person would have done anything like that much time. And who didn't make a few bucks in Nam wherever they could? There were a million ways for the savvy in Nam. So what if there a few bucks made? There were lots of ways to make bucks out of Vietnam without hurting anybody. Currency and narcotics meant no one was hurt. The probation officer said he had real problems to worry about.

So Wozniak was free. The feds gave him a little money and a suit. And he was on the move.

Hall was sure Wozniak was in Seattle. The clothes-pin on the judge's nose. Then the little Vietnamese girl. Just like Ap Thuy Tu. Wozniak had announced his arrival in a way only someone at Ap Thuy Tu that night would recognize.

He was recreating Ap Thuy Tu in Seattle two decades later.

And Hall was the only other person in the world capable of receiving the signal. Hall barely could remember the names of Wozniak's Backatya Boys. Well, except for Buu, of course. Was there a Nguyen? Many Vietnamese were named Nguyen. Ky? Phu? Hall remembered the helicopter. The night with the Chivas and then the execution. The claymore mine. God, they all were dead. He'd do it again.

The little girl. Also dead. He would never forget how she had waited beneath him as he had held her mouth. How he had let his weight push in the knife hoping the flak jacket would provide some absolution . . . .

Had he atoned? He had gone over the question a million times in his head. Mission was everything, the army had told him. He had defended the mission. Obeying orders was everything. He had obeyed his orders. What had he done wrong? What more could they ask of him? He had had to move on. Mary Kanawha was right about that.

All Mary Kanawha's handholding and counseling was wrong about that. It would never be over until Wozniak died like the little girl. There was no lawyer-made justice for what he had done -- what Wozniak, the army, the war had made him do. He had wanted to kill Wozniak in Vietnam, just as he had killed the Backatya Boys. For him, the Vietnam War had been one against Wozniak and his Backatya Boys. But Wozniak himself had been much more dangerous prey. Hall had stalked him, looked for the opening. But Wozniak was a careful man with many friends and more enemies

—

88

and he left no openings that Hall could find. At least not until the very end when Hall had landed the one solid punch at the Saigon airport. Maybe 20 years in a prison was worse than death. Hall hoped so. But still, one more death was necessary. More important than anything else.

Hall rose from the chair. He needed to walk to the window. Look out at the harbor and see the sailboats tacking, the freighters slow and link up with the tug boats. See Life. But he wouldn't see those things. The Dark Tower was out there now. In his face, just like the Black Virgin had been.

So Hall just stood in the darkened room. His eyes dropped. He could not even see the tips of his shoes. In Vietnam he had been 30 pounds lighter. He had been the terror of the low crawl course at Fort Benning. An animal on the bayonet assault course. A lean, yearling, resourceful coyote.

Now. Could he even crawl? Get a quarter of the way through the assault course?

"Asshole. You knew this day was coming. Why'd you let yourself go?"

Wozniak wouldn't have let himself go that way. Prisons had weights, running tracks and all the workout time anyone could want. Remember how he had killed Mary Kanawha.

Hall pushed the notes back toward the brass nautical lamp on the glass desk and walked to the window. There was the black building beyond the closed curtains.

The only question was: did he go looking for Wozniak or wait for him to show up, make him fight on his ground?

There was a knock on the door.

"Not now, I told you, Harriet," Hall called over his shoulder.

"There's someone here to see you, Jeremy. He says you'll want to see him," said Harriet's muffled voice. She didn't dare open the door without being invited to do so. She had learned that lesson once when he and Shiloh were together.

"Please come in for a minute," he called.

The secretary entered and shut the door behind her.

"Is his name Wozniak?" asked Hall.

"Yes. What should I tell him?"

"Show him in. After he is in, call security. Have them wait with you. Just have them wait."

"All right. Do you want me to call in Mr. Van Gelder or

anyone else to the meeting?" asked the secretary. She was asking if he wanted witnesses.

"No. Just show Mr. Wozniak in."

Hall sat at the desk and put his notes under the in-box pile.

"The desk a barrier? Or don't you want him to see what a fat shit you've become?" he muttered to himself.

And then Wozniak was standing in his office.

Hall studied Wozniak as Wozniak studied him. The former captain and major had changed. His shock of blond hair was gone. Now he was balding and gray. His face had lost his soldier's tan. Now he was white. White as a ghost. He had remained thin. He wore blue jeans, a light blue shirt open at the collar and a gray sports jacket. New Nike running shoes were on his feet. He also carried a battered brief case.

After Wozniak gave Hall the once-over, he walked to the window. He pulled the curtains open. His eyes immediately danced to the black building. "I like the view," he said. He turned and his eyes continued around the room, falling on Hall's glass desk and then finally back to Hall.

"Lootenant Hall. You've prospered."

"Please sit down, captain," said Hall, motioning to the chairs that faced the front of his desk. He was not going to refer to him as a major. Wozniak didn't appear to react to the slight.

Wozniak brought his brief case to the desk and sat. His hands massaged the expensive blue fabric of the chair's arms. "Yes, you have prospered." He sat relaxed, long legs crossed, hands at ease on the arms of the chair.

"The physical trappings aren't important, as you know. The mission here is what counts," replied Hall.

"Mission always is everything. Only here it's truth, justice, shit like that too?" asked Wozniak.

"Something like that."

"It's still real nice," said Wozniak. But his eyes now had settled fully on Hall. They twinkled, complimenting the smirk on his face.

"What can I do for you, captain?"

"Came for some information about our old unit, lootenant. You see, I've been away. Thought I might have missed reunions, shit like that. Do the boys still get together? Maybe sit around and drink that cheap PX Chivas, listen to that Dylan dude? The Dead, maybe?"

"Never looked back, captain," Hall responded flatly.

"A real shame. I still hear The Dead. And you don't get even a Christmas card from our colleagues, like maybe that little dink Nha?"

Hall shook his head, never taking his eyes off Wozniak.

"Really? I think about the old times a lot. Course I've had time to think. I didn't prosper, like you. But like you, I think a lot about truth and justice and that shit. Just like you. In fact, we must be alike in a lotta ways, lootenant."

"I hope not, Mr. Wozniak," said Hall, deliberately shifting away from the military rank.

"Oh, I think we are. More than you'll let on, lootenant. More than you'd like."

"What can I do for you, Mr. Wozniak?"

The merry eyes twinkled.

"I came to tell you that I know, lootenant," grinned Wozniak. "And to remind you: once you pull the pin, Mr. Grenade ain't no longer your friend."

"Know what?" asked Hall.

Wozniak ignored him.

"I figure it had to be that kid. That was the 'why'."

They had become the cobra and mongoose. Their eyes were locked. A fast move and a weapon surely would have been whipped from the briefcase or from beneath Wozniak's jacket. Hall's own hand curled around one of the heavy stone paperweights on the desk.

"I told you. Vietnam is very far away now. Water under the bridge. Water that has flowed out to sea now."

"You were very good," grinned Wozniak. "In fact, for a long time I didn't even get it. What finally gave you away were those kids. The ones that knocked over my elephant in front of all that law. My pals wanted what was in my elephant. But they wanted to get it away from me. They wouldn't have sent kids to knock it over in front of the law. Only a snot-nosed lootenant would arrange that. You ever know how much bread you were fucking with?

"Once I figured out the elephant, then the question became who? It became a process of elimination and I ended up with you. Course I walked backwards down that trail. Buu. I think that was a set-up. You and that little dink Nha cook something up?

"Ky. You were on the helicopter. Other gooks were on the helicopter. But only my colleague dropped out.

"Hau. We never did find who did him. Of course you ran the investigation into the bombing. And we were only looking for Cong. Never assume, lootenant. They always told us that. And I forgot the simplest rule. I never thought to look at my American associates. Just assumed it was the Cong.

"Nguyen. I heard he started up the road to Con Son with the White Mice. He never made it. It stunk to me like he was terminated with some of that extreme prejudice. You set that one up too? I think you did.

"Buu. My favorite set-up was Buu. You and Nha framed my gook colleague Buu, wrote that letter and leaked it to the Company. Then sat back and let me do my own dirty work. Nice, elegant touch. Elegant touch to use them kids at Tan Son Nhut. Revenge for the kid at Ap Thuy Tu, I suppose. Kids avenging a kid. In fact all that elegance confirmed it was you who had my elephant broken in front of the law."

Wozniak paused to smile. He resumed, "Did you know the rest of my stash is gone too? The fruit of three Nam tours sitting in a safe deposit box. I had been set. Then they found the key and the contract for the deposit box with my stuff. I lost it all and spent my best 20 years in stir. We truly do have some reminiscing to do, lootenant."

"I don't know what you are talking about, Mr. Wozniak. Maybe you'd better leave now."

"My business ain't finished," replied Wozniak, pleasantly.

"I'm afraid it is. I have other meetings. You'll have to leave."

"You'd better have that bitch out there block out a lot of time on your calendar for me, lootenant."

"I'm not a lieutenant, Mr. Wozniak, and my secretary is not a bitch. If you don't leave, I'll have to call the police."

"I don't think so, lootenant. I think you want to protect our little secret. What do you suppose that little chick's name at Ap Thuy Tu was? Ever think about that?"

"Get out."

"Yeah, that will play just fine in this citadel of truth and justice. Big Shot Executive Editor committed war crimes on children. Even beyond that, I think you won't call any cops because you aced the kid. You think you personally gotta resolve it. Atone for it," Wozniak said, his eyes laughing.

"The fact is, lootenant," Wozniak said, "You aren't ever

going to be happy until you've killed me. It's gotta weigh heavy on you. Man, that little chick was just trying to take a piss. And you killed her? For what? A handful of silver -- that's what the prison chaplain called the bread we felons killed for. You won't tell shit to anyone."

"Get out. Or I'll throw you out."

"Don't lose your cool, lootenant. A story is all in the telling, my friend. It's all in the telling. And that's how I remember it," grinned Wozniak.

"Get out," ordered Hall, rising, the paperweight in his hand.

"Maybe you're right. We'll be seeing a lot of each other. I don't want to overstay my welcome." Wozniak rose and walked to the door with his battered briefcase.

Then he stopped and turned, his eyes mischievous. "All this excitement about our reunion almost made me forget the present I brought for you."

He reached into his briefcase and pulled out a small tin candy box.

"God," uttered Hall, shrinking back from it.

Wozniak held it towards him with one hand. "A tin box. Just like the one in that kid's house," he said.

"Keep it and get out," ordered Hall.

"Sure?"

"Get out," repeated Hall.

"At least take a look at it," grinned Wozniak. He tossed the box so that it landed on the carpet several feet in front of Hall's desk.

Hall heard the door close quietly as Wozniak left. But Hall's eyes were riveted on the box as it bounced in front of the desk. The lid popped off revealing the hand grenade. Its pin had been pulled so the grenade's spring popped the handle as soon as the lid's confining pressure was gone.

The grenade rolled towards Hall's desk. It was too late to do anything. There was no shelter, no protection. In two seconds the shrapnel and shards of glass from the desk would shred him.

His last words on earth were to shout, "Get him!" Then Hall dropped to the floor, his arms wrapped around his head to wait.

One second.

Two seconds.

Three seconds.

Five seconds.

Nothing happened. Wozniak was playing.

The grenade was a dud.

Hall was surprised at how fast he vaulted his bulk over the desk. He raced through his door. He spotted the blue shirts of two security guards disappearing through the doorway at the end of the paneled executive corridor.

He followed, puffing already. He was through the door. There were four elevators and a heavy fire door labeled "exit." All four elevators were moving, according to the indicators above their doors. His eyes were drawn to the second elevator from his right. It was starting down from the 19th floor, according to the racing numbers. Hall's office was on the 17th floor.

He punched the up and down buttons beside the elevator's door. It was too late, the elevator passed 17 without stopping. It plunged toward the ground floor.

The door of another elevator opened and the two red-faced guards emerged. It was one of the elevators that had risen from the lower floors.

"The guy went to the stairs. We ran down after him but he disappeared somewhere. The guy is a ghost, sir," puffed one guard.

"Idiot. You just fell for the oldest trick in the book," spat Hall. "He ran upstairs, not down. And relaxed on his way down in the elevator."

Run, Now, 1986

"Run now. Disappear! Before it is too late!"

The Vietnamese man and woman sitting before Hall, both dressed in mourning white, blinked at him without any comprehension. He doubted they heard him.

The man was greasy fat. A merchant who apparently was doing well in Seattle's International District. At least the expensive house overlooking Bainbridge and Blake Islands across Puget Sound suggested success at something.

The father seemed useless to Hall. He sat and said little. Mostly he blubbered.

His wife was more in control and probably was the brains of the well-to-do family. She was perhaps 50. She was slim but was betrayed by drooping skin under her chin, puffiness around the eyes and thick Coke-bottle glasses. She was asking questions, but Hall was providing few answers.

"Sir. Please tell me your name?" she asked.

"I cannot," Hall repeated, answering the question the same way for the fourth time.

"This is a very difficult time for us. We do not understand why you have come here. Why do you trouble us now?" she demanded.

"I fear the person who killed your daughter may mean you harm as well," Hall said for the third time.

"Who is the person? Have you told the police? Why did he kill our daughter?" she asked.

"I told you. I cannot prove anything. I am trying to do my duty. I have suspicions. I cannot make allegations I cannot prove," said Hall.

"You are a citizen, as we are. You can help the police solve a terrible crime," said the woman.

"I cannot. I can only warn you to leave Seattle," said Hall.

"I'd like to see him come here." That was Luke speaking. He was the couple's son, who appeared to be about 19 or 20. He was slim, in good shape with a whitewall haircut. He wore acid-washed jeans and a tee-shirt. The photo of him on the mantle showed him in an Air Force Academy uniform. The picture next to his was of a thin girl with long black hair. That girl was sitting next to her brother. She was about 15. She had been introduced as Mary.

There were two other photos on the mantle. One was of a girl aged about nine. Smiling a dazzling smile. Very cute, eyes sparkling. No one had mentioned her.

The other was of Jesus. His hands were before him in prayer and he wore a crown of thorns.

Hall turned to the tough young cadet.

"If my information is correct, the person you must fear is very cunning, very resourceful, very evil. Please go away. Overseas would be best. Singapore perhaps, or Hong Kong or Bangkok, and disappear for a few weeks. You must beware."

The woman spoke again. "You want us to try to hide among yellow people. But we are Americans now. And we are used to adversity. I worked for the American Air Force Intelligence in Saigon." She rose and walked to a certificate on a far wall. She removed it and brought it to Hall.

It was a dime-a-million certificate of appreciation from some Saigon warrior captain in an obscure bomb damage assessment group tucked away in Military Assistance Command, Vietnam.

"The captain arranged for us to leave Vietnam at the last minute. The VC were already in Bien Hoa. Only one jet left Saigon after ours," said the woman.

"You must have been through much," said Hall. "But you have just suffered a great tragedy and you and your children are in dire danger of more tragedy. You must beware. Please go away. This person is much more evil than even the VC. *Your whole family is at risk.*"

Luke was on his feet in a fighter's stance. "I'll take care of this guy. Just tell me who he is."

"If you won't do as I ask, there is nothing more I can do here," Hall said rising. He had too much to do to listen to the bullshit bravado. "Thank you for your time."

The woman looked him in the eye. "Thank you for coming. I believe you are a good man even though you tell us so little. We will tell the police we have been warned this bad person may come back."

Hall shook his head. "It will do no good. You will be lucky if

—

the police have a patrol car drive by your house every couple of hours."

He looked at the front door. The lock was a hardware store-variety deadbolt. Then he glanced at the windows in the living and dining rooms. There was no way these people would keep Wozniak out.

"If you won't leave and can afford a security guard -- an off-duty policeman, someone armed and not a rent-a-cop -- I would do that. I believe you are in serious danger," he warned.

"Don't worry about us," said Luke. His fists clenched and shoulders squared. The boy's father and sister cried softly as Hall left.

Fair Lola, 1986

"Yeah, I remember Harry. But I'm trying to forget him," guffawed the bartender.

An appreciative crowd of pallid men wearing ball caps over their long, unwashed hair and chunky, middle-aged women joined in with their laughter.

"Course he turned himself into a pancake," added the bartender, drawing more laughter.

"Did he have any new drinking buddies, people he hung with?" asked Hall. He was uncomfortable conducting an interview with a tipsy audience. But he was the night's theater, probably as good as this joint ever got. And it was the bartender's rules. He seemed to want the crowd around. Hall didn't like it but maybe one of the drunks would slip and say something important.

"Who you again?" asked the bartender, a dirty, middle-aged man with a long moustache and shaggy hair. All the hair deflected attention from the man's head. An NRA cap was worn just high enough to reveal the skull was bald. The filth of the man and his establishment were revealed each time he opened the heavy wooden door to the built-in refrigerator. That was where he kept the cheap wine and canned beer.

"Just a reporter. And give me a bottle of your best imported beer. Plus a round for you and all your friends here," grinned Hall.

"Right, partner," said the bartender with a return smile. He moved to the fridge and removed an armload of Molsons. Hall slid two $50 bills over the bar, keeping his hand firmly on the money. All Hall's new drinking pals bellied up.

The bartender opened the beers, his eyes on the two $50s. Hall pushed one $50 his way.

"What do you know about Weird Harry?" asked the bartender.

"Not much," said Hall, after taking a swig and putting down his bottle of Molsons. "Just that he jumped out his window. I thought it might make a good human interest story. You know he was the city's 100th suicide this year, don't you?" Hall asked, making up the

—
98

statistic. "I think our readers would like to know what was behind it. What pressures drove him. That kind of thing. Real human interest."

"No shit? Harry was number 100?" asked one of the hags.

"Seems so," replied Hall.

"How'd ya know Harry hung out here? Not that we wanted him. Didn't spend shit. Didn't fit in. Just hung around. A major pain in the ass," said the bartender.

"I looked up the police report to get his address. You have the closest bar to his apartment," replied Hall.

The bartender looked around at his gallery. No one seemed to have any problems or questions with or about the explanation.

"He was a real asshole," said one long-hair in a sleeveless undershirt and greasy cap lettered, "Shit Happens."

"Sounds like he was, all right. But he is number 100. And the boss gave me the story. I gotta come up with something," said Hall. And to the barkeeper, he said, "Let's have another round." He pushed the second $50 towards the man.

After handing the second round of Molsons to the crowd, the bartender asked, "So, where were we?"

"This Harry. He have any friends?"

"Naw," said the bartender with authority and finality.

Hall waited but the man added nothing. Hall scanned the small crowd. Serial alcoholics guzzling free beer. Just slurping sounds.

Hall didn't know how. But the clothes-pins somehow linked Harry to this. It didn't fit the events at Ap Thuy Tu. Killing the judge did. Stabbing a little girl in the back did. Wozniak was playing a game, recreating Ap Thuy Tu. His next logical target was the little Vietnamese girl's family. Harry didn't fit in. Anywhere.

Then a blessed hag with a dirty white sweatshirt inscribed, "Honk if you're horny" crossed her eyes as if to focus on an obscure point somewhere in her fogged mind. She grinned in triumph and told the crowd, "That guy bought him a drink the night he jumped."

"That's right," acknowledged the bartender. He immediately added details, apparently to make amends for forgetting. "Skinny guy, white, like a spook, and balding, with gray hair. I remember now. Real white. Like he had been in the can or something. "

Several of the long hairs looked around defensively at the mention of the word "can." Hall took a deep breath. "You know where I can find this guy? Maybe he can tell me about Harry and

---

99

why he jumped."

"Never saw him before," said the bartender to his audience. It agreed with murmurs and shaking heads.

"This white guy with the gray hair. He come back here since that night?" asked Hall, turning on his stool to make sure Wozniak wasn't sitting in one of the dark booths. Satisfied he wasn't, he pulled another $50 from his wallet and moved his index finger in a circle over his right shoulder to indicate "here" was the dingy bar. As he waved his finger, Hall remembered how Wozniak used the gesture in Nui Ba Den's shadow. He quickly put his hand back on the bar.

"No, but he might," said the bartender, eager to be helpful in some way.

"Well, I'd better check back," said Hall, disappointed.

"Where you going, honey?" asked the hag with the horny sweatshirt.

"Out to talk to some of Harry's neighbors. I'll be back."

"Be careful, honey, that's a bad neighborhood," said the woman, referring to Harry's shabby apartment building only half a block away from the bar.

"I'll be careful," he said, patting her hand. He turned to the bartender. "Why don't you give me a piece of that jerky you've got there. I need something to chew on," said Hall, pulling another $5 from his wallet.

Rather than going to Harry's apartment, Hall took his hunk of meat to his car. He sat in the dark, scanning the buildings around him.

It wasn't much of a clue, but it was the best he had for the location of Wozniak's lair. The encounter with Harry probably was accidental so Wozniak might be living in the area. He had lost his Vietnam stash, couldn't have much from the prison. It made sense he would be in a downtown flophouse, maybe holding up mini-marts for a living while he settled his scores.

Hall settled back, shifted the pistol in his belt and studied the neighborhood, chewing and watching.

That's when the fingers slowly scraped the driver's-side window. Instinctively Hall ducked on to the seat then rolled to the floor.

"Baby, baby, be cool. It jus' me. Lola. I dough wanna hurt you" said a woman's voice.

Hall looked up. The nails and voice belonged to a very

young, almost child-like, black woman. The nails were too gnawed to effect the subtle and sexy come-on against the window the woman apparently intended.

"Go away," said Hall.

"You wanna date?" asked the woman.

"No," said Hall, firmly.

"Then why yo sitting here in dis fancy car?" she asked.

"I'm drunk. I'm waiting till I am sober enough to drive," replied Hall, reaching for his pistol and scanning the area around his car, refusing to be distracted by the woman and feeling foolish to be caught where he could not maneuver. Christ! His engine wasn't even running. He turned the key.

He saw no sign of Wozniak.

"Go away, I'm sober now," he told the woman. "I want to pull out."

She just stood at the window. He rolled down the window a crack. Her voice was practiced. She came on to men in cars professionally. She said her lines without thinking. Her rolling eyes and nodding head said her mind was somewhere else. Hall paused.

"You work here often?" he asked.

"Yeah, honey, dis is my corna."

"You see a thin white man, gray hair, new in the neighborhood?"

"I'll sober you up real quick," said the woman.

"No. I'm too drunk to get it up," said Hall. "You see that white guy with the gray hair?"

The whore apparently took the comment about the effect of the alcohol as a professional challenge. Her eyes focused on him briefly.

"You jus hop in dat back seat. You'll have a date you'll never forget. I don't care how drunk you is."

"You look a little young for this," Hall told the woman.

"Shiiiiii-it. I jus 30 years old," laughed the woman.

"You look like you should be in high school," said Hall.

"Man, I've been eating cum for . . . ." the whore stopped and tried unsuccessfully to think. "Cum keep me young. So how bout roun de world? Twenty bucks. You don't cum, you doan pay."

"No thanks. I just want to sober up. I gotta go," said Hall, turning the wheel and revving the engine.

"Baby," spat the woman, standing back unsteadily from the

car.

The car rolled slowly forward.

"Wait!" cried the woman.

"What?" asked Hall, ready to stomp the accelerator.

"Da man. He said give you . . . " The whore stopped, apparently unable to remember something.

The Man.

Who did she mean? The police? The white man? The Man. An authority figure. Blacks meant many things by The Man. It was slang. It was nothing to worry about.

"Oh. I knows," giggled the woman. "Da man. He gimme some o' de good stuff to giff you dis if you doan wanna fuck." She pushed her small handbag against her red miniskirt, struggling to open the snap.

"Here it is. Dis is what dat man gimme," said the woman. She was looking behind her into the dark shadows as though she thought someone was watching to make sure she concluded her side of a contract. It was an envelope. She stuck it through the small slit in the window and stood back, weaving on the sidewalk.

Hall pulled out, tires screaming and leaving rubber on the street.

He drove fast with abrupt turns. Several times he did sudden U-turns and backtracked. Finally, far from the whore, he pulled over suddenly on a narrow residential street and turned off his lights. Nothing pulled up behind him or passed him.

Satisfied he had not been followed, Hall turned to the passenger seat where the envelope waited for him.

He picked it up with the rag he used to wipe the windows. Then he opened it with the blade of his pocket knife. He was careful not to touch it.

Hall shook out the paper.

It was a school kid's lined paper. From a notebook. The closest thing in an American stationary store to a European -- or Vietnamese -- cahier book. Hall held it open on the seat next to him with the rag and turned on the car's interior light. In block letters the note read:

"Lieutenant. Starting at that bar was where some two-bit flatfoot would start. Obvious. Conventional. I expected better. You are going to have to pick up the pace if you want to play this game with me. By the way, you were wise not to consort with the fair

Lola. My specifications with the pimp were for a damsel with AIDS. Long, slooooowwwww AIDS."

It was signed: "Your brother in arms."

Luke's Death, 1986

"It's so horrible," said Shiloh Weeks. Tears brimmed and she hated herself for it.

"A shame," agreed Van Gelder, who clearly was nowhere near tears. "The boy sounded like he had so much promise, I understand," he tsked tsked.

The editorial page editor was lounging in his chair at the table of the Red Baron, a flier's hangout on Boeing Field, where Van Gelder kept his plane.

The "Baron," as it was known, served strong drinks along with sandwiches with macho fighter plane names -- Stuka, Zero and Warthog. Paintings of aerial dog fights between Spitfires, Messerschmitts, Sopwith Camels and other ancient planes adorned the walls. Weeks noticed a lot of the patrons wore long, white scarves.

Even Van Gelder wore an expensive leather jacket rather than his usual charcoal suit. A whitish silk shirt, expensive dark slacks and highly polished dress boots completed his outfit. Weeks never before had seen him without his immaculate suits and ties.

A Black Russian dangled from his mouth and a half-empty Scotch glass was on the table before him.

"We'll have to keep this short," he said, "I can't have another drink if I'm to fly.

"Where are you going?" asked Weeks. She was surprised he was leaving with so much going on. But then Van Gelder didn't deal with breaking news.

"California."

"Where?" she asked again, mostly out of her instinct for professional thoroughness.

"You need not worry about what I do with my free time. I'm the editor, remember?"

Van Gelder took another drag of his Black Russian and went back to the murder.

"While I concede it is a shame, I do wonder why it was so important for you to talk to me about it this morning? After all, tragedy is our business, it happens every day. I'm sure the night crew did a fine job." Van Gelder commented, looking at his Rolex impatiently. The glance was so fast Weeks concluded the gesture was to underline his impatience rather than to determine the time.

"Don't you see, Francis? He was the little Vietnamese girl's brother," Weeks said, unable to believe Van Gelder was so indifferent. The tears were gone and she was glaring at the man.

"To tie down this point, I assume you are suggesting Jeremy had a hand in this as well?" asked Van Gelder, opening his eyes wide.

"You bet I am."

"I'll agree with you that his relationship with Judge Kanawha bears examination. But the Vietnamese family? My God, Shiloh, there are gangs of South Vietnamese hoodlums in Seattle, Tong gangs, all manner of who knows what. Perhaps the store wasn't paying off the right war-lord or the rice bags didn't carry the right chop. Who knows? Work on the judge angle. I'll protect you as best I can . . . ."

"Jesus, Francis, you racist bastard. Vietnamese are different from Chinese who are different from Japanese . . . ." began Weeks. She saw Van Gelder's attention fading fast as she lectured.

Then he sat up straight. "Look, I am truly sorry. I understand this Luke was killed brutally. . ."

"His head was beaten in with a blunt instrument," confirmed Weeks.

"And he was at the Air Force Academy and all that. Very promising. Career down in flames. It is still very far-fetched . . . ."

Weeks slapped the table hard.

"Francis. I was out there before Luke's murder. I interviewed Luke's mother. Or tried to. She told me to leave her alone. She had already talked to someone from the paper."

"Not surprising," interrupted Van Gelder.

"She opened up a little. I pushed hard. One visitor was the cop reporter who called for the usual comment on the little girl's death," exploded Weeks. " But Jeremy was there. Or at least someone who must have looked a lot like Jeremy -- let's get this on the table. The guy would not identify himself. But the woman described Jeremy right down to his pot belly. Anyway, this guy came after the little girl but before Luke was killed. Jeremy was babbling about an evil man. He warned them to leave the country.

Francis, Jeremy seemed to know a lot about this evil man," Weeks said, her voice strident, urgent.

"Lon Chaney warning the townsfolk to run before he turned into a werewolf?" laughed Van Gelder. "Boo!" He grabbed at Weeks like a creep. "Come on, Shiloh. The man wouldn't even identify himself."

Weeks slapped the table again, wishing it was the editor's face.

"Don't be an idiot," she hissed. She looked around at the attention she had attracted from others in the room.

"If you must be theatrical, try Dr. Jekyll and Mr. Hyde. Francis, Jeremy WAS warning them about himself. I'm sure of it, damn it."

Van Gelder rubbed out his Black Russian. Finally. He was taking her seriously.

She paused so each could take a drink.

"Francis," she resumed, "I've looked into Post-Traumatic Stress Disorder. Lots of Vietnam vets got it. Developing a murderous personality fits right in. Multiple personality fits right in. Something has happened to Jeremy. He has snapped. We've got to do something."

Van Gelder sat back to think.

"Perhaps you are right. I think it is time to act. Is Luke's family still here?"

"No. As soon as I heard about Luke's death I tried to call the family. I've been calling every hour or so. No one answered the phone so I drove by. No one answered the door. The cops said the family took Mary -- she's their remaining child -- and left. Of course they wouldn't tell me where. But the mother told me Jeremy told her to disappear in Singapore or Bangkok. I bet that is what they did," said Weeks.

"I wouldn't go where Jeremy told me to go. I'd do the opposite," mused Van Gelder.

"Will you back me up with the cops?" asked Weeks.

"Shiloh. It is your theory and the police know you so much better than I," replied the editor with an evil grin. "Besides, I am planning a weekend trip, remember? I can't cancel it."

Weeks glared again in disbelief.

"You're really going to California after what I just told you?"

"Shiloh. The girl is dead. Luke is dead. The family gone.

106

Jeremy or whomever can't bother them anymore. Tell the police. They'll do what they must."

"You asshole," replied Weeks slowly. "Are you going to do anything at all?"

"I'll have a word about, ah, Jeremy's alleged ah, shall we say, outbursts and unusual behavior with the publisher first thing Monday morning."

"That's crazy," said Weeks, quietly. She gave up on Van Gelder.

She watched indifferently as his long arm reached over to her. His skinny yellow fingers curled over the back of her hand.

"Don't worry," he urged. "What else could happen now?"

Police Death II, 1986

The weirdo said he wanted to move up in life. Killing kids wasn't a challenge any more. Now he wanted to kill a cop. Make things interesting. "Come on, suckas," he said.

The weirdo's intimate knowledge about the murders of Luke and his young sister made things interesting enough for police Lieutenant Jerry Buck.

The caller had provided inside details only the coroner and cops had known. Buck had had to call and check. Yes, confirmed the coroner. The girl had been killed by a long, thin-bladed knife in the back. The brother with an odd-shaped instrument. Not a club or bat. If he had to take a guess, the coroner said it may be something with an elongated, thin surface. Like a rifle butt. That's what the caller said he used.

Buck replayed the key parts of the tape in his mind.

It was a man. He sounded drunk. Or high. Probably high, slurring his words. He kept forgetting where he was, kept asking the 911 operator to repeat what he had said before. He wandered, babbled, talked a lot but provided no solid clues about where he worked, what he drove, where he had gone to school, where a wife or parent could be found. The 911 operator had done a superlative job of asking questions, trying to draw him out -- and for a drunk, the weirdo had done a superlative job of not playing the game. He teased in his babble. But he gave nothing useful about his identity. The 911 operator also had done a superlative job of keeping the weirdo on the line. The trace had been easy. Especially since after about 10 minutes of talk, the weirdo stopped talking. But graciously, he had not hung up.

Buck checked the dispatch center by radio. Yes, the line still was open. There were no distinguishable sounds, however. No one responded to questions and entreaties to surrender. No background babbling, snoring, rattling, walking.

The captain wanted him to surround the seedy, West Seattle condo. Turn on the lights and speaker and wait for a surrender. Maybe -- after a lot of waiting -- use some tear gas if that didn't work.

But Buck insisted on doing it his way. Quick surprise. He'd bet his pension the caller had passed out. He wanted to move before the perp woke up.

The surprise was all ready. One team would batter down the door while a second team entered the bathroom window at the back of the condo. Everything would happen at once.

Buck turned on the small tape recorder again. He listened to all the nuances of the man's ravings. His detailed knowledge of the crimes. His threat to kill policemen. That was the clincher. The threat was so clear the judge signed the search warrant in an instant.

"I make it 2212. We go in at 2218 hours. On my order," Buck said quietly into his radio.

He sat back in the squad car's seat, closed his eyes and relaxed. He took a deep breath. His fingers moved across his Second Chance Kevlar bulletproof vest again, unconsciously probing for weak points or depressions.

Buck chuckled. And that little chick of a reporter was trying to convince him her boss was the perp. On Kanawha and the two Vietnamese kids. He was glad he didn't have to launch a major criminal investigation into the top editor of the city's biggest paper. Jesus, if women would just keep their noses out of police work. Shiloh Weeks was so much better at other things . . . .

The police lieutenant snapped his attention back to the mission. Quietly he exited the squad car and rushed in a crouch to the condo's door, his Glock cocked and held with two hands, barrel pointed at the sky.

SWAT team members waited on either side of the condo's front door. Their assault rifles also were aimed at the sky.

A two-man team stood ready with the battering ram.

"All ready?" Buck whispered into the radio handset attached by Velcro to the left shoulder of his blue, Second Chance bulletproof vest.

"Roger, Team 2." The team at the back.

"Roger, Team 3." The sniper team in the second story of the house behind him. It faced the front of the condo.

"Roger, Team 4." The sniper team on the roof of the house overlooking the back of the condo.

"Roger us, Team 5." The sergeant in charge of the team securing the scene.

Buck checked his watch. It was 2218. Time to go. He nodded to the guys with the battering ram and the cop who would follow the shooters with the video camera.

"Police!" shouted Buck as the thin, hollow door was smashed into splinters. The battering ram crew dropped to the ground at the right side of the door.

The unkempt living room was empty. There was a cheap couch which the SWAT guys immediately knocked over. No one was behind it. Lots of newspapers . . . couple of folding chairs . . . cheap, scratched coffee table . . . on it was a fresh bottle of Chivas Regal with a red bow . . . a TV.

Everything except the Chivas looked like it came from one of the pay-by-the week rental places.

Buck and the team took a quick swing through the kitchenette. No one there. The hand receiver for the red wall phone hung loose. Empty pop cans everywhere. That meant a sugar-hungry junkie. The SWAT guys would interpret the piles of pop cans the same way. Still, Buck warned, "Careful, we're dealing with a fry head."

They moved cautiously into the hall. The members of Team 2 were pivoting out of the bathroom at the end of the hall into a room off the hallway at Buck's left.

The room to his right was his responsibility - all prearranged based on the landlord's description of the condo. The door to the bedroom was closed.

Per the drill, the number two guy on the SWAT team kicked open the door. The primary shooter, M-16 ready, followed the kicker through the door.

The racket brought the guy on the bed to semi-consciousness.

"Watch it," shouted the primary shooter. "There's a shotgun by the bed. And the perp has a piece in his belt." The cop with the video camera dropped to the floor, camera still on his shoulder.

The other police officers shouted in drilled unison, "Police! Hands on top of your head. Police!"

The junkie on the bed didn't get it. He tried to sit up but the heavy pistol in his belt made it difficult to bend at the waist. Buck watched the junkie look down at the encumbrance. He seemed puzzled. The junkie attempted to swing his legs over the bed anyway.

His legs wouldn't go. His hand reached for the pistol grip.

110

Maybe he was going to move the gun so he could sit up.

"Hands on your head," shouted the primary SWAT team shooter.

The junkie looked up and blinked. The clouded eyes still didn't understand. His hand still was going for the pistol.

Nineteen years of experience told Buck the junkie wasn't going to shoot. He wanted to move whatever was keeping him from sitting up. This junkie was just a sloppy pig. An incompetent. The murderer was brutal, clever and left no clues. Something was very wrong!

"Leave the weapon alone," screamed Buck. His own finger left the Glock's trigger and he took a step toward the junkie. He intended to slap him across the head with the Glock so he ordered, "Hold your fire. . ."

. . . Just as the primary shooter fired fast three rounds from his M-16 which struck the junkie in a tight group in the center mass of his chest—just as the junkie still was pulling at the handle of the pistol with his left hand, still not comprehending.

The junkie jerked back and the SWAT team was on him. Two of the policemen drove their shoulders into the junkie's body while a third yanked the pistol from his waistband and then seized the shotgun. The officer immediately removed the weapons from the room. The two officers on the bed had flipped the body and cuffed its hands behind it.

The junkie's back, where the tumbling little M-16 bullets had exited, was hamburger. The raw meat told Buck the cuffs were unnecessary. Procedure but unnecessary.

Procedure also called for first aid so one of the SWAT guys, after a short argument, was attempting mouth-to-mouth resuscitation through a rubber mouthpiece. Procedure, but again, unnecessary.

Other SWAT team members crowded into the small bedroom. A couple of the cops slapped the primary shooter on the back. A couple more shared high-fives with him. Buck watched the primary shooter do a quick NFL end zone shuffle.

"All right!" shouted Buck. "You guys clear out. Don't touch anything you don't have to. Homicide will take it from here."

"Hey, lieutenant," shouted the primary shooter over the congratulatory din. "You suppose that bottle of Chivas is for me?"

"Might as well be -- after we check it for fingerprints," sighed Buck.

Buck walked over to the small table by the bed. There was a plastic sandwich bag filled with white powder. There also was a candle, matches, a spoon and a hospital-quality syringe. One taste of the powder told him the bag contained high-quality heroin. A lot of it. Several grand worth on the table.

The lieutenant leaned over and found a wallet under the bed.

"Let's see who we've got here," he said with a glance at the handcuffed corpse on the bed.

Gotta Run, 1986

"Jeremy! Thank goodness. Where are you? Are you all right? Tell me where you *are!*"

Van Gelder didn't give a damn about his health. Van Gelder wanted to know where he was.

"My note to the publisher explained all I can. I have some personal problems I need to work through. I'm going on a long hike. All alone. I'll keep in touch as best I can through voice mail. If someone needs to contact me, leave a message for me in voice mail. It's all in the note."

"I've read the damn note, Jeremy. You still need to come in. A lot has happened. You and I. . . and the publisher need to talk."

Hall looked around him. He was standing at a telephone kiosk at the terminal at Seattle-Tacoma International Airport. He was very open but that's how he wanted to be. He couldn't be cornered or easily attacked. Still, he didn't like standing so long in one place.

A woman's pleasant but no-nonsense voice came on the airport's loudspeaker system to announce the arrival of a United Airlines flight. Hall held the receiver toward the ceiling to make it easier for Van Gelder to hear the announcement.

"Jeremy. Are you at the airport?" demanded Van Gelder. "You must not go anywhere. We need to talk."

"Yes, I'm at the airport. My flight leaves in a few minutes. I've got to go. Just tell me what I want to know," lied Hall.

"Where are you going?" Van Gelder was demanding again.

"Can't say. I need to get away. Complete peace and all that. How's Anne doing?"

"Anne?" Van Gelder's voice sounded puzzled.

"Yes, Anne Fisher. I recommended that she take over as acting executive editor until I get back," explained Hall, allowing the irritation to show in his voice.

"Jeremy, Anne's not running the newspaper. The publisher has asked me to undertake that challenge." Van Gelder paused to let the hook sink in. Then he jerked hard to set it.

"Moreover, there are some things that simply must be

113

worked out. You have to come into the office. This morning. Now."
It was an order.

"What things?" Hall was demanding as well.

Van Gelder reversed field.

"Do you know about Ed Caldwell?"

"What about him?"

"Ed was killed by the police. Gunned down like an animal.
Last night."

"What?" demanded Hall.

"It's complicated. Please come in." Van Gelder was issuing
orders again.

"Francis, I'm not coming in. Tell me about Ed."

"Briefly, it appears he may have been involved in the
murders of those children, Luke and his sister. I stress the 'may'."

"That's ridiculous! Stay at your phone, Francis. I'll call back
in five. I have to check my bag." Hall hung up without waiting for an
answer or objection. He simply wasn't going to be a sitting target
that long. Maybe he ought to leave the airport and finish the phone
call from somewhere else. But he wanted Van Gelder to continue to
hear airport noise in the background as they concluded the
discussion.

So he raced up a back staircase to the mezzanine floor. He
waited behind a pillar for someone to open the heavy fire door
through which he had just passed. No one did.

Satisfied he was not followed, Hall explored an obscure
corridor past a row of hospitality suites operated by several foreign
airlines. The corridor came to a dead end except for a staircase that
would take him down a concrete and glass tube to a small ground-
level parking lot. Hall waited by the escape door, drawing the K-54
pistol he carried stuck in his belt in the small of his back. He held the
Chinese pistol under his sports jacket. No tail appeared.

Hall was fairly confident the precautions were wise but not
important yet. Wozniak still was playing his cruel game. Wozniak
was not after him -- yet.

Cautiously, Hall crept back down the corridor past the
hospitality rooms. He took a series of turns, doubling back several
times. Then he stopped at a pay phone on the wall near the airport's
USO office. The only person in the corridor was a young soldier in
uniform. He was sitting in a chair preoccupied with the small pay
television set on its arm. The airport PA system was very audible.

114

Hall dialed Van Gelder's direct number.

"Now, tell me about Ed Caldwell," snapped Hall.

"Take it easy, Jeremy." Another order.

"Tell me!"

Van Gelder said nothing, apparently to show he would not be pushed.

Then he began. "It appears Ed fell off the wagon, if that is the term that applies to substance abusers. At least the police found a large bag of heroin in his apartment. I gather a lot of the heroin was in him as well. It appears he may have called 911 to brag he had killed the Vietnamese children. And he threatened to kill policemen. Then he may have passed out while talking to the 911 operator. Police traced the call and something called the Special Weapons and Tactics Team went into his apartment. Ed may have been armed and was reaching for a pistol while ignoring police orders to put up his hands or whatever they order you to do. He was shot in self defense, the police say. They have it all on video tape. It happened late last night."

"You said 'may' a lot, Francis," said Hall. "What else is there?"

Van Gelder cleared his throat loudly. "I had a long talk with a policeman named Jerry Buck at -- God, you wouldn't believe the hour this morning."

"Go on," ordered Hall.

Van Gelder paused and turned the crank another notch. "I gather he is a rather special friend of Shiloh's. Anyway, you should come into the office to discuss this further."

"Tell me now."

Another of Van Gelder's pauses. "Jeremy. Lieutenant Buck wants you to volunteer to submit to some tests. Something about a voice test and a polygraph test. He also wants your fingerprints. He knows you were in the army and that means he can get them from the Defense Department. But that will take some time. He thinks it would be better if you would just come in and let them take them. It would clear things up very quickly."

"Say it, Francis, clear up what things?"

"Jeremy, to be candid, you have become a person of interest to the police. Officially in the children's cases. But in some police quarters there is interest in reopening the Mary Kanawha case." Van Gelder's voice was patient, factual, like he was a professional giving testimony. It was the voice he used in the presence of the publisher. Cool. Expert. Unflappable.

"Are the police looking for me?" asked Hall.

"I'm afraid so."

"You gave them a picture of me?"

"The newspaper cooperated with the authorities as requested. How could we do otherwise?" stated Van Gelder.

"It's bullshit. I haven't killed anybody. Neither did Ed."

"Then prove to them. Clear your name. Let them record your voice and take the polygraph."

Hall had to move. Had to get out of the airport.

Now the police, with Van Gelder helping as much as possible, were after him as well as Stephan Wozniak.

But he said, "I've got arrangements out of town that won't wait. Why isn't Anne running the paper as I requested?"

Another Van Gelder pause. "The publisher was . . . decided . . ."

"You mean he was persuaded," interrupted Hall.

". . . that you need to be placed on indefinite leave until this matter is resolved. It was decided, given the possible involvement of staff persons, it would be better to bring in someone from outside your newsroom."

"My plane is leaving. I've got to go," Hall said. "Tell people to use my voice mail. See ya. No! Wait!" shouted Hall.

"Yes?" asked Van Gelder, his voice calm and cool. The voice of a winner.

"What else did the cops tell you about Caldwell?"

"I'm not sure I should discuss it if you won't come in and face this like a gentleman."

"Don't be an asshole. What about Caldwell?"

Now Van Gelder was harumphing. "Just that he was under the influence. Well, good heavens, we all knew he had a history of substance abuse. No surprise there. He should have been cashiered long ago in my opinion. Lieutenant Buck wasn't sure where the guns were from, though. No record that Ed ever bought or used guns. Murder also was totally out of character. It takes a special person, in my view, to commit murder...."

"Cut the shit, Francis," ordered Hall.

"Well. Ed was lazy and incompetent, not to mention the drugs. But in my view, not a murderer."

116

Hall looked around nervously. No sign of anything unusual. But he knew the airport cops depended on a lot of television surveillance. Now the cops had a picture of him . . . . He saw no cameras aimed at him. The enlisted man had not lifted his eyes from the TV screen. The corridor remained otherwise deserted. Hall didn't like it one bit.

"That it?" he asked.

"Well, Ed lived like a slob. No surprise there. Looks like he must have had a visitor, or was planning to visit someone," Van Gelder replied. He sounded like he actually was trying to search his memory.

"Why do you think that?" asked Hall, his attention now riveted on Van Gelder's words.

"Well, Lieutenant Buck said the only clean thing in Ed's condo, or apartment -- whatever -- was an unopened bottle of Scotch with a bow on it. The police doubt it was Ed's, given all the heroin in him."

"What kind of Scotch?" demanded Hall.

"Chivas. Chivas Regal, I believe Buck mentioned," replied the new executive editor. "Why?" he asked. "Do you see some significance in that? That is why we need you to come in. Please come see us, Jeremy."

"Thanks for everything. Enjoy your paper," said Hall, slamming down the phone.

He strode boldly down the corridor and followed the heavy stone steps that brought him to a large rock, a piece of unidentifiable but expensive modern art. He assumed the persona of a busy executive in a hurry as he moved into the main terminal crowd. He also checked reflections in windows and mirrors he passed for any sign of Wozniak.

The fast, preoccupied walk of the busy traveler suited him now. He *was* preoccupied, trying to work through Wozniak's game. Wozniak was recreating Ap Thuy Tu. This time he was after more than a tin box of money.

There was the woman on the berm. Wozniak killed her and pinned her nose. Life stunk, he told her corpse. Read his former friend, Judge Mary Kanawha. Probably chosen just because she was an important woman. Wozniak must have heard distant rumors of their past . . . .

Then the little girl who walked to the berm to pee. Read

117

Theresa, the little Catholic Vietnamese girl. Both with the knife.

Wozniak then had moved to Theresa's family in Seattle, just as the Backatya Boys had slaughtered the little girl's family with their rifle butts in the shadow of the Black Virgin. Luke was the first. Hall hoped what was left of the family truly disappeared in Asia.

But Harry, the man with the clothes-pins. He didn't fit at all.

Wozniak threw the man out the window and planted the clothes-pins. What was the point? Hall remembered the sense of relief he felt when he thought Harry had killed Kanawha. If Harry was the killer, then Wozniak wasn't really back.

Then the sense of absolute horror he felt when Anne said little Theresa had been stabbed in the back. Just Stephan's Wozniak's way of saying, "Howdy, I'm really here. And I'm going to fuck with your mind before I kill you."

Where next? For Wozniak, certainly the game just was becoming interesting.

"Gook colleagues." That's what Wozniak had called his Backatya Boys. But did Wozniak know the Backatya Boys had been repaid in full for Ap Thuy Tu?

Caldwell. Wozniak was starting on his colleagues. Shot by police. Just as he had arranged for the police to execute Wozniak's colleague, the Backatya Boy Nguyen.

Hall had used Chivas to prepare Nguyen for the set-up. That was why Wozniak left the Chivas at Ed's apartment after getting him high, planting the guns and calling 911 and impersonating the reporter to set him up to be killed by the police.

How could Wozniak know about weak links among Hall's colleagues? He must have watched the paper, done his reconnaissance. Caldwell was as weak as links came. No doubt Wozniak made Caldwell a heroin offer no junkie trying to go straight could possibly resist. Wozniak probably befriended him. Debriefed him about who was who at the paper. Tell me all about your boss, Jeremy Hall, Wozniak would have urged Caldwell. Where did he live? Who did he love? Who were Jeremy Hall's closest colleagues? Wozniak would have asked a lot of questions when Caldwell was good and high. Promised lots more dope if Caldwell was a good boy and answered all the questions. . . .

Who were his closest colleagues?

That would have been a tough question for Hall himself to answer. Hall just wasn't close to anyone. He admired Anne Fisher's competence and insight. Francis Van Gelder had been his rival for years. Van Gelder could be good, when he focused.

But his association with the people at the paper had been simply professional. They were just colleagues.

Which is what the Backatya Boys had been to Wozniak. That meant anyone would do. Caldwell had been good enough. Wozniak would want three more colleagues.

Then Hall felt a chill. There was one person who was more than a colleague. What did Caldwell know about his relationship with Shiloh Weeks?

There were plenty of rumors. Van Gelder made veiled but open references to them in story conferences, for God's sake.

So Wozniak had to know too. Hall had to assume that.

Then Wozniak would go for her. Probably as payment for Buu, if he discovered their special relationship.

After Shiloh, Wozniak would come for him.

Well, he had to warn them. Shiloh. And the others. Especially Shiloh.

He stopped at another open phone kiosk and dialed the publisher's telephone mail box. His mouth back from the phone and a handkerchief over the mouth piece -- hoping to frustrate any voice testing by the police -- he left a short message marked "urgent". He asked the publisher to issue a general warning to all employees at the paper that there had been threats and they could be in danger. He urged the publisher to ask employees to report anything suspicious to police.

It was a stupid call. One he had to make but stupid. Wozniak's targets would not see anything suspicious until it was too late.

And the call would simply convince the publisher, if Van Gelder hadn't successfully done so already, that Hall was sick and possibly dangerous. The recorded call also would give the cops a muted sample of his voice. That might relieve the police pressure on him if they had a tape of the 911 call from Ed Caldwell's apartment. Or it might simply convince the cops there were two or more killers working together.

That left Shiloh. She rated much more than a phone call. Not just for the old times. Could something good come out of all this? This provided every reason for them to get back together again.

They had shared so much before. He would explain Wozniak

to her, just as he had explained so much about Vietnam to Mary Kanawha. He would have an ally again. He would have Shiloh again.

Hall's pace picked up as he walked across a crosswalk leading from the terminal to one of the airport's spiral parking garages where his car was parked.

His car. He dared not go back to the car.

Hall made an abrupt about face and returned to the terminal and took the busy escalator to the street level. He waited near the bus stop, again the busy, impatient traveler, scanning the traffic for his ride.

At the last minute he jumped through the closing door of a Seattle-bound bus. The bus was nearly empty.

It gave him time to tie down one more loose thread. How did Wozniak link Nguyen's disappearance with Chivas? It wasn't much of a trick. Chivas was cheap at the PX and the drug of choice of Hall and his fellow officers as they waited each night for the VC rocket attacks.

Besides, plenty of people witnessed Nguyen getting shitfaced on the Chivas Hall had poured repeatedly into his glass.

Going Home, 1986

Despite the bullshit shown on television, effective covert surveillance requires teams of people.

Some spooks in front of the subject. Some to the side. Some behind. They must be constantly shifted so no one becomes familiar to the subject. The army had taught Hall all that. There were no teams following him. Not even Wozniak was following him. Hall was sure. He'd pulled all the tricks: abruptly jumping from cabs and buses; ordering meals at restaurants and leaving suddenly through back doors before the meals arrived; walking against the traffic on one-way streets; hiding in crowds and making discrete turns into buildings and using confusing, abrupt combinations of their elevators and stairs, bursting into store staircases and running up the stairs rather than downwards as a nervous subject would be expected.

And always setting up quick ambushes to catch any tail coming too fast or too close. Finally he walked down to Alaskan Way, beginning a slow saunter to the south from Pier 70. The area was open. He stopped in the drizzle of the early evening to watch the ships and ferries. No one passed him. No one matched his stop-walk-stop-walk pattern. He still seemed to be alone.

He arrived at the Aquarium on the waterfront. He turned east towards the city. Above him was the Pike Place Market. Then his condo. And looming high above both was the Dark Tower which dominated the city with its curved black, reflective sides.

Hall climbed the steep stairs to the market. The stairs provided many abrupt turns and corners which he turned into ambush points. Still no tail. He might as well risk going home.

Walking dead slow now, Hall exited the market, following Pike Street through the junkies and drunks, punks, street kids and homeless people with their earthly belongings in backpacks and old suitcases and black garbage bags piled in stolen grocery store shopping carts or stacked on old bicycles.

Finally, he was at his apartment building. The condo was new and was a marvel of electronic security gadgets. Probably as secure as a federal courthouse.

The gadgets might keep out the cocaine addict burglars and street kids. But they would prove no barrier to Wozniak. This had to be his last trip to the condo for a while. Until this was over. Even this trip was a gamble, but a necessary one.

There was no avoiding the confrontation with his wife, Beth. That was coming. It was one that had to be handled face-to-face. And he needed some things.

Hall circled the building, staying in the shadows as much as possible. He studied the street people. Passing drivers. The windows in the surrounding buildings.

Finally he walked swiftly to the garage entrance, the K-54 pistol in his hand. He was entering a killing zone. The entrance was below street level. He had to walk several feet down a steep driveway before he reached the gate and the security box that would open it. He could be trapped in front of the heavy steel metal security grate with no chance of escape. He reached the box and punched in the security code: 6-6-6. The metal gate rose at an agonizingly slow pace. It was so slow Hall was a dead man if Wozniak suddenly appeared at the sidewalk, about 10 feet uphill from the gate.

Hall might be dead but Wozniak would die too. Hall was ready.

No twinkling eyes appeared and then the gate was high enough for Hall to slip beneath. He waited behind a parked car until the gate dropped again before he moved through the garage. A series of cameras marked his progress.

Then he was at the elevator. Another code box. He punched in 9-9-9. The elevator whisked him to the fourth floor. The door opened, and the world was transformed from street garbage and smells and metal and punks and cars to carpets, paintings, wall paper and mirrors.

Hall stopped, weapon ready, and checked the doors to the garbage chutes and to the stairs. No one waited. He made sure the heavy fire door to the sterile cement stairway was locked so that it could be opened only with a key from the stairway side.

There was nothing else to check. He was at the door to his apartment.

He checked the handle to make sure the door was locked. Then he opened it with his key and entered the dark hallway. He slid against the wall of the hallway to the archway and into the living room. There he waited, allowing his eyes to become accustomed to the dark. The tall, arched windows over-looking Elliott Bay collected natural and city light, which flashed from the metal and glass furniture. Then, systematically, he searched the room. His gaze stopped abruptly at the wooden wine rack. There were a couple of bottles of Chateau St. Michelle Merlot. A couple of glasses of the red would help. . . . or a chilled glass of Adelsheim Vineyard Chardonnay, the one with the picture of the lovely Barbara Setsu Pickett on the label. Long dark hair, Asian -- Vietnamese, maybe. Vietnam -- that snapped him back. He saw nothing to warn him that Stephan Wozniak awaited him.

Light was visible under one of the doors in the dark hallway that led from the living room. Carefully, Hall navigated the treacherous path between his wife's black leather Scandinavian couches and the metal and glass tables and display case in the room. But before he opened the door to the lighted room, he searched all the dark rooms of the apartment. Then he went to the door to the room with the light. He didn't hesitate. He walked in boldly.

Beth was reading on her side of the low, broad rosewood bed. Even occupied, her side looked neat. The light green sheet with the dark green lines folded neatly over the blanket just beneath her arm pits. Beth read by the light of a tall, elegant lamp that look like a Grecian column. The jade-green shade was almost flat. Hall hated the lamp which was the only thing, except for a slim green cordless telephone, that was on Beth's bed table. Beyond Beth's side of the bed were two expensive rosewood dressers. She had filled them both, as well as a large, walk-in closet. There was nothing on the top of either dresser except a framed photograph of a dog.

The opposite side of the bed, and bedroom, was chaos. The sheets and blanket were pulled out at the bottom of the bed where he had kicked them out during fitful attempts at sleep. His night table held a lamp made from the heavy brass of a lantern from a British cruiser badly damaged in World War II. The base of the lamp was covered in all manner of clutter -- books, papers, an old-fashioned wind-up clock and a box of tissues.

Beth didn't look up from her book. But she gave her customary sigh of disapproval.

Hall long ago had given up trying to explain his hours. After some searching in the rubble of his closet he found a small running bag. In silence he filled it with the things he needed. Might as well

123

postpone the battle as long as possible. Even better to get the packing done in silence. He might forget something if he packed under battlefield conditions.

Into the bag went underwear, toothbrush, toothpaste, traveling razor. He opened the handkerchief drawer and took several handkerchiefs.

Then it was time.

"Beth. There's something up. I need a big favor from you."

He had spoken first. That meant Beth considered herself the Round One victor. Her eyes locked on the bag and she opened with a broadside.

"I can guess what's up. You and the little bitch Shiloh Weeks on again?"

"No," Hall replied. "I want you to go to Europe. Go low and fast. You never took the Hall name. Don't refer to it, don't refer to me when you get there. Stay invisible. I'll pay."

"Alone? You want me to go alone?"

"Yes."

"Ha!" And then, "What the hell are you up to now, Jeremy? Why do you need the little wife far out of the way?"

"I can't tell you. But it's not what you think."

"Don't tell me what I think," snapped Beth, slapping her book shut for effect.

Then she was silent. Hall waited for the next Encyclical.

"Okay," she said finally.

Hall was surprised.

"You'll go to Europe? Tomorrow?"

"Yes," she said simply. "You're paying."

"I said I would." Hall was surprised. Beth normally demanded a battle over every issue. He could see no reason why a free trip to Europe shouldn't be worth a fight.

"But things have to stay within reason. I'll give you a check now. That will be for a month. I'll send another for the same amount if you stay a second month. Anything you put on your card or write on your account is yours," he added cautiously. His original warrant was much too broad for a woman like Beth.

Now the war would begin.

But again, she said simply, "Okay."

"If you need to talk to me, call my voice mail box at the paper and leave a message and phone number. I'll have to call you. I won't be going into the paper for a few days."

Beth gave a short, contemptuous laugh.

"You can tell me where you and the bitch de jour will be playing. I'm not going to be alone for very long."

"It's not like that. There is no one. Call it work. I've got a job to do. A dangerous one."

She studied him and then said, "I'm not coming back." Her voice was soft, low-key.

"Let's not make any radical decisions until we have to. But thanks, though."

Beth looked puzzled. "Thanks? For what?"

"Just thanks." He opened the dresser's handkerchief drawer again and unwrapped the long, thin Gerber stabbing knife. He added that to his bag, blocking the movement with his body so Beth could not see what he was doing.

Then he crossed the dimly lit room to his wife's side of the bed. He leaned over and kissed her on the forehead. She had reopened her book without responding to the kiss. He took from his pocket the check he had written and put it on her immaculate bed table. Still, without looking up from the book, Beth reached out for the check. Her hand snapped it in front of her eyes. Beth put the book down long enough to reach over and stash the check in the bed table's stylishly narrow drawer.

Hall stopped at the door. "Please leave tomorrow on the first flight you can get. And remember, low and fast. Be CAREFUL!"

Beth held the sigh until just before the door closed.

Hall stood in the dark of the living room with the small bag. The obstacle course of sharp steel and glass corners of Beth's furniture was before him. And beyond that, Captain Stephan Wozniak.

Heading South, 1986

No doubt it was Wozniak's voice. An upbeat, jivey almost black spin to it. But Wozniak's voice.

Hall punched the "2" key on the phone at the prompt to hear the voice message again.

The pleasant female voice mail operator began, "The following unheard message was received at 9 a.m. today."

Then Wozniak:

"Well, My Man. Jeremy. This is your long-lost pal. The one that's been away. We didn't have this newfangled jazz where I was. Hope the message gets through. I'll know if it doesn't. Then I'll try again, okay, My Man?

"Why don't we get together for a drink some time. Talk some more. You got the bottle of Chivas I sent, didn't you? Bring it along. We'll drink it clean, maybe just an ice cube, just like the old days. I'll get a second bottle just in case one is not enough. Or maybe you already drank the one I sent. I know you've got a lot on your mind now.

"Anyway, I've rented a place. It's hard to find, so listen carefully. It's south of Purdy. On the peninsula where the women's prison is. Turn south from Highway 16 on 302. Go over the Purdy bridge. Go on 302 until you get to South 95th Street. Hang a left, toward the water. Drive a mile. Take your time, it's real nice country back here. Man, I'll tell you, I'm sure not used to so many big trees, you know, My Man?

"Anyway, just after a sharp curve you'll see a driveway on the right. My place is about half a mile in. It's the only place on the roadway. I doubt even you could miss it, you old trooper, even if you broke into the Chivas on the way. Ha, ha. You'll know it from the clothesline I got. I'll hang a sign on the line. I know, I've got an old sheet. I'll hang the sheet and write on it. 'Truth and Justice.' That's what I'll write. In big red letters. You won't miss that. Anyway, it's an area called Devil's Head. That's what made me decide to rent the joint. That name. I like it. Just like I like the name of that big black building in Seattle. The Dark Tower. That just draws me. You know what I mean?

"I'm home every evening. I like the chance to be alone. Eat whatever I want when I want. Little shit like that means a lot, when you've been away, like me.

"Just come when you can. Tonight would be okay, I'll get a couple of crabs. But no big deal. If you and Beth have other plans, drop in any time. I know how busy and prosperous and important you are. Truth and justice, that's what you do. And me too. Gives us lots to talk about. Well, hope you can make it. I'm supposed to push the "pound" key when I'm finished. That's the ticktacktoe one, isn't it? All I've got to do is pound that little sucker and this hot news flash is filed away in your telephone. Man, I'll tell you, it's a new world. Here goes, pound away, hope to see you tonight. Truth and Justice."

And then the voice mail operator was saying, "Press seven to erase this message. . . ." Hall pushed it. "Message erased, Next unheard message. . . ." began the automated voice.

Hall pushed the "star" button a couple of times to exit the voice mail box.

He paused to scan the area around the phone booth before exiting and rushing across Marginal Way in the rain to the cheap south Seattle motel. Most of its clientele appeared to be hookers working the docks for longshoremen and sailors.

Hall saw the motel manager, a pot-bellied, balding man with heavy gray sideburns and thick ear hair, spotted him as soon as he jogged past the motel sign promising "free hot movies". The manager clearly was suspicious, he apparently didn't get many solo men who appeared only interested in making phone calls from phone booths.

The manager watched Hall until he had reached the orange door to his room. Hall had no intention of staying in the room, or anywhere else, for more than a few hours.

His current problem wasn't the motel or its manager. It was the message.

Obviously a trap.

But what kind? And was there really a chance Wozniak would be there? Hall had been unable to track him. His only lead had taken him to the debacle at the bar near the apartment from which Wozniak had tossed the unfortunate Harry.

Wozniak was right. He had to pick up the pace. Plodding

gumshoe work wasn't worth squat. He had to get two or four jumps ahead of Wozniak. The only answer was to go to Devil's Head. Where Wozniak was waiting.

Ambush the ambush.

Hall generally knew the area. Devil's Head was a point of land in South Puget Sound. Mariners probably gave it the name. Its broad exposure to the prevailing southwest winds across the wide-open waters probably gave under-powered boats serious trouble.

More important to him was the land route. Only one road, Highway 302, led through the narrow Key Peninsula to Devil's Head. And from Seattle, just about the only way to drive to Highway 302 was to cross another narrow bottle-neck, the Tacoma Narrows Bridge.

There would be no surprise if he took the conventional route across Puget Sound. Somehow, Wozniak would see him come.

Move one jump ahead.

Take the ferry from Seattle across Puget Sound to Bremerton. Rent a car or hitch a ride. That still left him exposed on the highway. But it was better.

Move another jump ahead.

Hall would come from the south. By water. Low and slow.

Move another jump ahead.

An amphibious assault. But not to Devil's Head. To a point a mile or so away. Then overland, from an unexpected direction.

Hall checked the Chinese K-54 automatic pistol. It was well oiled, its action smooth. It should be. He had been babying the weapon for 20 years. He pushed the gun into his belt in the small of his back.

With relief, Hall shut the orange motel door for the last time and walked into the chilly, gray drizzle.

It took him several buses and several hours to get to Olympia, which would be his starting point south of Devil's Head.

The bus time gave him a chance to think about Wozniak's call. The operator had said the message was "unheard." Presumably, that meant he was the first to call it up and no one else had done so. Or could the cops have had the message reinstalled in the computer's memory with the "unheard" notation? Assume the worst, that Buck, the detective who seemed interested in him, had heard it. Surely the cop had thought to monitor his voice mail. And if the cop didn't, Van Gelder certainly would have suggested it. Anyone listening would assume the caller was a friend of Hall's. Wozniak seemed reasonable, friendly. He clearly had been away, traveling or living abroad maybe. The cop probably would conclude that -- editors would be expected to know exiles, writers or whatever. Wozniak certainly didn't sound like someone who had been in prison.

There had been no reference to Vietnam or the secret only the two of them now shared. No hint that Wozniak planned to continue climbing bodies until he reached Hall's throat. With Ed Caldwell's death, Hall presumed that meant three more murders, for Hau, Ky and Buu. Then Wozniak would come for him.

Wozniak may have made one slip. He had mentioned the bottle of Chivas.

"You got the bottle of Chivas I sent, didn't you?" he asked. "We'll drink it clean, maybe with an ice cube, just like the old days. . .."

Buck could link that with the bottle Van Gelder said Buck found at the unfortunate Ed Caldwell's place. If the cops were that far along.

The bus drew onto the Olympia's Plum Street off-ramp from Interstate 5. Hall hoped he had gotten to the message before the police. The reference to the Chivas could be enough to bring the police to Devil's Head too. Wozniak wanted to play this game with him, so why would he risk bringing in the police? Probably to stir the pot, if nothing else. Throw in a wild card, jazz things up. Besides, how else could Wozniak send him a message?

The important thing was that he had to watch for the police as well as Wozniak at Devil's Head.

"Low and slow, low and slow," Hall muttered the words like a mantra as the Intercity Transit bus slowed on the ramp.

Of course, Wozniak had used Beth's name as though he knew her. He didn't. Probably a tidbit picked up from Caldwell. Well, he had done as much as he could for Beth. All he was willing to do.

"Farewell, Beth," he whispered to his reflection in the bus window.

Olympia's weather remained promising for a water crossing. Drizzle, poor visibility but no wind. Hall walked to Percival's Landing, Olympia's yacht harbor. On the way he stopped at an outdoors store to buy a small Silva hiking compass.

He soon spotted the boat he wanted. It was lashed to the side of a houseboat among Percival's Landing's yachts. The houseboat looked empty. No one seemed to be around the docks.

The next three hours were spent paddling the stolen Easy Rider Eskimo kayak up Budd Inlet. Then more paddling right up Dana Passage to Johnson's Point. That was his last known point of land. Before him were the open waters of the Sound. His best guestimate was he had to head about due east through the dark drizzle. Something over two miles. He had no lights and would not dare to use them if he had.

A yacht or one of the rare log ships bound to or from Olympia could cut him in half if they didn't see him. A ship probably would cut him in half even if the watch did see him. The tonnage rule of the road.

It was a risk he had to take.

It was all a big risk. He was already tired from one three-hour trip from Percival's Landing. Hall sat breathing deeply in the black drizzle. Ahead was open water. No coast to hug.

He dug the starboard blade of the Finnish Kober paddle into the black water with a hard stroke. Then a twist of the wrist and a hard stroke with the port side.

The power of the stroke was long gone three hours later when Hall saw lights. Then a beach loomed in the black rain.

The stroke was just mechanical now. Bloodless, blistered hands barely were able to hold the paddle. Hall shivered and he knew he was in the early stages of hypothermia. The Gore-Tex parka was soaked through as were his jeans. He had found no spray skirt for the kayak at the house boat. Cold water inside the boat sloshed over his legs and feet.

Only the scraping of the kayak's hull on the beach made him realize the misery of the paddling routine -- right side, twist, left side, twist -- was over.

Gratefully, Hall climbed out and held the kayak in the shallow water. He could no longer feel his feet. He just stood in the water. He couldn't focus . . . . Finally he worked out a vague plan. He pulled the two plastic float bags from the bow and stern, deflated them and threw them and the hated paddle on the beach. He carefully placed the damp pistol on one of the float bags and used the second bag to protect the weapon from the rain.

Then he backed the kayak out into the water. The cold water reached his waist, then his armpits. Hall was preparing to tip the kayak so the water would fill the boat when suddenly his feet found no bottom. His head went under the cold salt water. His only hope was his hold on the kayak. Instinctively, he wrapped his arms around the boat's bow and kicked with his legs until he had drawn back from the steep drop-off and his feet again were on solid bottom.

Coughing, he tipped the boat and sank it, giving the leaden, submerged craft a push with his boot, hoping it would drop hundreds of feet to the Sound's bottom.

But he was too tired to care. The shivering was much worse when he reached the beach again. He knew he had to do other things. But what? He rubbed his hands up and down his body. Then he saw the air bags and paddle.

Hall unhooked the rainbow-colored bicycle cuff strap that held Wozniak's Gerber stabbing knife against his right calf under the soaked jeans leg. Carefully he pulled the sharp knife from his Danner hiking boot. The sharp blade quickly reduced the two plastic air bags to what would pass as general beach garbage. He buried the bags' hoses in the sand. Then he stuffed the wooden paddle under a beach log.

His hand shook violently as it replaced the knife. He had difficulty re-attaching the cuff strap. Then he stuck the Chinese pistol in his pants. He was as cold as the steel of the weapon.

Shelter. Warmth. Nothing else mattered now.

Rubbing his sides, Hall moved cautiously up the beach. He had no real idea where he was. Vaguely, he was aware the cheap compass should have brought him somewhere to the vicinity of Devil's Head. He had tried to refer to it often during his dangerous trip. But who could know?

Get warm. Get dry.

Or die.

Where he was, where Wozniak was, where Shiloh was -- nothing mattered.

Hall slipped through the beach logs. Most of the houses in front of him had outside lights. It was unlikely anyone would be awake, it was after 1 a.m.

His freezing body screamed to go to the first house. He wished he hadn't stashed his gym bag back in Olympia. Knock. Ask for help. And if they said no . . . . well, he had the pistol. . . .

But Hall stopped and tried to focus. Not any house would do. It had to be a certain kind of house. But what kind? He couldn't think . . . .

Hall stumbled through the logs hoping he would see what his mind would not recall. There were big houses ahead filled with many large picture windows, balconies, cedar siding, outdoor lights. He didn't want them. Why? New mansions would be filled with jumpy, suspicious people who made money in cities. They would have alarms, locked doors and big dogs.

He wanted something else. But what?

He saw it. An old house. Two stories and a dormer attic. Peeling, single-glazed windows. Shingled in decaying asbestos. You knew where the bedrooms were. People would be sleeping upstairs.

Country people would sleep in this house. Country people with no alarms, who might even leave their doors open. . . .

Somewhere a dog barked halfheartedly as Hall circled the building. He found the outside door to the basement. It was warped. The white paint faded and chipped over decades. Only patches of putty still held a single pane of dirty glass in place.

The lock looked rusty and old.

Hall stood stupidly before the door. He tried to remember the lock-picking instructions. No use. His hands and body shook too much for that kind of delicate work. And he couldn't remember anyway. He tried the knob with his hand, but his shoulder ready to smash the old door. . . .

The knob was stiff and didn't turn. He tried harder and it squeaked in protest. But it turned.

Hall rushed in.

It was dry. And it was warm. Through the cobwebs and boxes and bicycles there was a large, octopus furnace ahead in the gloom. Hall moved carefully to it and stripped off the soaking parka and rag wool sweater. Then his burgundy lycra turtle neck. He sat and pulled off the soaking hiking boots and wool socks. He draped the clothing over the hot protruding arms of the furnace and crammed the boots against it. He wanted to remove the wet jeans but was fading into sleep as he pulled the pistol from his belt and the knife from his leg. The shivering was beyond control as he curled his body as close as he dared to the huge, warm furnace and then he slipped into darkness, into sleep or death, he really didn't care which.

He knew it was sleep when the gulls called him back with their raucous shrieks.

"Wake Up!"

He listened motionlessly. The sunlight coming through the

high, small window on the basement wall had that early morning luster and glow so loved by photographers. This morning the gulls -- and was there cawing too? The gulls' fellow travelers and foes, the crows -- were exploiting the light and probably a low tide, searching the exposed tidelands for shrimp and tiny crabs and clams.

There. Hall heard the gang shrieks and caws.

The alarms of the gang of scavengers and predators had awakened him just in time.

For there was another noise too. A quiet, sinister one. Someone just moved, just shifted position slightly. Someone was inside the basement room with him. . . . .

What basement was this? Where? Why? He remembered.

Noise inside was danger. No doubt about it. He felt the hard lines of the pistol and knife hilt below him under his belly. Slowly he moved to bring his hand down to the knife. No hurry, no panic, just a sleeping person shifting. . . .

Now. What was the danger? It could not be Wozniak. There was no way Wozniak could know.

The good news was the shivering was gone. But he felt like hell. Sore, still tired. Scared.

The danger was behind him. His tortured hand palmed the handle of the knife, concealing the long blade against the inside of his forearm.

Then the slow, contented turn of a person in a deep sleep. Knees drawn up, ready to kick, knife at the ready, pistol under his body.

Hall peered through a slit in his eyelids. The oath almost escaped.

A little girl was sitting patiently on the lowest of the rough lumber basement steps. The door at the top of the staircase was shut.

The little girl held a bicycle helmet on her lap. She was a bright-eyed doll. Brown, curly hair. Brown, inquisitive eyes. Ruddy cheeks.

"For breakfast I'd like a bowl of steamed clams with strawberries on top, a Mars ice cream bar and to drink, a strawberry milk shake with crab claw," said Hall, formally opening his eyes.

The girl giggled. "You can't have that for breakfast."

"Then I'd like a bowl of geoduck cereal, avocado juice and a carrot."

"We don't have that either," she giggled again. The laugh was infectious and Hall felt the corners of his mouth turn up.

"What kind of hotel is this then?"

"This is a house, not a hotel, silly," laughed the girl.

"It has to be a hotel. I've just slept on the softest bed I've ever had."

"You're sleeping on the floor, can't you see that?" demanded the girl.

"It's the softest floor I've ever slept on then," replied Hall.

"Why aren't you sleeping at your own house?" asked the girl.

Hall had to think about that. "I don't really have a home," he said finally.

"Where do your children live?" asked the little girl. "They have to live in a house."

"I don't have any children," admitted Hall.

The pretty head and brown eyes drew back in disbelief. It was a concept the child apparently had to think about.

Hall needed a break as well. He had almost killed himself to sink the kayak and keep his arrival secret. Now a talkative kid knew he was here. A talkative little girl in a slow, small beach community where everyone knew everyone. And talked about strangers.

And Wozniak, the master of stealth, had warned him years ago, "Surprise is our only advantage. . . ."

Wozniak surely knew he would come. The only thing he didn't know was when and from which direction the attack would come.

And now. There was only one sure way to preserve the secret. . . .

"Why not?" the girl demanded.

"Why not what?" asked Hall, blinking.

"Why didn't you have any children? All my uncles and aunts do. My mommy and daddy do. All my mommy and daddy's friends do. You're old enough to be a daddy."

"Your mommy and daddy and uncles and aunts must be very special people. It takes very special people to have children. And take care of them."

"Don't forget mommy and daddy's friends."

"They must be special people too," said Hall.

"You seem like you would like to have children too," said the girl.

"I don't think that would be a good idea."

"My mommy and daddy never spank me but some of my friends get spanked," said the girl. She held her head high and proud.

"I can tell that. Listen, what's your name? No, don't tell me," said Hall. "Do you know a place called Devil's Head?"

"Yes, and I'll tell you my name if you want me to."

"No," barked Hall. "I'll try to guess in little while. How close are we to Devil's Head?"

"Well, we live near Taylor Bay. That's pretty close. But it's too far for me to ride on my bicycle. I could do it but my mommy wouldn't let me. That's my bicycle." She pointed toward a small, neon green bike near the door through which Hall had entered.

"So, what is it?" she asked.

"What?"

"My name."

"I'll tell you what. It was dark when I arrived at this hotel last night. I'll guess the name of the hotel."

The girl rolled back her eyes to ponder the offer.

"Okay, what's the name of this hotel?" she giggled.

Hall furled his eyebrows as if in deep thought.

"I think it is 'Ye Olde Groggrewoggle Arms'," he said.

The girl laughed. "That's not it. Not even close."

"Then it's the Taylor Bay Hiltonia-Romando-Gooey Duckling Toad and Frog," he said.

"That's it," the girl confirmed, exploding in uproarious laughter.

Hall waited anxiously for any noise on the floors above to indicate the paroxysm of laughter had waked others.

He heard no telltale squeaks in the old house. But he said, "Well, I've got to be going. I've got to swim to Olympia by 3 o'clock. So I better pay my bill."

"Silly, you can't swim to Olympia. The water is too cold. I'm not allowed in it," she said decisively. And she rose from her step and approached him, helmet under one arm. She held her other hand towards Hall.

"That will be 75 cents," she said, giggling.

Hall had to keep his arrival secret. And there was only one way to be sure. His hand tightened on the knife handle.

Wozniak's Lair, 1986

Wozniak's lair was a triumph of American trash-tacky.

A clearing had been hacked from a forest of tall, lovely Douglas firs. The surviving trees kept the clearing gloomy and dark.

The small dark brown house, its paint peeling, was cheap ticky-tack: T-111 exterior siding; aluminum slider windows and curling roof shingles that once had been white but had weathered to black with accents of green moss spreading from the shingle grooves.

Scruffy weeds served as grass. A couple of old cars rusted on concrete blocks. Treadless tires, beer cans and other rubbish accentuated the look.

There were probably a lot of these cheap houses hidden in the woods of the area. But there was no doubt this one was Wozniak's.

A sheet had been stretched between two firs. Large red letters said, "This is the place for truth and justice." Numerous clothes-pins festooned the sheet's edges.

Hall observed the sign and the clearing from 30 feet up in a tree located about 25 yards from the house.

He clung to the thick trunk, his back covered by thick foliage. Someone would have to be looking right at him to see him.

He was motionless, exhausted. It had taken seven hours to find the house via the overland route through nettles, blackberry brambles, large wet ferns and huckleberry bushes. All the plants were heavy with moisture. So again, he was wet. Even with the compass, Hall had had trouble keeping his route straight. It was like he was back in Wozniak's element: Vietnam.

He avoided even the smallest trails and moved slowly as his eyes and hands and feet searched for tripwires, booby traps and anything else the jungle fighter may have pulled from his bag of tricks.

While his jeans and parka again were soaked, his wool sweater was still dry and the temperature had risen to the low 50s.

If he made a conscious effort to ignore the cool air, the

shivering stopped. Maybe it helped that he still was carrying the insulation of fat.

And maybe he was draped in a tree like a damn fat python. But the paddling, crawling and crouching was over. He was resting, finally.

Scouting the house for several hours had produced no information about Wozniak except for his banner. Wozniak wanted him to find the house. But, as far as Hall could tell, it was deserted. No lights appeared as darkness encased the woods.

So where was he? Was Wozniak concealed somewhere in the wet brush along the narrow driveway or around the clearing? Rifle ready so that with one quick burst he would have his truth and justice?

It wasn't going to be that easy. Wozniak had expressed pleasure at the ways in which Hall had extracted his justice for the family in Ap Thuy Tu. Wozniak had called the killings of the Backatya Boys "elegant." The hooker with AIDS, Caldwell's murder -- they had Wozniak's fingerprints. He wanted to show off the gossamer touch.

Move another jump ahead.

Something waited for him in or near the house. But it wasn't Wozniak with a rifle.

There also was no sign of the police. Hall suspected he was not yet a full-fledged suspect. He wasn't worth a SWAT team. That meant a couple of deputies might be sitting on the house in a squad car, engine and heater running. They would be fortified by large thermoses of hot coffee, sandwiches and donuts. There was no sign of a squad car.

Hall stopped at the thought of coffee and sandwiches. He hated coffee. He was surprised he hadn't thought of hot tea or food. He should be craving them. But he wasn't. Food and drink were superfluous, irrelevant to him. Everything had become irrelevant except this blood hunt. He hurt and he was too heavy. But his body was alive, alert, as it had been when he was a young man when he had hunted in the Central Highlands and other VC strongpoints. He had survived then and he would survive now.

Through the night Hall heard a couple of cars speed down a nearby road. Once there was a crashing somewhere in the dark. Dog, cougar, bear, deer, it could be anything. Wozniak wouldn't crash in the dark. He would wait as motionless as death itself, as long as it took for the victim to enter the killing zone.

And that's how Hall waited, dozing a little, but still alert for any sound, any movement.

Gradually the darkness faded into gray mist and fog. Nothing had changed at the house. Hall pressed against the tree trunk and urinated into his pants. The warm pleasure it produced soon chilled his legs and crotch and made it more difficult to control the shivering.

Dawn crept towards mid-day and still nothing moved in the clearing. And then the wind came.

About 10 a.m. a breeze put a shimmer into the tall tops of the surrounding firs. By 10:30 a.m., despite the dense tree cover around the house, there was enough wind to whip Wozniak's truth and justice banner. The sheet strained desperately at its tied corners. The great strain couldn't free the corners but suddenly an audible rip separated "truth" from "justice". Soon the sheet was in half, flapping wildly. The weight of the clothes-pins did nothing in the fury of the windstorm. No one emerged from the house or forest to remove or repair the sheet.

But a white Acura rounded a corner in the narrow lane bulldozed through the forest. It stopped as soon as the driver was in view of the house.

It resumed the remaining 50-yard journey to the clearing at a hesitant crawl.

Hall watched Shiloh Weeks survey the house and its trashy surroundings from behind her car's steering wheel.

The white door opened and she emerged. She wore tight blue jeans. The slim legs of the ironed jeans covered pointed, shiny footgear of some kind. Probably cowboy boots. Cowboy boots were Shiloh's idea of outdoor gear.

Despite the cool, blustery, rainy weather she wore only a light blue jacket over her white blouse. The jacket stopped at the waist to underscore the effect of the jeans.

Weeks paused by the car and placed a narrow reporter's pad on the roof. The wind seized its pages and sent them flapping. Weeks recovered the pad and stuck it high between her thighs. Her hands gathered up her flying hair into a bun.

Hall watched the slim hands work in unison to capture all the strands until her hair was pulled tight against her head, accentuating, even at the distance from which he watched, her high cheekbones, her long, Mediterranean nose, her lips . . . the distant image summoned up before Hall's tired eyes memories of the many times after their lovemaking they would lay entangled and he would gently gather her hair and pull it back from her face and they would look into each other's eyes, not speaking, until her hand would reach out and caress his face and then pull it to her. . . .

Weeks' eyes left the house and scanned the surrounding forest. Her gaze seemed to stop in his direction, on his tree. It was impossible for her to see him but still . . . .

She was looking again at the house. She craned her neck as if the extra inch or two would help her see something she had been unable to see before.

"Hello?" she called.

There was only the wild flapping of the banner and the "WHOOOOOOOoooooooooo" of the wind in the trees.

"Anyone here?" she called, removing the notebook from between her legs and holding the bun with one hand. She took her first prim and cautious steps toward the house.

She stopped. "It's Shiloh Weeks. Anyone here?" She waited, clearly losing patience with someone who had missed an appointment.

She pivoted and walked directly to the ripped sheet. She seized one flapping side with her notebook hand and held it so she could read the banner. She released it and grabbed the other.

Someone must have told her to find the house in the woods with the truth and justice banner. She had talked to Stephan Wozniak!

Now Weeks was no longer tentative. She was a beautiful, successful reporter who had been stood up.

"John. It's me. Shiloh Weeks. Where in hell are you?"

No response.

She freed her hair and shook her head in the wind. And marched on the house, reporter pad in her left hand, and a pen she had drawn with her right hand from the tight pocket over her right buttock. She put the pen in her mouth and ripped off the cap as she approached the house.

Then Shiloh was gone, the shack concealed her.

Scream a warning! Get her out of here!

Hall's body clung motionlessly to the fir but his tired mind was in overdrive and panic.

Thoughts, emotions, memories and instincts cascaded and tumbled together and he pressed his forehead into the tree and closed his eyes and tried to sort them.

Shout to her!

Rush to her, gun at the ready, throw her into the Acura and speed from the trashy clearing.

For God's sake! You love her. Get her out, Wozniak doesn't matter now. You have a gun. So it's you and him, you know you wouldn't hesitate to shoot him or anything that moved now.

Just get Shiloh out!

But wait.

You are both in Wozniak's killing zone and this is war and this needs a resolution and there was a little girl who wanted to take a pee in the middle of the night in Ap Thuy Tu. And then her family. . . . and Caldwell and the others . . . . The worst thing you can do is panic. You've already made one big mistake after giving the kid at Taylor Bay $5.

You let her live.

The kid knows you are here. So Wozniak knew, or soon would know. Fool. Chump. You can't afford a second mistake. One is enough with Wozniak. Get smart now, after all this. Turn this into an opportunity to flush Wozniak.

Let Shiloh be bait.

That isn't it. Wozniak isn't here. There is a trap but Wozniak isn't here. And the math isn't right. Wozniak isn't ready for her, or you. So let Shiloh scout. No, that isn't it. The truth is: let the bitch scout. Shiloh is just a bitch who's making love to a policeman who wants to arrest him.

And this is just Wozniak mind-fuck.

With a very sharp point.

Hall's mind spun. He couldn't focus or decide.

Then Shiloh came around the house. She was peering in windows and then knocking on them.

"Where are you, John? I'm the reporter you called. I found your banner. You were going to tell me all about Jeremy Hall. What the hell is going on here?" shouted Weeks.

The window tapping became loud pounding.

"All right, God damn it, I'm coming in. You better be here," she shouted. Hall watched Shiloh give up the window pounding and march back around to the front of the house.

140

"You told me you'd tell me everything I wanted to know about him," she was shouting. "So let's have it. We made a deal!"

He might love her. But there was no doubt about it: God, she was a tough bitch.

"I want the truth about Jeremy Hall," Weeks was shouting at the house. "And I want it now!"

More Wozniak's Lair, 1986

The peeling shack was not at all what Shiloh Weeks expected to find amid the dancing shadows at the end of the rough, wooded drive. For her, it was not even in the right part of the state for a recluse to live.

She knew some very interesting recluses, most of whom she met on weekends with Jeremy Hall at Orcas, Lopez and other of the beautiful San Juan Islands. They were artsy-craftsy refugees from Manhattan and Beverly Hills who built a pile of money before disappearing in the islands. And they had the good taste to build hand-hewn log cabins in the remote islands. There they would write or compose or paint and take their occasional visitors on tours of the mortise and tendon joints and nail-free construction of their furniture and homes as they babbled about how good the acid used to be in the 60s.

But this trashy, cheap place! Down on the South Sound, for Christ's sakes! Probably owned by a logger. Was John a logger? She called his name a few times and got no answer. She checked the clothes-pin festooned sheet flapping in the wind. It was John's banner all right.

"Shit," muttered Weeks when she tripped on a log. She stopped and inspected a snakeskin cowboy boot. Yep, the damn thing was scratched.

"Shit!" she repeated, this time loud enough for anyone in the house to hear. She had reached the door and pounded on it. Then she waited, listened and scanned the clearing and the surrounding trees that shuddered in the gusts of strong wind.

It was a logger or truck driver's dump. But the caller who had brought her to the place certainly had not sounded like a pig. He had called her Ms. Weeks. His voice was calm, methodical, pleasant, even merry at times, sad and apologetic at others. He was knowledgeable, helpful. And there was a hint of something else. Like he was unsure of himself. There was a hesitation when he called her "Ms. Weeks." He had had to remember the proper means of address. Well, he was a recluse. John had said so himself.

But he certainly seemed to know about the string of strange murders afflicting the city. None of them -- except for perhaps Ed Caldwell -- associated with the usual motives -- drugs, insurance fraud or intra-family abuse. The caller seemed to know somehow the murders were linked -- a judge with a clothes-pin on her nose; a strange fat man with an apartment full of guns and clothes-pins; a little Vietnamese girl and then her brother. And then the cops working the cases kill a reporter who reached for a gun while he didn't even know where the hell he was. It was all so strange. Buck and the boys kept thinking they had things figured out and then something came out of nowhere at them.

Weeks knew the link: Jeremy Hall.

And when John called as soon as she arrived at work this morning -- when she thought he was just another nameless kook -- she realized he knew something about Jeremy too, although he had started out slowly. He had started out bemoaning the violence of the era and specifically the crime wave in Seattle. She was about to tell him to fuck off and hang up when the caller moved toward the point.

"Are you the reporter handling the story about the string of murders?" he had asked.

"Yes," she had answered without hesitation as she scanned the City Desk file on her computer to see what other reporters were turning in for the next day's paper.

"Then there is something you should know," the caller said.

"Yes," repeated Weeks.

"I knew a man once. You know him now. There are things you should know about him."

"You know him now!"

The caller's words sent a chill up her back.

"Tell me!" ordered Weeks, punching a button on her keyboard that cleared the City Desk file and provided her a blank screen for note taking.

The caller paused. She was pushing too hard.

But he began.

"This man I knew was very evil. But he didn't seem that way. He was very tricky. He seemed as normal as you and me. Something must have snapped in Vietnam. Did I tell you that is where I knew him -- in Vietnam?"

"No, you didn't."

"What are you typing?" asked the caller.

"Just what you are saying," responded Weeks. She recited a familiar drill. "What you are saying is important to me. I don't want to miss any of it. I can write much faster on my computer than I can with my pen and pad."

"Okay," said the caller. "As I said. It was in Vietnam. This person -- he was an officer, a lootenant -- killed someone -- a child, just like the one the other day -- for no reason except personal enjoyment. Very brutally, he killed her. She was very close. So close he could feel her blood on his evil hands. This was no bombing or artillery strike, no unfortunate casualty of war. It was a knife in the ribs, just like the other girl . . . ."

"I get your point," Weeks said, her fingers flying on the keyboard. "Why do you think he liked what he did?" She already was sure she knew where the conversation was going to end.

"Because he then killed several people. People who were on our side. People who never hurt him in any way. People who took part in the Chieu Hoi program -- do you know what that was?"

"No, tell me."

"Chieu Hoi was a program for Viet Cong and North Vietnamese Army soldiers to give themselves up and join our side. Our enemies became our scouts. Kit Carson Scouts they were called. They were very helpful. Usually friendly, helpful people."

"Go on."

"Ms. Weeks. I believe this lootenant learned to love killing and he may be involved in these unfortunate events we are now witnessing."

"Tell me the details," said Weeks, her fingers way behind her thoughts. "Start with the Seattle killings and then what happened in Vietnam. Who is this man?"

She waited, furious that excitement was creeping into her voice and her questions were tumbling out in a disorganized way.

"Unfortunately, I can't think of another way to do my civic duty. Like this man, I had some terrible experiences in Vietnam. Some of the people this man killed were my friends. I've had a terrible time since. Frankly, I've been shattered. I've become a recluse. My counselors tell me I have Post-Vietnam Traumatic Stress Disorder. Therefore I don't want any police hassles. I just couldn't stand that or the publicity it would bring. If I could just tell you what I know . . . but you must promise you won't reveal my name to anyone or bother me again. You cannot quote me or refer to me. Is

144

that okay?"

"Deal," said Weeks. She would agree to anything now and make whatever adjustments were needed later.

"But how do I know you are legit? You have to give me specifics about this guy," she added.

"Well, let us see. He learned what thrilled him in Vietnam. I told you that. He is in Seattle now. He was an intelligence officer in Vietnam."

"His name. I want his name," Weeks urged.

"I'll tell you what I know. But I am distracted by your typing. And I want to see the person with . . . ah . . . whom I am speaking. I feel we are developing a rapport, don't you think?" the caller asked.

"Where shall we meet?"

"Here. At my place. I don't like to leave my home. I am very uncomfortable elsewhere. I'm sorry about that. But my government made me the way I am. I have little use for my government. But I now am what I am. In many ways, my life has been wasted. I am very bitter about that."

"I'm on my way, Mr. . . . sir, you never told me your name."

"It's John. If I don't tell you my whole name, I can be more confident our bargain will be kept."

"Fine," said Weeks. Once she knew where he lived, it would be easy to find his whole name in the county property tax records. Then she could find out everything there was about John. Police records, military, financial, credit, court, the works. The kind of research she did all the time.

"Tell me where you live."

"Listen carefully, it's hard to find. But you'll know you are in the right place when you see my banner. It's something I have believed more sincerely than anything since Vietnam. It is why I am calling you now. It says, "This is the place for truth and justice.""

"Tell me how to get there," said Weeks, "I'm on my way."

And here was this horrible shack. The instructions had been clear. Over the bridge and down the highway. The banner proved this was the right shack in the woods. So where was John?

The wind was terrible. It turned her hair into a rat's nest. No one answered her calls.

She was at the house. More calls yielded no responses. She saw no one moving through the windows.

"Hey John!" She pounded on the door.

"All right, John, It's been a long drive. Grab your socks and haul 'em up cause I'm coming in!"

Weeks turned the door handle and pushed.

The door swung open without resistance. The interior released a powerful odor that made her flinch, shake her head violently and back into the wind.

"Jesus, what have you been doing in there, John?" she called.

No answer from the house.

After another quick look around, Weeks held her nose with the hand holding the reporter's pad and stuck her head in the door to scan the foul-smelling room.

It was filthy, just like the clearing. More beer cans, cigarette butts, cheap, crappy furniture.

Maybe this was it.

She had finally gotten there. The point where she would give up on a story. No matter John had seemed to have some solid information, he clearly was a kook. Who else could live in such a shack? Maybe she just didn't need this story this badly. Goodbye Pulitzer, goodbye New York.

She hesitated at the threshold. Maybe the thing to do was to return to the office and get someone -- maybe one of the big male photographers to return with her. But that would mean letting Anne Fisher know about the lead and what she was doing. Fisher would tell Hall, if she could find him. It would also mean letting the photographer have a bite, even a very small bite, of her story.

No way.

Maybe a call to Buck then. Get him to come out. She could withdraw in the Acura to the highway, maybe find a place with hot coffee, and wait. . . .

No way.

If she could break this one -- unveil a mass murderer who also happened to be her own boss and distinguished newspaper editor -- and deliver him to the cops trussed like a pig on a silver platter, the Pulitzer would be a shoo-in.

"Awwwlll raaaiit, Iaammn kombing iinnn," she announced, her voice distorted by the pressure of her fingers pressing on her nose.

Her left snakeskin boot just crossed the threshold when something had her jacket and yanked her back.

Weeks swung around, ball point pen held securely, with

about three inches behind the point exposed, ready to slash at eye level.

She checked her hand when she saw it was Jeremy Hall hauling her backwards by her coat. He was actually pulling her towards her car.

"You? You're John?" she shouted. "You scared the shit out of me!" She brought her hand down in a chop to force the editor to release the jacket.

"Don't go in! Get out of here," Hall ordered.

Weeks ignored the order and inspected her boss. He was dirty, unshaven, his face gaunt, eyes fierce and blazing. He was holding a pistol in his right hand.

"What the hell?" she demanded. "I'm not going anywhere, you psycho."

Hall's eyes and attention had been everywhere except on her. Until he heard "psycho."

He gave her a contemptuous look before striding past her to the door of the shack.

His back was against the cabin, pistol held up with two hands, police style. Hall was peering around the door frame into the small house.

"This is a joke, isn't it? Just what are you playing at? Rambo, is that it?" Weeks's hands automatically had begun to take notes of the psycho's actions.

"If you won't leave, at least make yourself as small as possible," Hall said from the side of his mouth.

"Oh, come on. This is just too ridiculous." Weeks joined him at the door, her back against the opposite side. She continued to take notes.

"Did you call me and identify yourself as 'John'?" she asked. She had begun to interview her boss. She found it hard to believe her boss and lover could have passed himself off as a reclusive stranger named John. But here she was, standing in a filthy clearing with an urbane and cosmopolitan man who insisted on acting like a damn elk hunter after weeks in the boonies.

"Jesus, just shut up, will you?"

"Really!" said Weeks, again entering the house in a full, upright-position.

Again, the psycho son-of-a-bitch was grabbing her jacket and pulling her back.

147

"All right. Is this your place?" she demanded. "This is all for the record." She shook herself free and resumed writing.

"Shut up."

"Did you call me and pretend to be John? What is the matter with you?"

But now Hall didn't seem to hear.

"I didn't bring the police, if that's what you think," she said. "This is my story."

Hall was paying no attention to her at all.

"What does this place smell like to you?" he asked finally, still scanning and sniffing the filthy room, from his position along the building's outside wall.

She inhaled deeply through her nose.

"Like my cat's litter box," Weeks said. "Or maybe it's you who smells like cat piss. Jeremy, you do smell like piss! What the hell have you been doing? You look and smell like hell!"

"Cat piss. Doesn't that mean something? Didn't you write a story about drugs and cat piss or something?"

Weeks shut up and thought. Somewhere there was a story about drugs and cat piss. A couple of years ago. It was about methamphetamine and the labs that made it. Jesus, she remembered now.

"Jeremy, be careful. If this is a meth lab, it is very dangerous," Weeks warned. She moved along the wall so she could view the inside of the room.

"Look at the table -- back in the kitchen," she said, pointing.

Hall dashed across the open doorway to her side. She felt his body against her back, his left arm around her waist, the hand holding the gun over her other shoulder, the pistol pointing into the house. He was using her as a firing post and shield.

"See the stuff on the table?" she asked. She pointed out to him a variety of chemist's glassware, most of it blackened at the bottom. Two Bunsen burners also were visible. Below the table were several large bottles and containers. She could read "ether" on one container. Another was labeled "solvent."

"Back off," Weeks whispered. "It is a meth lab."

She turned from the room and dashed for her Acura. "Come on," she called.

"Not that way," Hall shouted. She stopped and turned. Hall was hurrying towards the treeline at one side of the clearing.

148

"God damn you," she shouted but, after a glance at the car, turned in Hall's direction, vaulted a bald tire and followed him at a run.

The executive editor didn't stop in the trees. He dropped into a crouch and moved quickly, batting through bushes like a wild animal. Weeks followed. Brambles grabbed at her legs. She slipped repeatedly on the slick-soled cowboy boots. Her jeans, then jacket, dripped mud and moss. She moved through a group of tall, single-stalked plants and immediately felt stings on her face and backs of her hands.

"Jeremy, those were nettles, watch where the hell you are going!"

But Hall just turned with a finger across his lips. He abruptly changed directions. After a few yards, zagged back into another direction.

CRAAAACK!

Weeks responded instinctively, following Jeremy's dive into the underbrush at the sound of what -- a shot?

She lay still and low as she watched Jeremy roll and disappear in a clump of large ferns. His pistol emerged at an elevated angle, apparently following his eyes as he scanned the trees.

Then he was up and moving again. Weeks rose, slipped and fell, and rose again.

Jeremy zigzagged. She followed in a straight line, trying to keep up. She didn't believe he was capable of this much energy.

Then Jeremy went into a wide arc that returned them to just about the point where they had entered the woods. There he lay in his green parka, breathing heavily. He held the pistol in a two-handed police grip, the barrel aimed generally at the clearing and house.

Weeks crawled up and turned immediately on her side to examine the knees of her sharply pressed jeans and the elbows of her jacket.

"Was that a shot?" she demanded when she recovered the breath to ask.

"A tree breaking. I think," he replied.

"You are a crazy psycho, Jeremy," she panted, turning so she faced him.

"Shut up." It was a cold, don't-give me-any-bullshit order. She glared at him but shut up. She turned to watch the clearing. She

149

saw nothing.

After about half an hour that seemed like hours, Hall turned and crawled back into the brush. Obediently, she followed his green parka.

Hall stopped several hundred yards into the brush. He lay on his stomach, pistol aimed down the rough and temporary trail they had created through the vegetation.

"Here's the story," began Hall. He was still cold, authoritative. "We are going to circle back to that clearing. You are going to get into your car and drive back to Sea-Tac Airport. Get on a plane and disappear. I'll cover you at the clearing."

If she wasn't still panting so hard, Weeks would have laughed in his face.

"You don't really think I am going anywhere, do you?"

"It's the smartest thing you can do," he replied matter-of-factly, his attention still elsewhere.

"If I don't do as you say, are you going to kill me the way you killed all those people?" she asked, trying with her gaze to hold his roving face still.

"Don't be a fool. Do as I say. If you don't leave now, I'm taking off. I'll leave you here. Get out while I can cover you. I don't think you are in danger yet. But soon you will be. So leave. Go to Iowa, anyplace. *You* especially must disappear."

"I'm not in danger? What about that God-damned house? Just getting some of those meth solvents on you can kill you. Cops who have handled it have died. The stuff is probably in the walls, on the floor, even the outside walls. The furniture. And if the fumes don't get you, the chemicals have a damn good chance of exploding. If you had fired that gun of yours who knows what might have happened. Cops use moon suits and whole fire departments to go into places like that, for Christ's sake. And if that wasn't enough, here's my ex-boyfriend . . . my boss running through the woods looking and smelling like an animal with a loaded gun.

"You know there are a lot of people who think there is a long trail of bodies behind you. And you say I'm not in danger?" Weeks realized she was shrieking. And she was still holding her pen like a small knife.

"Run, Shiloh. Run for your life," Jeremy snarled, disappearing in the underbrush.

Icy Death II, 1986

Anne Fisher checked the Mickey Mouse watch on her left wrist as her right hand gave her apartment door an unnecessarily hard shove. She waited a millisecond for the impact against the wall. CRACK!

Then she uttered the oath that had become part of the tradition of coming back to this empty apartment. She refused to think of it as home.

"Shit! 9:45" She knew the woman across the hall didn't like the cursing. So she said it again, even louder. "*SHIT!*"

Just as she had every other weekday for months, she had arrived at the paper -- just five blocks away -- at 6:30 a.m. -- almost 15 hours earlier -- to prepare for Hall's, and now Van Gelder's, 8 a.m. story conference.

After the daily story conference battle it was one crisis or skirmish after another, especially with this strange murder spree. And there were the usual mini-crises -- prima donna columnists and reporters bitching about cuts and changes in their copy by assistant city editors; advertisers and public officials bitching about the "tone" of this or that; the unending political correctness bullshit from just about everyone inside and outside the paper and finally, the unending onslaught of personnel problems.

Fisher shut the door of her apartment, again, harder than necessary.

At least the personnel problems had abated about 50 percent since Ed Caldwell got himself shot.

But Caldwell's personnel hassles were replaced by the outrage on the staff and throughout the press across the country that police would shoot a reporter. And some commentators were already suggesting it never would have happened if the paper's management -- read Anne Fisher -- had intervened in time. Ed Caldwell, troubled victim, substance abuser, would still be alive if only senior management had . . . . blah, blah, blah.

Already The PBS News Hour wanted her to appear to defend herself.

Whatever his faults, Jeremy Hall would have absorbed all that shit and protected her and the rest of the staff. It was becoming clear Francis Van Gelder intended to hang her out to dry -- alone.

Well, here she was again, alone again in the empty apartment, after another 15-hour day.

She marched straight to the kitchenette and took a Manhattan glass from the cupboard. She opened a bottom cabinet to study her liquor collection. Red wine, Vodka, cheap Scotch. And Chivas Regal. It was a Chivas kind of day.

She placed the bottle next to the glass and glanced at the freezer portion of the small refrigerator. All she needed were the two ice cubes and she'd be on her way. . . .

But she turned and walked to the sleeper couch where she sat and removed her white Reebok walking shoes and tossed them at the apartment's locked front door.

She sighed and looked back at the glass and bottle. Then around the minimally furnished apartment. No knickknacks, no paintings, no photos, although she had bought a $4.25 bunch of Safeway tulips and had put them in a beer mug on the cheap coffee table. The flowers were beginning to wilt.

She lived lean for a hell of a good reason. One day -- someday soon -- she'd have the bucks all saved. And then she and her computer were heading for where? The Caribbean? Greece? Goa? Right. Goa's nude beaches. Show some sag. If not Goa, somewhere. And the novels would pour out. No more story conferences. No more political correctness crises.

And she'd meet the right guy. Almost any guy.

Fisher rose from the couch and walked to the small bathroom, allowing herself one more glance at the liquid relief waiting on the kitchen cabinet.

She braced herself on the sink and removed her thick walking socks and stockings. The rest of her clothing joined them in a heap on the floor.

The routine in this empty apartment was getting so old! As usual she turned on the vanity light and examined her face. The hair color kept the gray at bay. But the lines around her eyes! God. She pulled back her upper lip with one finger to examine the gums over her chewing teeth which already were covered by or filled with too much gold and silver.

The gums looked they must have receded even more during

the day. A friend -- ha, she had no time for friends -- an acquaintance told her surgery could restore receding gums. Maybe. For how long? She was going awfully fast. She ought to check the management dental plan for that option. If she did it, she certainly wasn't going to cut into her collection of certificates of deposit for dental surgery. That stash was for escape.

Fisher spent several minutes examining her face from several angles. It was slim. Eating like a damn bird and long weekend walks and a little jogging kept it that way.

But it was plain. The nose too big, the lips too thin, the hair too stringy.

"Jesus, you make me sick. Get a cat or something. That's about the best you'll ever do. You're the only 40-year-old woman I've ever met who dreams about running to a sunny island with a computer. Get a life," she scolded her reflection.

Fisher slapped out the light and her eyes returned to the Chivas bottle and glass on the kitchen cabinet.

Just a couple of pieces of ice and two, maybe four -- fingers of Chivas, some music. Maybe Jimmy Buffett singing of the islands. Or Pavarotti. That man had a lock on rocketing, at least vocally, above the daily grind. His voice virtually escaped the pull of gravity and floated free . . . .

Fisher's hand reached for her robe and her eyes turned to the kitchen. "If you are going to drink," she told her reflection, "at least put it off as long as possible. Take a shower. The drink will taste a lot better when you're clean."

She slipped into the small shower and pulled the spigot, standing as close to the back as possible to wait for the water to flow from cold to warm.

Then she stood in the dark as the gentle water and hot steam enveloped the small stall.

Standing and wondering about Jeremy Hall. How could she have so misjudged him. A murderer? It just didn't seem to fit. He had all the qualities she admired. Loved.

And that message from him to senior staff via the publisher. The warning to be alert for danger. Was he really warning people about himself? That was the spin Van Gelder was putting on it.

But that was work. That wasn't what she wanted to think about in this steamy, warm shower.

She wanted to think about Jeremy, the man. She wanted him

to be in the shower with her.

Fisher shook her head in more disgust with herself. Married Jeremy. Beth and Jeremy. Shiloh and Jeremy. That beautiful, talented bitch Shiloh.

They've certainly been in showers together.

Well, Shiloh had sent Jeremy and Beth's relationship to the rocks. And he had chosen her, not Shiloh, for city editor.

Fisher knew she was competent, coldly competent. Incisive. Thoughtful. She cut through the bullshit, that's what Jeremy liked to tell her. He told it to her often even in front of the reporters, anyone. It didn't seem to matter who heard that stupid compliment. He even said it in front of that idiot Ed Caldwell.

What a thing to say! If only he knew what she wanted him to say. But maybe there still was a message in his choice. Turning her face into the water's flow from the shower head she replayed selected scenes from story conferences and other contacts with Jeremy. Any hints? Any glances? Anything?

Face it. Everything had been professional. Jeremy wouldn't do anything unprofessional. Shiloh must have made the first move. Jeremy had by-passed Shiloh and selected her for city editor because she was the most competent; able to cut through the bullshit; willing to put in the hours; willing to give up her life . . . .

Until she surprised everyone and said goodbye. When she had the money . . . and it was coming in much faster now with the city editor's job.

Time for that drink. She soaped and rinsed.

Fisher turned off the water and stepped out into the fog that consumed the small room. She toweled herself without turning on the fan concealed in the light or opening the door because she didn't want the fog to lift and reveal the damn mirror and its foul truths.

She put on her robe and wrapped her hair in a turban and made the bee-line for the kitchenette.

Fisher unscrewed the bottle and tipped it over the glass but lifted again just before the liquor began to flow.

"Ice first, you goose."

Her hand closed around the handle of the freezer section of the white Kenmore refrigerator.

Then she pulled the hand away. At least she had to throw something to eat in the microwave before she had the first drink. "Rummy," she muttered.

She pulled open the refrigerator door. Not much. A quart of skim milk. A quart of pineapple juice. A jar of olives.

A Domino's pizza box. It contained half a medium pizza. The remnants of last night's dinner. Not again.

So Fisher methodically went through the small cabinets below the sink. Nothing to eat. The cabinets above the sink had a few crackers, plates, glasses. She slammed cabinet doors with increasing violence.

The choices were to get dressed again and go sit alone somewhere, order Chinese or eat the damn pizza.

Fisher looked at the bottle and glass. It was going to be the pizza. Part of her routine, boring life was to eat a salad for lunch. So she had had her veggies and maybe could take the calories.

She returned to the refrigerator, ripped open the door, removed the pizza and pushed it into the microwave. She gave it three minutes.

Okay. Now it was time for the drink. First the ice cubes.

Three steps brought her to the freezer door. She took the handle and jerked it open.

And there was a great flash. She was flying backwards. She felt a stinging in her left forearm. Felt the unraveling towel turban fly from her head. She felt the impact of her shoulders on the floor and then her head snapped against it and the light was gone and she wasn't sure. She wanted to get up but her legs and arms weren't responding. Her ears rang. She just wasn't sure what the problem was. She relaxed her neck muscles and let her head roll sideways.

She heard someone asking, "So how come I always pull the ugly bitches, anyway?"

Then there was a mouth pushing against hers. She shook her head violently and the mouth pulled away and someone's hands released her chin and nose. She felt panic, desperation.

Hands pushed her back when she tried to rise.

"Don't move," ordered a voice.

Fisher opened her eyes. She was on the floor. A black fireman in a yellow helmet was leaning over her. She turned her head. A white man with a strange image of a staff entwined with snakes on his dark jacket was wiping his mouth with a hand covered with the membrane of a white surgical glove.

"No offence, lady," said the white man. "I didn't know you'd come around so fast."

155

"You want some of this?" the black fireman was holding a capsule covered in gauze in front of her face.

Fisher didn't know what to say and didn't reply. So the man broke it and stuck it under her nose.

She felt her body jolt as she tried to spin and escape from the sharp smell.

But the hands held her down.

"Take it easy," said the black fireman. "There's been an explosion. You'll be all right." She watched the man raise his head. "You ready?" He was talking to someone else.

"Let me just get an IV into her." It was the man whose mouth had been against hers and who had called her an ugly bitch.

"Can I talk to her?"

Fisher turned her head to find the new speaker. It was a tall man with red hair in a suit.

"Sure," said the man who had called her an ugly bitch. "She wasn't hurt too much except for the cut on her arm. Mostly it was shock. Another minute won't hurt."

"Miss Fisher, I'm Lieutenant Jerry Buck. . . ." began the tall, red haired man.

"Of course, we'll have to X-ray the head to know for sure," interrupted the man with the snakes, defensively.

"Sure," said the man calling himself Buck.

"I'm a police officer," said Buck. "Do you feel up to answering a few questions?"

Fisher thought about that. She had had little success getting her body to respond. And she felt so light-headed.

"I'll . . . I'll try," she whispered.

"You're Anne Fisher, the editor who works for Jeremy Hall, aren't you?"

"Yes," she replied. "What happened to me?"

"Miss Fisher, an explosive device of some kind was planted in your freezer. It was rigged to explode when you opened it. We're investigating," Buck said.

"An explosive device?" The words were so strange, so bureaucratic. "You mean a bomb?"

"Yes, a bomb," said the policeman.

"Why?" she asked.

"We are trying to find that out. Was anyone here today at any time to your knowledge?"

Fisher didn't have to think about that. It was that damn empty apartment of hers.

"No. Unless someone from the super's office. . . ."

"No, miss, the janitor, no one else was in here. Did you notice anything unusual when you came home?"

"Unusual?"

"Door open. Furniture moved. Anything missing. Anything new. Stuff like that."

"No. The apartment was just as it is every night," she replied. "Nothing different."

"Well, you had a visitor."

"Maybe it was just an electrical short or something like that. Who would want to hurt me?" she asked.

"It was an explosive dev. . . a bomb, Miss Fisher. We've found the wiring."

"It couldn't have been much of a bomb." She raised an arm weakly and pointed a finger generally in the direction of the man who called her an ugly bitch. "He said I am okay." There she was. Cutting right through the bullshit again.

"Ah, Miss Fisher, either this guy was a blithering incompetent or the bomb wasn't intended to kill you," said the policeman.

"Why?"

"The bomb guys say there was no shrapnel involved, you know, no nails, ball bearings, that kind of thing. Just blast. Probably a combination of aluminum powder and potassium perchlorate. Makes an impressive bang, but that's about it. I guess you got a sliver of ice or ice tray in the arm."

"Lucky she didn't have a tray of frozen herring in that freezer. They'd a made a hell of a missile," said a voice behind her as if she wasn't there. It was the one that made the ugly bitch remark.

"Who'd do something like that? What's the point?" asked Fisher, annoyed that a bomb had gone off in her face and she was still cutting through bullshit.

"Who do you think, Miss Fisher?" asked Buck.

"Could you make it Ms. Fisher?" she replied.

"Sorry. You are lucky you don't keep much in the freezer. Any idea who'd want to play that kind of a game?"

"Of course not!" she snapped.

The cop looked at someone beyond her, probably the medic

with the big mouth.

Then the cop asked, "Maybe a boyfriend, ex-husband, someone like that?"

"I'm very involved in my work," replied Fisher. "What I mean is, I don't have an ex-husband or a boyfriend."

"Could this be something?"

Fisher looked in the direction of the refrigerator. A man with reading glasses perched on the end of his nose and white rubber gloves was asking the question. One of the gloved hands held a piece of paper.

Buck, who also was wearing white surgical gloves, took the paper and read it. "Where did you find it?"

"On the floor. It looks like it was one of many papers that had been held on the front of the refrigerator door by those little magnets. Until the explosion, of course. The boom scattered them pretty well. I found it in the debris on the floor," said the man in the reading glasses.

"Are you suggesting this bomber left a note?" Only she would get an incompetent bomber who left notes. She couldn't believe how ridiculous her life had become. She didn't wait for an answer. "What does the note say?"

Buck raised the note before his eyes. He read: "Dear Anne. I know you like to cut through the bullshit. You're making a damn career of it. Does this little missive make my point? Get out of my face."

Then Buck looked up at her. "It is not signed. Any ideas?"

Fisher felt the panic rising again and she tried to sit up. But couldn't. Hands and something else held her down. For the first time, she noticed she was strapped on a gurney, its legs collapsed.

"I don't know," she said sullenly.

"If you know anything, this is the time to talk about it," said Buck. It sounded like a warning.

"The 'cut through the bullshit' phrase. My boss often uses it. In reference to me."

"That boss would be Jeremy Hall?" asked Buck.

Fisher hesitated before saying, "Yes."

Buck handed the note back to the man with the reading glasses. "Put a priority on this at the lab. Check writing, fingerprints, the chemical stuff, everything. Let me know as soon as you do."

"Right," said the man, putting the paper in a plastic bag.

Buck waved and another man in a police uniform with three stripes on his arm appeared within Fisher's view.

"All right, let's pull all the stops. Let's find Hall. Put out an all-points bulletin. Check with the feds to see if he has left the country. Also Oregon, Idaho, Montana and B.C. Mounties for special emphasis. Give them his license number, check for rental cars, see what his credit cards are doing and subpoena his phone records. Freeze his bank accounts and notify the banks we want to be notified if he goes near them. We're finished playing fool around," said Buck.

"What's the charge?" asked the cop in uniform.

"Aggravated murder. The judge, the two kids and we'll think up something in the contributing area for Caldwell. Felony assault on this one. Get on it."

Fisher shook in fury against her bonds.

"What did you say?" asked Buck.

"Hall. That fucking bastard. Get him."

Hiding Out, 1986

The image in the Rescue Mission's mirror was becoming the truth. Hall was becoming someone else.

His freshly shaved face was alien now. Red, puffy eyes. Skin drawn and gaunt. A nasty scrape received while hurrying down the big Devil's Head fir tree to get to Shiloh was still ugly but finally healing. The hair hadn't been so long since college.

But after weeks of living on the street the change wasn't just in the way he looked. He no longer was a liberal, upper middle class editor. He was becoming a homeless outcaste in the way he thought, the way he acted, in the daily routine of his life. Was he becoming too much of a harried bum who craved charity and slinked from confrontation?

Could he still kill? Would desperation serve him as well as hatred did in Vietnam?

He stood amid a crowd of homeless unfortunates and bums in the barracks-like community bathroom. He got jostled once or twice for his spot at the sink by those still healthy enough to push.

He felt murderous fury mount with each jostle and shove. But a fight in the center would just draw attention and probably the police.

So he gave a little, holding enough position to finish washing and shaving. But he relished the sense of rising fury.

Yes, he still could kill.

He got out as fast as he could. He was clean and wore a new shirt, parka and slacks from the Five and 10. He didn't like the creases where they had been folded on the display table. The pants -- waist down to size 33 from the size 40 he wore just weeks earlier -- looked new, and might attract attention. But they also might be right out of a suitcase. That was cover. He was a traveler.

But clean clothes, a shower and 15 harried minutes in front of a Rescue Mission mirror wasn't enough to give him what he really needed and he knew it. He was just too tired. Deep, deep bone tired. Too many nights of trying to sleep amid bums and thieves, pickpockets and young punks.

He could make a serious mistake without sleep. He had to get some. And maybe food, although that did not seem to be very important any more. The soup kitchens' white bread and lukewarm, gristle soup and piles of macaroni and cheese sustained and revolted him. Meals had become annoying but necessary danger zones where he was compelled for a minute or two to shift his attention away from Wozniak to a paper plate and its miserable contents.

The skies outside the Mission were gray and chilly. As he studied the skies, he immediately saw the refuge he needed: The Executive Crest. A big, fancy, ask-no-questions-if-you-looked-okay hotel that was built in anticipation of a renaissance that never came to Tacoma. The hotel was directly up the hill from the Mission.

Stopping at a good hotel appealed because it broke the pattern he was setting: rest at a cheap dive or homeless shelter for a few hours and then slip back into the crowd. The Crest was a place that would observe a "Do Not Disturb" sign.

Although the hotel was directly up the hill, he turned right, shuffling like a drunk who'd stayed dry for a couple of days and cleaned up. He shifted to aggressive out-of-town businessman in mufti after he was convinced he had no tail. Finally, he went to the hotel.

He strode rapidly to the front desk of the hotel and asked for a single room.

"Please fill out our registration card. And may I have a credit card?" asked the pretty blonde desk clerk, her hand out for the card.

Hall kept his face on the registration card and replied, "I operate my finances the way I operate my business -- no credit. I'll pay cash in advance."

"No credit card?" It was clearly a new problem for the fresh-faced clerk. "Our policy is to have a credit card number on record in case . . . ."

"I'm not going to tear up your room. I just want to get some sleep." He opened his wallet for the money, making a big mistake.

The young clerk pointed across the counter at his wallet where portions of several gold-colored credit cards were visible. "We can take either the American Express or Visa," she said.

"They aren't credit cards," he snapped, shutting the wallet. Mistake number two. "How much is the room?" Hall held out the cash he had.

"May I see your driver's license?" asked the clerk.

"Lost it for DWI," snapped Hall. "How much is the room?"

The woman studied his face, his new shirt and his dirty parka.

"It's irregular sir . . . $60," she said finally.

That was the signal his hunch was right. The fancy hotel probably didn't have too many guests. Ultimately money was the most important thing and maybe the place would take good care of the people it did get.

Hall handed over three $20s. He was getting dangerously short of money. And he had no idea of how to get more. He didn't dare use a credit card or go to a branch of his bank. Phone, bank and credit card records formed the foundation of any law enforcement agency's hunt for a fugitive or missing person. Money was a problem that had to wait until he was rested.

"Room 614. Will you need assistance with your luggage?" the clerk asked.

"I'll bring it up myself after I check the room and get something to eat," replied Hall. Mistake number three. He was implying he had a car after telling her he had no driver's license.

"Sixth floor, turn right from the elevator," said the woman's voice behind him.

He took the key and walked through the empty lobby to the elevator. The ceiling was a big glass skylight except where huge ducts cut off the night sky. Large flower displays were arranged on several tables. In one corner a computerized black grand piano enthusiastically banged out ragtime to an empty lobby. A bored, uniformed concierge waited for business.

The room was spacious, clean and boasted a clear view of steam or smoke spewing from a waterfront paper mill.

Hall sat on the bed. He was afraid to lie down.

Even drowsy, he knew had made too many mistakes. If the police were looking for someone acting suspicious, he had set himself up nicely.

Maybe any paying guest was too important for a call to the cops. That didn't work. There were times when any hotel needed the cops. Even the fancy hotels couldn't afford to piss them off.

Maybe the Seattle cops weren't looking this far south.

Don't be stupid.

He couldn't stay in the room. But he had to stay somewhere safe. For at least eight hours. He had to sleep deeply.

162

Hall rose and walked to the bathroom. He splashed cold water on his face. God, his face alone was enough to arouse suspicion, forget the debacle over the credit cards, forget he was the classic hotel red flag -- the guest without luggage. He should've lifted the best looking bag at the Mission. He had long ago trashed the running bag he took from his condo for fear it would give him away. That was smart. But now he was making too many mistakes. He had to sleep.

He rubbed his face with a luxuriously soft, clean, white towel, an artifact of a previous life. Be smart. Be careful. Forget about that shit. He replaced the towel, hoping it looked unused.

Hall took the elevator to the first floor and, showing little face, waved at the desk clerk as he exited. He made a purchase at a nearby mini-mart and returned to the hotel, entering through the side door at the parking lot. He descended to the basement.

Where he found a door marked "Employees Only." He turned the knob boldly, prepared to be the drunk looking for a bathroom.

It was open and empty. And it was the chambermaids' supply room.

Shelves were stacked with towels, toilet paper, bars of soap, and bottles of abrasive cleaning supplies.

Behind the door he also found a mounted set of hooks. A sign belabored the obvious. "Keys."

After checking the hall, Hall took out the roll of transparent packing tape he had just purchased. He pushed in the wedge-shaped latch on the door and taped it back so it would not engage. He covered the latch hole on the door frame with more transparent tape as extra insurance.

Hall gently pulled the door back. It might work. A tired maid might set the lock on the inside handle and pull the door behind her and not realize the door still could be opened from the hallway. And the transparent tape across the hole and across the latch was almost invisible.

Hall left The Crest through the parking lot exit and found an open Japanese restaurant. Too tired for chopsticks, he insisted on a knife and fork. The Japanese waitress was surprised. Another mistake. He had wandered into a yuppie restaurant where customers ate sushi and insisted on authenticity.

"Just a fork," Hall repeated and looked away. He drank all the weak tea in the tiny cup before him. The whole pot would do nothing to keep him awake for the next few hours.

"Miss?" he called after the waitress. "Black coffee, please." He shuddered at the prospect. But maybe it would keep him awake long enough.

The big plate of fried noodles reduced him to $5 and change. His next big problem: he had to find some money. After sleep. Then it would be easy. Somehow.

His watch said 7:03. He had to keep moving at least two more hours. Three to be sure.

Hall fell into his cleaned-up-bum-for-a-day shuffle and returned to the Rescue Mission. A piece of paper taped on the closed door said "full." He joined several other men and a woman who waited with piles of possessions in plastic garbage bags. Hall didn't have a stack of stuff, but he waited in the line with the hopeful.

He stood with his back against the yellow walls of the Mission, hood pulled up to conceal most of his face, watching the patterns in the night life around him. When the cops were circling, the hookers, both female and male, moved on. Then the hookers would come back and the procession of cars and pick-up trucks would resume their reconnaissance. Occasionally a driver would pull to the curb and there would be talk of dates and money and bargains reached and the hookers were so skinny and ugly wearing flashy, ugly, short clothes and their hair was stringy and they smoked and the kids were so young and the cops were coming again . . . and it was so hard to stay awake.

Hall shook his head.

Wake up!

The police car slowed and stopped. The driver used the search light on his door to study each person in the short line.

And then the beam was on him. The parka's hood covered his eyes but the light illuminated the tip of his nose and his mouth. The beam lingered on what the cops could see of his face. Then the beam dropped along his legs and to his hiking boots. And then to the wall on either side of his feet. The cops were looking for his bags.

Hall went into a paroxysm of coughing and his hand slipped to his stomach, then into the parka and around the handle of the K-54 stuck in his belt. Maybe the police would see the gesture as an effort to rein in an ulcer or tuberculosis or whatever winos did to maintain control of their failing bodies. Or maybe they'd think he was reaching for a weapon..... . . . .

The beam moved on to the next person in line.

Hall raised his eyes to The Crest up the hill.

A clear pattern emerged.

He counted 25 floors with guest rooms. The 26th had big windows, probably Plum's Place, a restaurant advertised by a banner in the lobby.

Lights were on in rooms on floors five through nine. With the exception of the 26th floor, floors 10 through 25 remained as black as the night sky.

Hall waited until 10 p.m. to be sure. A few more tired travelers still might pull in from Interstate 5 and a few guys would get lucky with dates. But it was clear the hotel was filling up from floors five through nine. Maybe 10 would get some people. And maybe there was a penthouse or very large room on 25 if someone special showed up.

He bet floors 11 through 24 would remain empty.

He made the slow ascent from the Mission to the hotel. He tried the parking lot door. Locked.

He had to enter through the front door.

He was the aggressive out-of-town businessman again as he strode through the lobby, waving his key at the same clerk who had rented him the room.

She gave him a corporate smile. "Need help with your luggage yet, sir?" she called.

"Thanks -- no," he replied.

And her eyes followed him to the elevators. And probably watched the digital display above the elevator as the lift traveled to the sixth floor where he got off.

Cautiously, Hall walked down the stairs to the basement. The basement hallway was empty. The blue metal door to the "Employee Only" room was closed.

Hall paused and looked back at the stairway. He doubted he had enough energy left to do what he must. It was getting hard to focus. Why the hell was he even going through this? He was ready to sleep under a bridge.

Where he would be rousted -- and checked -- by a cop. He needed certain, safe sleep. That's why he was about to make ascents that would be comparable to a rested person climbing K-2.

Hall pushed on the door. It opened. The tape gambit had worked.

There were two sets of keys hanging from the hook behind the door. Hall took both sets and made sure one of the keys would open the blue door. Then he removed his tape and left the door locked.

What did he have left? An hour, maybe two. Then oblivion.

The exhaustion of the long climb towards the top only helped to confuse him. He couldn't be sure which floors were dark. How large a buffer of empty rooms should he leave between himself and the occupied floors? How many floors could he climb?

He just kept his head down and focused on the steps before him. One step after another. Counting steps worked for a while then he couldn't keep track any more. Finally, he looked up. Floor 22 chose him. He couldn't go any higher.

He walked to a room at the end of the hallway and opened it with the maid's passkey. It was dark and empty. He taped the lock with an excessive amount of transparent packing tape. Then he stared stupidly at the number for several minutes. 2219. Could he remember it? He pounded his forehead. 2219. 2219.

Then he tried the door. The latch wouldn't engage. He returned to the stairs and walked down to the basement. He was surprised at his speed. Well, the end was in sight.

After replacing the keys on their hooks, Hall began the second ascent to Floor 22.

Just focusing on each step wasn't enough this time. He had to sit and rest frequently. He gave himself five minutes to advance each floor. Several times on his rest breaks his head slumped to his chest but each time he shook himself and got back on his feet. There was a buzzing in his head he could not control and his eyelids felt like anvils. If Wozniak had followed . . . he didn't even have enough strength or even the interest left to pull the gun and fire it . . . and he knew it.

Finally, the number on the wall said 21. Only 25 steps to go. Hall gave himself 10 minutes to make the floor. He was crawling now.

Then, with his back supported by the wall, Hall edged his way towards Room 2219.

The door opened and he remembered to pull off the tape and stuff it in his pocket. But he stood stupidly in the open doorway looking at the "Do Not Disturb" sign on the door's inner knob. He was confused. Put it out or not? No. A do-not-disturb sign on an empty floor was a clear red flag to a passing chambermaid. Wasn't it? But what if the hotel put guests on the floor? In Room 2219? Without the sign, a maid might come in the crack of dawn. Hall couldn't decide, couldn't think. He left the sign on the door knob and stumbled to the bed. He could figure it out if he could just lie down for a minute . . . .

There was light through the window when Hall opened his eyes.

He immediately remembered the dilemma of the do-not-disturb sign. The answer now was clear and straightforward and totally meaningless.

Because he sensed a bigger problem had arrived. The only sound was the hum of the heater or air conditioner, whatever it was. Otherwise everything in the room seemed clean and in order.

The problem was more a disharmony. Maybe a distant noise as well. But mostly he sensed the disharmony. That was the only name he could give the feeling. But then he had been neither hunter -- nor prey -- for many years.

He moved slightly. The bed springs squeaked some so he reduced his effort to dead slow. No alternative but to risk the noise -- he slipped the pistol's safety to off. And rolled off the bed. He moved across the thick beige rug to the door. He listened but heard nothing. Not even a distant vacuum cleaner. Still -- there was disharmony.

Quiet as a shadow Hall crossed the room to the window. He pressed his chest to the plain brown industrial grade wallpaper. Making sure the drape did not move, Hall looked down at the street.

He was too high and the angle was too great to see it. But across the street was a large building whose windows were made of gold reflective glass.

The slightly distorted scene he viewed in gold was more pandemonium than disharmony.

Several police cars were in a line in the narrow street in front of the hotel. Red and blue lights flashed on the tops of the white cars. The line also contained a blue and white squad car of the type used by Seattle police.

There also was one unmarked car. That was where several men had gathered.

Hall was surprised at the detail he could see in the gold building. Several of the men were in uniforms and he spotted a couple of shotguns. Four cops seemed to be in jeans and parkas that were lettered "POLICE."

They were waiting while a man in a suit was talking on a radio handset.

The man in the suit -- did he have red hair? -- returned the radio to the car. The move seemed to precipitate an animated discussion among the cops.

The cops gestured and talked. What brought them? The pretty little receptionist. She had taken the $60 and what? Called to report him?

Or just told a canvassing cop with a photo, "Yes, there is a man who looks like that picture in Room 614. I think he was hiding something too."

Maybe a beat cop had come in to flirt and asked the throw-away question as he always asked -- "Anyone interesting check in?"

If only he hadn't been so tired, that crap with the credit cards, and the DWI and having no luggage would never had happened. . . .

The problem was the gleaming gold street scene before him. Clearly the cops had pounced on Room 614 and found it empty. What else had they found? He had handled the door knob with his hand in the parka pocket. So no fingerprints there.

But he had sat on the bed and used a towel. Maybe the bed was mussed or the towel not quite right. Maybe the cops knew for sure someone had been there. Would hair, lint, mud from his shoes tell them anything? Would they bother to look? That would take time.

They'd given up on surprise. But did they have the hotel sealed? Was a search of the building under way? Were they coming to Floor 22? Was it safer to stay or move?

One thing was sure now. He was being treated as a serious suspect. There was a lot of firepower on the street below. A lot of commitment.

A search, at least at the beginning, would be careful and systematic. By the time a search team got this high, if it had started at the bottom, it might be sloppy. Or were they starting from the top to flush him down to the cops on the street? . . . .

Hall checked the street again. All but one of the white prowl cars were pulling away. Probably the local cops, maybe pissed about Seattle coming down and using up all their resources on a wild goose chase.

But two men from one white car and two cops from the

Seattle car walked into the hotel. The man in the suit put his car between himself and the hotel's front door and leaned, arms folded, across the auto's roof.

So. There was going to be a half-hearted search. A couple of Seattle uniforms and the Tacoma cops along for jurisdictional turf-protection. Probably all the side doors to the hotel and doors to its staircases had been locked, all elevators but the one being used by the cops shut down. If he slipped out the front, the red-haired man waited. . . .

There was no point in trying to sneak out. The best hope was to find a place to hide in the room. And hope the cops started at the bottom and were tired and bored from searching scores of rooms before his.

They had to be sloppy. Hall did not want to become a cop killer to find Wozniak.

But he would.

The room offered few possibilities. Under the bed. The closet. Behind the bathroom door or the shower curtain.

Or there was the window ledge. But the window didn't open, there was no real ledge and the cop below would spot him in a minute.

So how about the window drapes? They were loose and hung to the floor. He might be able to hide in their folds.

Hall straightened out the bed and moved into the folds of the drapes in the corner.

His hiking boots had to be sticking out the bottom!

Hall leaned down and yanked the rug. It had been secured to the concrete floor with screws. He pulled the rug and its underlying pad free of three screws. He had enough slack to conceal the toes of his boots. Then he arranged the folds of the drapes around him and waited, pistol cocked and ready.

The voices arrived in the hallway approximately an hour and a half later.

That had to mean they had started on the first floor. And they were moving fast.

"PLEASE!" Hall whispered into the cheap cloth in his face. He pleaded for help but couldn't think of where to deliver the cry he mouthed.

In five minutes the voices became distinct outside the door.

"It's locked too, just like all the rest," confirmed a voice.

"Open it," said another.

"Here you are," said a bored female voice.

"Stand back," ordered a male voice.

Several people came into the room.

"See anything out of place?" demanded the male voice which had ordered the female to stand back.

"No, it looks just like all the other rooms," said the woman.

"How many more floors?" asked a new male voice.

"Just three," said the woman.

"I think our boy is long gone," groaned the man who had asked about the number of floors to go.

"He was in 614. Someone used a towel," said the first male voice.

"No one has used this bathroom," said the complainer. "I think Buck is wasting our time."

"You checked everything?" asked the first male voice.

"Except the window," groaned the complainer.

Through a crack between the wall and the curtain Hall watched a heavy-set, middle-aged policeman step up to the glass and look out.

"There he is, that red-haired asshole," said the cop, evidently the complainer. "I can see him in the reflection of that yella building."

He waved into the glass and smiled, "Top of the morning to you, you shithead." He said the words but mouthed them as though he was shouting them.

"Can it. We've still got more floors. Don't forget the curtains," said a man's voice in the room.

Hall watched the complainer use his nightstick to poke the drapes on the other side of the window.

The drapes quivered. The complainer turned to unseen people in the room.

"I'm telling you sarge, this Hall guy ain't here no more. At the rate he is killing people, he can't spend no time in hotel suites. Seems like he's got a damn quota to fill."

"Methany, if you had any sense you wouldn't be so quick to poke things with that stick. Hall is one tricky, murderous dude and he's real handy with booby traps."

Hall watched Methany, the complainer. Hall sucked in his stomach and waited, gun ready.

Methany stood where he was, continuing to face the center of the room. His arm moved and his wrist flicked the stick so its tip raked the drapes about half an inch from Hall's belly.

"How's that lady from the paper?" Methany asked. "The one that found the bomb in the refrigerator?"

A pain ripped Hall's stomach as if Methany had clubbed his gut with all his might.

"It was in the freezer. And I guess it was just meant to scare her. She got off with some burns and a bad headache. Damn lucky."

"I guess," said Methany. "Well, this room's clear. Let's go hit the next 400 empty rooms. Jeeeeez." The fat cop moved out of Hall's line of vision.

People moved and a door closed and the voices receded down the hallway.

But Hall remained frozen in the drapes. Sweat poured down his face. He needed to collapse on the bed and double up and hold his stomach. But he couldn't move.

The lady from the paper, the fat cop said. A bomb in the freezer, not the refrigerator. Hau's claymore had been in a refrigerator and it had been very lethal.

But Wozniak's had been in a freezer and it hadn't been meant to kill.

What was Wozniak's game?

And who was the lady from the paper?

Shiloh?

True Love? 1986

"Mr. Wozniak?"

The lanky, gray-haired man, who dressed with the comfortable informality of a college professor, ignored her and followed several lines on the page of the open paperback with his finger, apparently finishing a point. Only then did he look up. His expression was bemused, his eyes twinkling, so Shiloh Weeks looked at the book to see what was so funny.

The man had closed the book over a finger so the title was visible. It wasn't a humorous book. Wozniak was reading "Rebuilding Relationships: You Can Do It!" It was one of the latest, and hottest, self-help books.

But it was also a book Weeks expected to find a neurotic woman reading. Not Wozniak, a reasonably good-looking man sitting in a Seattle counseling and rehabilitation center for soldiers who had served in Vietnam. It was the third center she had visited that day. A lot of the vets had relationships they had to rebuild. Who cared?

She was tired, her temper frayed. She had a found a couple vets who had been in the 303rd Special Services but neither had been of the slightest help to her. If only she had been able to find the caller John -- if there was such a person. The confusing incident in the woods did not improve her mood.

"Yes? I'm Wozniak. Stephan Wozniak."

"Hi, I'm Shiloh Weeks. I'm a reporter at the paper. Do you have a couple of minutes?"

"For you, lovely lady, all the time in the world," grinned the man.

Weeks's defenses went up. He'd better not come on to her. The question came out in a bored deadpan: "One of the counselors told me you were in the 303rd Special Services unit in Vietnam. Is that correct?"

"Shiloh. That's an interesting name," said Wozniak. "Why did your parents name you after a very bloody Civil War battle? Perhaps even the first battle of modern warfare? Ever wonder about

172

that? Or did you choose the name yourself?"

"My parents gave it to me and I haven't really thought about it. I like it because it is poetic." she replied.

"Shiloh. Shiloh. A little church. A refuge, a place of peace. Over which 25,000 men shed their blood. Shiloh. That's an interesting, pregnant name."

"Pregnant?" asked Weeks. Who the hell did this guy think he was?

"Pregnant in the sense it is filled with interest and meaning for me. Shiloh is not a boring name, Ms. Weeks."

"You know a lot about the Civil War," she said.

"War is a hobby, I suppose you could say."

"Is the Vietnam War part of your hobby? And the 303rd Special Services Battalion?"

"Join the 303rd, bigger by a third," replied Wozniak affably, smiling more broadly.

"What?" asked Weeks, surprised at the response.

"Just an old joke."

"Sounds dirty," replied Weeks.

"It was intended to, I believe," replied Wozniak, shyly. "How can I help you?"

"I'm doing research for a story. I have to admit it's like looking for a needle in a haystack."

"If I can be that needle, I'd be charmed," grinned Wozniak.

Weeks couldn't help a big smile. This guy really did look and talk like the college prof. He certainly seemed to be educated. She liked him already. A little old and a little gray, maybe, but then not much older than Jeremy Hall. Quite an improvement over that pig, Jerry Buck.

"Thanks. I'm looking for information about another 303rd guy," Weeks flashed the smile of someone sharing an inside joke. "Someone who was bigger by a third in approximately 1966."

"I reckon there were thousands of intelligence people in Vietnam in 1966," replied Wozniak.

"Really? So why did the U.S. get its ass kicked?" asked Weeks.

"Army intelligence—a contradiction in terms. I'm sure you've heard that one. As I said, lots of folks in Vietnam in intelligence work. There were scout platoons, aviation recon, LRRP's -- sorry, Long Range Recon Patrols -- any number of units...."

"None of those sound right."

"Then, of course, there was the 303rd, a very special intelligence battalion, designed to provide coordinated, accurate information to MACV and the American front-line units. It had people in order of battle analysis, counter-intelligence, prisoner interrogation. . . ."

"That sounds like it," said Weeks.

"Well, then, maybe I am the needle you seek. I *was* in the 303rd in 1966," said Wozniak, smiling helpfully.

Weeks felt the excitement rising but tried not to let it show.

It wasn't just that she might have found the needle for which she was looking. She liked this unassuming Wozniak. She looked around the day room of the counseling center. It was filled with scruffy furniture and scruffy, smoking men who kept sneaking furtive glances at her. Wozniak certainly didn't seem to fit here . . . .

"Really?"

"Yes, ma'am," said Wozniak. He seemed so sincere. So helpful.

"I was in the Order of Battle section. Kept notes on what the NVA -- North Vietnamese Army -- and Viet Cong were doing and where they were. I'm pretty good with numbers. Pretty futile exercise, it turns out. But at least it kept me out of the field, most of the time."

Weeks noticed Wozniak's merry expression turned pained as he ended his sentence.

Why that was so would have to wait. Another question was bursting out.

"Did you," Weeks began, her voice dropping as she leaned towards Wozniak, "Know a man named Jeremy Hall when you were there?"

Wozniak drew back from her. An expression of horror shattered the friendly grin.

"Please leave," he said, reopening his book and staring at its pages.

Jesus. What had she done?

"I'm sorry. I didn't mean to upset you. Did you know Jeremy Hall?"

Wozniak at first ignored the question and then looked up. "I asked you to leave, please do." Then he turned his attention back to

"Rebuilding Relationships."

"Mr. Wozniak. I'm very sorry if I offended you. But this information is very important to me. To this city. You have to talk to me."

Wozniak closed his book without attempting to save his place.

"Look, Miss Weeks. Those of us who come to this place do so because we were wounded in Vietnam. I don't mean physically although some of my new friends here have suffered in that way as well. We see this as a place of refuge, where we can be among others who experienced the same horror and who share the same pain. The most important rule we have is that we do not stress each other in any way. When we feel stress, we ask the person inflicting it to back off. And they do," scolded Wozniak.

"Now," he continued. "I have asked you to leave. Please do so."

Wozniak reopened his book and studied a page. It wasn't anywhere near the part he had been reading.

Weeks felt so close now. There had to be a way.

"Mr. Wozniak, I'd like to buy you lunch. We can talk about anything but Vietnam. I won't ask you about that person."

Wozniak looked up again. His expression had changed.

"I have to admit I'd like very much to have lunch with you." The twinkle was back.

Wonderful. Now, just proceed at dead slow . . . .

She suggested a fashionable place on Fifth Avenue. "I'll drive," she volunteered, pointing at her white Acura as they left the center.

"That would be very nice. But I'd prefer something more utilitarian and vegetarian. I'm a simple man," said Wozniak. He told her of a Capitol Hill place.

As they drove, Weeks asked Wozniak the basic questions. He was the college professor he appeared to be. He had just taken a one-year position at the mathematics department at the University of Washington to do research in calculus. He had spent the last 20 years teaching at a small college in Kansas.

"It sounds silly, but adjusting to the big city, especially with some of the emotional luggage I carry, has been quite a challenge. That's why I recently sought the counseling offered by the veteran's center. To tell the truth, I feared seeking assistance through the university's facilities because, no matter what they say, you can pick up a 'psycho' label very easily even in these enlightened days. 'Sought counseling' is no plus on your academic curriculum vitae," said Wozniak.

Weeks smiled. She enjoyed the company of this soft-spoken vegetarian's unassuming simplicity and trust. Here he was already telling her his secrets. Telling them to a newspaper reporter he hardly knew. He was so unusual. She couldn't imagine such simplicity from Jeremy Hall. She bet there was much more she would be learning about Jeremy Hall from this man than she ever did in her relationship with him.

"Here we are," she said, nosing the Acura into an end parking space, to protect at least one door against dings, at the vegetarian restaurant.

"You'll like it -- I hope. I found it only recently," said Wozniak. "I recommend the yaki soba. Organic and whole grain."

"Let me ask you something, Mr. Wozniak. You go to organic vegetarian restaurants yet you are a smoker. I can smell it a mile off. What gives?"

"Call me Stephan. You're right. I smoke a lot. Learned it, as many did, in the institutional environment of Holy Mother army. One of its many benefits. I now regard it as part of my neurosis. I've tried to shake it. I can't. Simple fact. Our Mother promoted smoking—giving us free cigarettes with our C Rations and VERY cheap cigarettes at the PX, although I never could go to them—too dangerous. Jeremy got his cheap PX Chivas from a corrupt supply sergeant, the same one who got me my cartons of cigarettes ... but that's another story."

"Let's try the yaki soba. And call me Shiloh," said Weeks, opening the car door.

They ordered and made small talk. Weeks tried to get Stephan to talk about his calculus. But he brushed off the questions, claiming his subject was boring and arcane to everyone but himself.

"And I certainly have no intention of boring a beautiful woman if I can help it," said Stephan, his eyes twinkling brightly. Weeks found his eyes very attractive. Little, simple things, such as her incompetence with chop sticks -- delighted both of them. She liked watching his eyes give away reactions and feelings he would not verbalize. Maybe she shouldn't be in such a big hurry to run off to New York after breaking the Hall story and pulling down that

Pulitzer.

Whooaa, lady.

"If you won't tell me about calculus, tell me about Vietnam," smiled Weeks. Her hand crossed the table and landed lightly on Stephan's forearm. She gave the arm a light squeeze.

"Do it slowly and easily," she smiled.

Stephan smiled weakly. His free hand went to his forehead and his thumb and middle finger rubbed his temples hard.

Shiloh noticed Stephan's arm under her hand was still and relaxed.

"Miss Weeks . . . ."

"Shiloh," she said softly.

"Shiloh. I want to help. More than anything I have wanted to do in a very long time. It's just . . . . you don't understand. It's very painful. Very stressful. I'm not sure I can maintain my, well, my dignity."

The twinkle was gone, the face sad, grayer.

"We'll do it together, slowly and easily," she said softly.

A weak, forced smile.

"All right, Shiloh, I'll tell you."

Both her hands moved to the backs of Stephan's hands and she felt his thumbs wrap around hers. She squeezed and he squeezed back.

Stephan began slowly, continuing to hold her hands.

"As I said, I was in the order of battle section. My job was to sift through reports from all kinds of imaginable and unimaginable places --prisoner interrogations, captured documents, the LRRPs I told you about, the Special Forces, aerial sightings and even very secret radio interception and electronic sensor reports and make sense of it all. I tried to account for all the enemy units thought to be in each area of Vietnam on a huge map and I kept cards summarizing information about each of them. The cards said where they were. How many men they had. Casualties. What they were eating, if anything. Ammunition, supplies -- that sort of thing. Each day I prepared my estimates of enemy strengths and capabilities and intentions and briefed them to the generals."

Stephan stopped to take a long draw of the herbal tea in his cup.

"In other words," he continued, "I had a desk job. My biggest problems were getting enough sleep -- there were a lot of attacks on the camp -- and keeping my uniforms clean and pressed and boots shined for the generals' briefings."

"What did Jeremy do?"

"Pretty much whatever he liked. And what he liked was horrible. Criminal. Officially, he was in our counter-intelligence section. Called 'CI'."

"What's that?"

"They are the spy catchers and the people who defended us against internal attack, you know, fifth columnists." Some terrible memory must have surfaced in Stephan's mind because he pulled back his hands and buried his face in them.

"Take your time," Weeks whispered. Her left hand reached across and stroked the side of Stephan's head.

Stephan rallied.

"It was more than just the job of a CI spook. You have to understand the environment. CI by definition puts a person in a very gray world where the spies of both sides seek out and exploit moral corruption and decay. Deception and trickery reign. Cruelty is a prerequisite. Torture, blackmail, intimidation, murder, you name it. Nothing is what it seems. It was a world where you had to be willing to take two people out in a helicopter and throw one out to convince the second to cooperate. You can't really blame the people in it. I didn't like what they did, but then I didn't like it when colleagues pulled booby-trapped eating trays from mess tent racks and set off huge, deadly bombs. It was kind of like those B-52 strikes. I hated what they did. But if they killed the people trying to kill you, you tend to applaud even undeclared war in neutral countries like Cambodia and Laos."

"If Jeremy was just doing an ugly job that someone had to do, why did you react so to his name?" Weeks asked.

"Jeremy did, and enjoyed, things even the Phoenix people -- they were murderers too -- never would have dreamed of doing. Jeremy took the necessary black arts, double cross, triple cross, blackmail, murder -- you name it -- to a high art form and labor of love. Soon doing the army's dirty business didn't satisfy him. He and a small gang of thugs soon branched out to all kinds of crimes. He used to sit around at night waiting for the incoming and drinking his Chivas Regal -- it was always Chivas Regal -- and brag he was going to get rich in Vietnam."

"Incoming?"

"Incoming artillery. Rockets, mortars, that kind of thing."

"He sounds like the original war lover. Did you know any of his victims?" asked Weeks.

Stephan's right hand went to his eyes, which he rubbed hard.

"Yes. Many. You know, Shiloh, I should have been in the Peace Corps, but that's another story. I really tried to get to know and help the Vietnamese. There was a village near our base. I used to go to it. To help the people. I had friends with whom I used to have dinner. I found out what Jeremy was really up to when my Vietnamese friends would ask me to intervene. Find people who had disappeared suddenly and mysteriously, that kind of thing. Then, one time, I witnessed Jeremy in action."

"Tell me about it, Stephan."

"I went to the field on a mission. I was young and stupid. Even though I had a fairly safe job, I wanted to get war souvenirs like the other people. So I figured I could risk one mission. Jeremy thought it uproarious. He took me along as a joke. He treated me like a joke too." Stephan's hands were back on his eyes.

"This is very difficult," he said.

"It will do you good to talk about it," Weeks said softly.

Stephan looked at her. He seemed surprised.

"Don't be stupid. I'm telling you this because I like you. It certainly is not good for me."

"I'm sorry."

"I won't go into details. But I witnessed Jeremy kill a little girl with a knife in the back during an armed robbery he committed. Please don't ask me about it beyond that."

"Stephan, why didn't the army stop Jeremy?"

"Remember the environment I told you about. Jeremy and the other CI people by necessity had to operate in much secrecy and with much freedom. The other thing you must know is that the most important empirical measure of success in Vietnam was body count. It was not an empirical measure for very long. Enemy body count became the greatest compilation of lies, and the greatest incentive to lie, any modern organization produced. Promotions, plum assignments -- everything depended upon it."

Stephan paused and averted his eyes.

"Hall," he continued, "became one of the genuine body count production machines in the unit. His numbers came to rival the body counts of some infantry battalions. They -- the bodies -- were just

Vietnamese, after all. Gooks. And if they weren't armed and in uniforms, that didn't matter. The army dreamed up a special category for the dead civilians. They were called VCI. Viet Cong Infrastructure. They were supposed to be the spies, the couriers, the laborers and others who gave aid and comfort. The line between a VC courier and a person walking down a rice paddy minding his own business soon became very thin indeed. VCI became a veritable ash-bin of the innocent. They counted VC cows. VC haystacks. It was absurd. And horrible."

"Stephan . . . ."

"That Hall," erupted Stephan, "He even counted the little girl he murdered as a VCI in his body count. Does that show you what I mean?"

"Stephan," asked Weeks softly. "Did you know Jeremy Hall lives in Seattle now? He is a very influential person."

"God, no!" Real horror crossed Stephan's face.

"Yes. I think he may have committed several recent murders here. The police are looking for him."

"He's on the run? Maybe he left the area?" asked Stephan.

"He's around. I saw him a few days ago at a meth house. He looks and acts like a wild animal. And he's got a gun."

"Shiloh, beware. Jeremy Hall has a blood lust. He is a cruel and clever murderer. Oh God! Oh God! Oh God! I should never have talked to you."

Stephan was shaking.

Weeks reached out and collected Stephan's hands. She squeezed them hard.

"It will be all right," she said. "Jeremy will be caught. The police have a massive manhunt. They almost caught him in Tacoma."

Stephan shook his head. "They'll never catch him. He is a cunning animal with special skills the army taught him and more he learned in murder and confusion and blood and moral morass and treason and . . . ."

"Stephan!" shouted Weeks. "They will catch him. And I'm going to break the story."

Stephan was no longer paying any attention to her. He was looking nervously around the small restaurant as if he expected Hall to walk through one of the doors.

"I can't stay here. I must return to Kansas. I'm sorry, but I can't stay here. He's the reason I live in this torment . . . ."

"Stephan. Relax. You can't, you mustn't go."

Stephan responded with a look of what? Contempt? Not quite. But close.

"You're a reporter," he said. You'll do your story and move on to something else. I've got to live with what I've seen. I thought if I just got lost in my equations it would all go away. But it never has and never will. And then I move west and he's here and he's doing it again. . . ."

Stephan's eyes shifted nervously. He could no longer look her in the eye.

"Please . . . ." Weeks began.

"Who has he killed here?" Stephan demanded suddenly.

"I don't think I should tell you."

"Damn it, Shiloh!" Stephan's eyes finally were looking into hers. His burned.

"The police think he killed an ex-girlfriend who became a judge. Then . . . ."

"Who else?" demanded Stephan.

"A young Vietnamese man. And he may have set up one of our reporters to be killed by police. And last night it appears he put a bomb in my city editor's refrigerator."

Weeks looked away.

"You're not telling me everything, Shiloh. After what I just went through for you!"

"The police think he may have killed a young Vietnamese girl."

"God . . . ." gulped Stephan. He buried his head in his hands. Then he looked up. "How . . . how did he kill her?

"Listen, Stephan . . . ."

"How? Damn it, how?"

"She was stabbed. In the back."

Stephan just shook his head. "Just like Vietnam. Just like Vietnam," he sobbed.

Suddenly, his hands reached out for hers.

"Shiloh. You said you saw him. I don't care where or why. Please, never go near him again. Go away until the police have him."

She noticed they were gripping each other's hands.

"I'll be all right, Stephan."

"If you won't leave, let me help. I'm not a brave man, in fact

I'm a coward. I've been running for almost 21 years. But I feel driven now to help. I know I'll never find peace until he is arrested and punished. I'll do anything. Should I go to the police and tell them what I know?"

"No!" Weeks's answer was delivered like a karate punch. "There is plenty of time for that. Frankly, Stephan, if I can be truthful with you, I'd like everyone, including the police, to read about Jere. . . this monster in my story."

Stephan squeezed her hands again.

"Whatever you say. Look, I've got something to do tonight. But maybe we could get together for dinner tomorrow night. Eat and talk some more. And a walk? I like walks."

"I'd like both things," Weeks replied.

"Great, I know a great little restaurant," Stephan said.

"Tell me!"

"It's called the Captain Whidbey Inn. On Whidbey Island. It's a wonderful place to walk."

"Stephan," Weeks said softly. "That's a hotel too, isn't it?"

"It is, if you want it to be."

High Death II, 1986

"AIEEYEEEEE!"

Francis Van Gelder emitted the war whoop as the strong updraft shook his Beechcraft Bonanza while he slashed, starboard wing down, through the narrow valley created by Mount Rainier's white bulk on his left and Little Tahoma peak on the right.

He soared, as if in God's hands. And that is how he felt.

He glanced left, wishing he could skim the deep, icy-white half-mile-wide cone at Rainier's summit and take the wild ride in heavy turbulence down the Emmons Glacier. His plane didn't have the power and he didn't have the oxygen along to fly over 10,000 feet. The summit was at 14,412 feet. And a summit ride would be foolish. Very foolish.

But what a ride!

He'd just have to get something with the power to take the summits. Soon . . . but first he had another kind of power in mind . . . . And then there would time for all kinds of power.

"POWERRRRRRRRRRR. . . .," He howled.

Van Gelder rode the edges of the mountain's rough downdraft wave over more ice and snow. The impotent huge maws of the crevasses on the Emmons waiting below.

He passed a roped climbing party working its way down some 50 feet below his Bonanza. He made a silent approach at 160 miles per hour.

The surprised climbers shook their ice axes at him as he buzzed them.

"Disrupting your peace and quiet, eh? Foolish earth-bound scum!" Van Gelder yelled. He banked into a chandelle and buzzed them again, tipping his wings to match the steep glacial contour below.

And gave them the finger yelling, "Fuck you!"

They couldn't hear him, of course. But that was how he felt. Fuck everyone. He was in God's hands.

He had never felt so good. The mountain was his. The day sunny and blue and beautiful. The Bonanza was running like the

Mercedes in the showroom that soon would be his. The day was his. The paper was his. He was on top. Finally.

The announcement had come from the publisher that morning. Francis Van Gelder was replacing Jeremy Hall as the newspaper's executive editor. Permanently.

It looked so easy. But it had been a difficult campaign. Wisely he had not taken the position Jeremy should be permanently ousted from because of the crimes he appeared to be committing. The old buffoon of a publisher would have babbled indefinitely about innocence until proof of guilt.

But Jeremy had disappeared at a time of major crisis for both the city and newspaper. His mysterious voice-mail message that he had personal business out-of-town wasn't washing. The captain had left the bridge on his watch in the hurricane. All hell had broken loose on Jeremy's watch. That's how he argued it. In those terms. *Jeremy had left the bridge on his watch.* The buffoon, an old naval man, had bought that one. Not immediately, but he had bought it.

"AIEEEEYEEEEEE!" whooped Van Gelder.

He had crossed the stumpy, wind-bent trees at timberline and now was over thick forest. He pushed the plane over and pulled her out of the dive just over the tree tops.

He hummed "Treetop Flyer," Stephan Stills' song about flying choppers low in Vietnam.

Van Gelder howled, pulling the control column forward and back and alternately stomping the rudder pedals so it would appear to the deer and bears as though a drunk was in command.

As in the song, he followed the contours of the hills and valleys of the Cascades.

The prototype of his own career. Little hills and valleys in the choking exhaust of Jeremy Hall.

The next hill of his career was going to be like the damn mountain the Bonanza had almost climbed. And the hills like Mount Adams and Mount Hood and all the white peaks that lay before him. One mountain after another. Circulation was going to sky-rocket. He would blow away Oprah and David Letterman and television itself. People were going to be lined up outside the building to buy that newspaper each morning.

First step: Change the format to USA Today. Lots of color pictures and charts and graphs. Short, punchy stories. Lots of criminals, animals, gossip, sex and violence.

The old buffoon would grumble. Until the fool saw the revenues.

Of course he would have to make personnel changes to make that cash roll in. A lot of them.

"AIEEEEEEYEEEEE!" whooped Van Gelder at the prospect.

Anne Fisher would be at the top of his hit list. She would be a real problem. She would fight change. She was Jeremy Hall's man.

Given Jeremy's insane outburst of violence, she already was politically suspect.

But he couldn't flat fire her.

One strategy would be to create a parallel position for one of his men. Call it metro editor. And gradually shift all power to the metro editor.

How long would it take for Fisher to get the message and bail out? Maybe she wouldn't bail. Maybe she'd force a power play.

Better to create the new job and then submarine her. At every turn. Slip her the old perfumed ice pick and walk away leaving her bleeding and flopping on the ground.

And keep his powder dry for the big massacre that would follow as soon as she was impotent or gone.

God.

He was thinking so small. He had the opportunity to act boldly. He had to start thinking like an executive editor. He only need use his brain, and the old publisher would do whatever he wanted.

Conduct a massacre -- Fisher included -- on his own authority. Why not? The old buffoon would be angry, but he might not countermand the order. Big risk, though. At least he would have to wait until he brought in enough new people to get the paper out the day after the axe fell.

Speaking of axes. And bombs and murder and death.

Why had Jeremy only put a big firecracker in Anne's freezer? Because she was his protégé? Why attack her at all?

If only Jeremy had killed her. Then the massacre could begin immediately and the paper rebuilt. Trust Jeremy to botch things.

"Seattle Approach to Beech November three niner two. Beech N392 come in," said a crisp voice on the radio.

His plane's number. The call was for him.

Had the Park Service gotten his plane's number as he played

on the mountain? He better answer. It was unusual for Approach to call unsolicited.

"This is Beechcraft N392, over," replied Van Gelder.

"Beech N392, this is Seattle. This is urgent. Someone from your office is in the tower and needs to talk to you. Over."

Someone in the tower? Highly unusual procedure. Of course now that he was executive editor he had had to leave word about his whereabouts. A definite downside of the job.

"Seattle. This is Beechcraft N392. What is the emergency?"

"N392. Stand by, over."

Bureaucrats!

"Seattle, this is N392. Can you tell me more about the nature of the emergency? Over."

"Mr. Van Gelder?"

"Use procedure, identify the plane and say 'over' when you are finished," cautioned the tower guy.

"Van Gelder! What's so damn important, over?"

One of the rawest assistant city desk editors on the weekend daytime shift, a kid named Jack Somebody, again, said, "Mr. Van Gelder, the police want to talk to you. Please call Lieutenant Buck at pager number 723-8972."

"What happened? Over." Van Gelder snapped.

"It appears Anne -- Anne Fisher -- has been involved in a bombing . . . ." The kid was trying to report calmly but the strain was evident.

"Say 'over'," said the tower guy.

"Another bombing, over?" demanded Van Gelder.

"I'm not really sure. Buck -- Lieutenant Buck -- wants to talk to you. She may be dead . . . I'm not sure. Over," replied the junior editor.

"Jesus," snapped Van Gelder, Then he snapped, "November 392 out!"

He would have to land and call the cop.

The twit would be number two on his hit list. Didn't he know how to ask questions?

Anyway. What was going on? Another bombing? Or had the idiot just gotten the message garbled? There couldn't possibly have been two bombs, the second fatal for Anne.

Van Gelder couldn't resist a long glance at the blue heavens. A tragedy if it was a second bomb. A shame. A real God-damned shame. And a Godsend.

Van Gelder sang loudly of helicopters and Vietnam, plucking at the steering column like it was an acoustic guitar.

Screw singing. Even the hope that Jeremy had struck again made Van Gelder want to dance for joy. At least the plane could dance.

Van Gelder pulled back on the controls and the nose of the Bonanza came up instantly.

"It's an Immelmann. I'm a jet," he giggled as the Bonanza labored for altitude in the maneuver designed for a fighter jet, turned slowly upside down and then, nose to the ground, banked back. Van Gelder returned to his southern course with an aileron roll.

He was jazzed.

So where was he? 6,000 feet. Van Gelder's eyes studied the landscape through the whirling prop, looking for something to inspect or buzz. He was flying the southern spine of the Cascades. An hour out of Boeing Field -- and he was almost on the great gray hulk of Mount St. Helens. Probably spent too much time playing. But it was fun. Vietnam. Helicopters. Trees. Something. Something.

His gaze left the dark greens of the remaining forests and light green squares and rectangles and triangles of the clear-cuts to the whirl of the prop to the thin black-brown lines streaking back along the white engine cowling and the specks of brown dotting the windshield.

Jesus.

Lines? Specks?

His eyes focused on the cowling. No doubt about it. It was streaked with thin, elongated lines.

Oil.

The plane was leaking oil. Not too much. Had he checked the braided nylon oil hose in the pre-flight check? No. It was new and he hadn't bothered. So maybe a problem with manifold pressure? A crack in the aluminum case?

What if it was the oil hose? And it was broken or had developed a slit? It couldn't. It was new.

But what if it wasn't screwed tight to the engine block? As the oil heated and thinned, more would escape if the hose wasn't screwed on tight.

Was it so loose it could work free before he could land?

Yes.

The cowling was turning brownish-black. The black-brown fluid was covering the windshield.

He couldn't see.

The Bonanza carried only six quarts of oil. The joint must have come unscrewed. If only he could reach forward and check. A few twists with thumb and forefinger and the deadly black rain would stop!

Van Gelder checked his dials. The news was bad.

The oil temperature gauge was rising. The oil pressure gauge read 45 pounds. It should be at 70!

Van Gelder was all pilot now. He flicked the dials. Of course the readings were accurate.

The oil pressure gauge had dropped to 43 pounds.

How about the cylinder head temperature gauge? 480 degrees. It should read 400.

"Mayday, Mayday, This is Beechcraft N392. I have developed severe engine problems. I am losing oil fast," shouted Van Gelder. "Come in, Seattle Approach. I'm declaring an emergency!"

"Roger, Beechcraft N392, we have you," said the crisp voice.

"Seattle, this is an emergency. I am at seven thousand about . . . thirty-five klicks due north of Mount St. Helens. I am losing oil pressure and may lose power at any time, over."

"We have your position, Beech N392. We are scrambling Mountain Rescue and a MAST chopper from Fort Lewis. Keep us informed about your condition and position. Switch to emergency frequency 121.5. We will monitor all transmissions."

The prop continued to blast oil at the windshield.

The numbers said the oil was just about all gone. Oil pressure at 30 pounds, cylinder heads at 550.

Soon, almost immediately, the engine would seize and the prop would freeze.

Oh God!

He needed to find an airport. A highway. A straight stretch of logging road. That's all he needed, 300 feet. He could land in 300 feet. He would try in 200 feet. One hundred fifty.

But he could see nothing through the blackened windshield. There couldn't be much left.

Trees. Nothing but trees and mountains and steep valleys and stumps and twisted logging roads below. The fear was rising.

The Bonanza shuddered as the guts of the engine fused. Through the blackened window Van Gelder saw the prop freeze.

Desperately Van Gelder rubbed the inside of the windshield. It did no good, of course. He had to glide to a landing.

The altimeter showed 5,500 feet, which meant just about 3,500 feet separated his falling plane from the stumps and trees. Air speed at 73 knots. Van Gelder estimated he could keep the plane aloft for about three minutes.

Was there a straight logging road? Just 300 feet. Just 150 feet.

How about a clear-cut? They looked fairly open but Van Gelder knew they would be filled with killer stumps.

A school yard? Anything?

Just black-tinged green hills and valleys.

The Beechcraft was gliding towards them.

He had about 2,000 feet and a minute and a half left.

And he was going to die in this cramped, blackened world.

Van Gelder's head dropped back against the head-rest and he closed his eyes, although his hands still held the wheel steady.

He listened to the silence. It wasn't really silent. The wind caused a quiet, whooshing around the black void. The blackness must be thinning in the wind because Van Gelder felt more of the sun's warming, bright rays penetrate the cockpit.

He was close. He had been so close.

And a simple hose connection. . . . A bizarre thought occurred to him. Could it have been sabotage? Could Jeremy have unscrewed it just enough to get the plane airborne and let him play for 90 minutes . . . ? It had the simple but diabolical touch that could very easily be Jeremy.

It was almost funny.

God. Jeremy had killed him.

It was true.

Jeremy killed him. Just like the others.

Just when he was so close, he became Jeremy's victim.

Van Gelder yanked the radio mike to his lips. "Seattle Approach! Do you read me, over?" he shouted.

"Beech N392, this is Seattle. I read you," said the crisp voice. "What is your condition?"

"My condition is dead. That is my condition! Now make sure you have your tape recorder going, roger?"

"Beechcraft N392, this is Seattle. Affirmative. All radio transmissions are routinely recorded, over."

"It was Hall. It was Jeremy Hall who killed me. You tell them to look for sabotage. Jeremy Hall killed me, Seattle, you read that?"

"Roger, Beechcraft N392. You are claiming someone named Jeremy Hall sabotaged your plane. Is that a roger?" Neither the pace nor the tone of the man's voice had changed.

Van Gelder forced his voice to sound calm. He didn't want a felony murder jury to think a madman was making accusations from the doomed plane just 45 seconds to impact.

"November 392. I say again. Jeremy Hall sabotaged Francis Van Gelder's plane! Jeremy Hall did something to my oil supply. Check the oil! Out!"

"N2392. Stay on the air."

"Fuck off, Seattle. Don't have time for you now. Out."

"Stand by. . . ." ordered the voice.

Van Gelder switched off the radio and took a Black Russian from the pack in his shirt pocket and put it in his mouth. He dropped his head back on the seat. And again closed his eyes.

So close to prestige. Influence. Power. So much power. So close.

And now the trees.

So close.

But he held the control column steady. He really was a hell of a pilot.

In God's hands.

The clear-cut stumps reached up to him.

My Love, My Lamb, 1986

"Stephan! Have you been in prison or something? You are insatiable! Those Kansas girls must not take care of their men!"

"You're a very special woman, Shiloh Weeks. I could never get enough of you. Or give you enough pleasure."

"Naaaaaaayaaaaa," she groaned. "That's got to be the corniest packet of lines since . . . It was very corny."

Nevertheless, she ran her fingers through Stephan's short, rough gray hair. "That shit really work with farm girls?"

Stephan continued kissing her neck gently in a heart-shaped pattern. He was in his third lap around the design.

She was trying to sound tough but doubted Stephan bought it. He had gently nibbled away so much of her tortoise shell veneer in the last four days she doubted she had any shell left. Might as well be honest and see what happened. Stephan was so full of surprises.

"Seriously, Stephan. You'd better be careful or this sophisticated, hard-nosed lady reporter could fall in love with you and your stupid numbers."

"Fraid it's already too late for this hick professor. All his numbers add up to just one thing, Lamb Chop," Stephan whispered into her neck between kisses.

Weeks lay still and enjoyed Stephan's explorations. She couldn't remember when she felt so at ease and peaceful. She was in the proverbial quiet eye of the hurricane with him. Fear was all around her, throughout the city and particularly at the paper. Many of her friends who abhorred guns were buying them. Others were demanding the right to take extensive leaves. Everyone searched their memories for anything he or she might have said or done to Jeremy Hall that could be interpreted as a slight or insult, although most of her colleagues felt the Jeremy they knew was such a nice guy they had a hard time believing he would hold any kind of grudge. Yet he clearly had a nasty side. What happened to Van Gelder showed that. Anne's death in the second refrigerator bomb showed it didn't help to be on his good side. No one knew for sure what to do.

Van Gelder had kept up a steady drumbeat of editorials demanding the police capture the murderous lunatic terrorizing the city -- even if it turned out to be a newspaper employee even he wouldn't name -- and calling for reorganization and new blood that would bring "some measure of competence" to the force.

It was mere months earlier that the "dangerous lunatic" Jeremy lay in her arms just as Stephan was now. Then something snapped. Jeremy picked Fisher over her for the City Desk promotion. Something awoke his old instincts. His lust for blood. The judge. The two Vietnamese. The police were convinced Jeremy had given Caldwell a lot of heroin and then set the poor man up by calling 911 and providing information about the murders of the Vietnamese children himself before slipping out of the condo.

Then Jeremy hit his murderous stride.

The bomb in the freezer part of the first refrigerator just burned Anne Fisher. Then the second bomb in the refrigerator at Joan's place. Joan, a copy editor, had offered Anne a rollaway until Jeremy was caught. Jeremy found her first and Anne was turned into hamburger by the second refrigerator bomb filled with nails.

And then Van Gelder's death in the plane crash. The cops were sure the National Air Traffic Safety Board would find the crash was no accident. Jeremy Hall had struck again.

Stephan had been right, as usual. Despite his reign of terror and the resources the police were putting into the search, Jeremy remained elusive, apparently moving, and killing, at will.

Weeks's fingers danced lightly down Stephan's neck to his slender, hard shoulders. They were drawn to a familiar scar on his back. Slowly her fingers circled the outline of the kidney-shaped indentation on what she knew to be a very white back.

He was so white Weeks wondered if her lover ever had been to a swimming pool or beach. This quiet, cigarette-smoking vegetarian was such a puzzle to her. Shy, unassuming, diffident, trusting -- all so nicely leavened by a fine mind and a clever, self-effacing sense of humor. How his eyes gave him away! Sometimes he acted so serious yet those eyes were so merry it seemed he would burst.

She wished she knew more about his ethereal world of numbers. It was so obscure she didn't even know how to question him about it and he volunteered nothing.

His body told a different story. The kidney-shaped scar on

his back was just one of several scars on his back, arms and legs. Stephan wouldn't talk about them, except to say he once had a confrontation with a combine and the combine won. Whatever a combine was.

The small dagger tattoo on his arm also seemed out of place for this academician.

Stephan attributed it to a wild, teenage weekend trip to Kansas City.

She had to buy that. She was a veteran of quite a few wild weekend trips as well. They hadn't resulted in any tattoos -- but plenty of emotional scars. Especially the wild weekends with Jeremy Hall.

"Stephan," she whispered.

He mumbled and wrapped himself more tightly around her. Then his hands joined his mouth on the move.

"Stephan! We'd have to use the slide rule or whatever it is mathematicians use to count the number of times we've done the dirty deed. We've got to talk about Jeremy!"

"Computers have replaced slide rules, my Lamb," Stephan said, up for another round.

"Stephan! Jeremy could be out killing someone right now!"

"I doubt it. I think the action is here, now, my darling." Stephan indeed was getting very serious.

"Professor Wozniak!" squealed Weeks more in surprise than pleasure. They had been in the bed for hours. "How do you get that thing to do that?"

"When you've lived in Kansas as long as I have, the sheep start to look pretty good. And when you've honored one sheep, you've got to honor them all. The rest of the flock expects it."

"Silly, they don't have sheep in Kansas," she protested, but not very hard.

"Heads up. I mean down," Stephan said, pulling the covers over them.

"Baaaaaaaa," Weeks bleated softly.

Later, Weeks reached out sleepily as the insistent line of warming sunshine crept up her face.

Stephan was no longer beside her. Reluctantly, Weeks opened her eyes. He wasn't in the bedroom and the bathroom door was open.

She was going to have to put more effort into teaching

Stephan all the wonders of bed. He had mastered some of them, but beds also were for sleeping. And he used it for very little of that. She definitely was going to have to break this early morning farmer routine of his. The man must rise at 4 a.m., although she never heard him get up or leave the room.

Weeks pulled a pink silk robe around her naked body and padded to the living room-kitchen area. There was no hint of coffee perking, eggs frying, toast popping or anything. No lights were on. It was funny. She had never seen Stephan turn on a light. Ever. He seemed comfortable in the dark and shadows. Even when they came to her place late at night he never turned on the lights. One night she even tested him. She didn't turn on the lights to see how long it would take for Stephan to throw a switch. He didn't.

As usual when they came in, he had only one thing in mind. He always approached the subject seductively and lovingly and without haste. But always in the dark.

Weeks found Stephan in one of his favorite places, sitting on the living room carpet with his back against the wall, arms across his knees.

"What are you doing?" she asked, kneeling before him and allowing the robe to fall open. She ran her fingers up his arms.

"Thinking, Lambkins," he responded, eyes on the wall in front of him.

"Bout what?"

"Odds. Making things even up."

"Is that calculus?"

"Sure, my Lamb."

"You need more rest. You'd think better. Come back to bed, you'll see."

"Can't. I'm in the middle of something."

"Stephan, why don't you write things down? It must be easier to do equations on paper -- and use a calculator."

"It's easier to work things out up here, Lamb Chop," Stephan said, gesturing vaguely in the direction of his head. He still was distracted.

"Want something to eat?" she asked, running her hands along his arms to his chest and then to his stomach. He was wearing jeans, nothing else.

"No."

"I don't think you'd eat at all if I didn't insist," Weeks pouted.

"I can take it or leave it."

"Just like smoking? I know you smoke, but I haven't seen you light up a cigarette. How come no nicotine fit?

"I know you don't like it," he replied, still lost in his calculus.

"You can turn it on and off, just like that?"

"Yes, my Lamb," replied Stephan ignoring both her and her dancing fingers.

Weeks stood up, wrapped her robe around her and went to the fridge for juice.

"How about you stop calling me lamb and various lamb parts? If I've got to be an animal, how about something more interesting?"

"What interests you?"

"Oh, I don't know. Eagle. Lioness. Maybe a cat. Like you. You're like a very tough Tom cat. Sly. Noiseless. Night hunter."

"I haven't been able to find anything tough on you after quite a bit of prowling. Where did you see him?"

"Who?" asked Weeks.

"Hall. The other day you said you saw him recently."

"Out at Devil's Head near Longbranch. I got a call from someone who said he served with Jeremy. I drove out to see the guy."

"What happened?"

"The guy wasn't there. You know, he told me stuff on the phone that sounded like some of the things you've told me about Jeremy. Did you know anyone named John . . . ." Weeks paused to turn and face Stephan and let the robe fall open again . . . "In the 303rd?"

"Not to remember," replied Stephan without looking at her.

"But Hall was there?"

Weeks closed the robe and turned on the Mr. Coffee Machine.

All right. If Stephan was going to be all business, so was she.

"The house or cabin or whatever it was turned out to be empty. Apparently someone had been making meth there. It was real dangerous. Those places have poisonous fumes and chemicals and things that explode. Anyway, I'd forgotten my story I wrote about meth labs. I was about to barge right in and dig out this guy John when Jeremy . . . . Hall . . . appeared out of nowhere and grabbed my jacket. He pulled me out and pointed out what a dumb shit I was."

"Then?"

"He must have thought the cops were near. He had his gun out and wouldn't talk until he had run in circles through the woods and hidden like a mongoose."

"What did he say?"

"He warned me to go away. That's all."

"You sure?"

"I'm a reporter, remember? A very good one. That's it in a nutshell."

"You think Hall was pretending to be this guy John to get you out there?"

"No, John didn't sound like Jeremy. Frankly, he sounded more like you."

"What kind of gun did Hall have?" asked Stephan.

"A pistol."

"Other weapons?"

"Not that I know of."

"How was he dressed?" Stephan asked. He was beginning to sound like a cop.

"Jeans, rag wool sweater. Green parka. Red shirt. Why does that matter?"

"Just curious. Did he tell you how to contact him?"

"Of course not. I told you, he told me to leave town."

"Did he look good? Strong?"

"A lot skinnier. But he pulled me away from the cabin very strongly."

Stephan finally looked at her.

"Did you tell the cops about seeing him?"

"Don't be an idiot, Stephan. I told you I'm breaking this story. The cops will have to do their own gumshoe work."

"Idiot? Please don't call me an idiot, my Lam . . . oh, that's right. You don't want to be a lamb or lamb parts. Isn't that right, my little pussy?"

Stephan, My Love, 1986

The Korean woman finally was alone at the cash register. It appeared the last stragglers had come in for smokes and half-racks when Hall had made his fourth pass by the small First Avenue grocery some 15 minutes earlier. By the fifth pass two drunk Indians had picked up their Styrofoam begging cups, wrapped themselves in filthy blankets and huddled against the security bars of a closed store. Hall knew they were drunks -- identifying them with skill and instinct honed during weeks of ducking police and hunting Wozniak -- and not undercover cops.

Between passes by the store, Hall had scouted the area looking for cops and cop cars. There were a few blue and whites that passed but he blended well. No one showed any interest in another slow-moving bum in this seedy part of Seattle.

Hall found no unmarked cars with a vertical "XMT" for "tax exempt" on the plate to the left of the license numbers. No cars with two-way radios visible under the dash. None with glass or wire protectors between the front and back seats. No car with two people sitting silently in the dark waiting to back up another team of cops.

So it was unlikely this little Korean store had a couple of cops with shotguns lying in wait for junkie stick-up artists -- a stake-out technique in vogue with the Seattle cops. At least while still editor he had seen several stories about hold-ups that suddenly had gone very sour for some bad guys because of cop ambushes.

Hall paused in an unoccupied doorway to slip the safety off on the K-54 hidden in the right-hand pocket of his plaid overcoat. He had selected the plaid coat at Goodwill after ditching the parka because the coat's pockets were large enough to conceal the gun and his hand. And because he had been wearing the parka too long for safety.

The Goodwill coat cost him his last folding money.

His last meal had come at a soup kitchen serving breakfast the day before. It would be several more days before he would risk another soup kitchen handout.

He was setting no patterns.

197

Certainly Stephan Wozniak had set no patterns that Hall could discern as he searched Seattle's mean streets and flophouses.

It was possible Wozniak had made some big money on a robbery or a drug deal and found a comfortable hideout. Without money, the paroled felon had few other alternatives beyond the flophouses and missions. The house on the Longbranch Peninsula suggested Wozniak had some knowledge of, and entree into, the area's drug culture. And he had been smuggling heroin when he was seized at Tan Son Nhut. If Wozniak had linked up with the drug crowd and big money, Hall had no idea where to start looking. No entree or bona fides to prove he even should be admitted to that world.

And he was too hungry and tired to even think of a way to set a trap for the elusive phantom. At least soon, very soon, Wozniak would be ready to find him.

Who else would have to die before Wozniak came for him?

Hall wasn't going to be tired and hungry when that time came.

The cash register was open. The woman was closing.

He had to do it now!

Hall strode boldly into the store like a harried suburban husband running to the 7-11 for whatever brands of baby formula and diapers were available at midnight.

The Korean woman bowed slightly but said nothing.

Hall walked the aisles, stroking his bearded chin, examining the scrubbed, but almost empty shelves. There were a few cans of Spam, Vienna sausages and some 16-bag boxes of Lipton tea in one section.

Hall stopped at the rectangle-shaped Spam cans and picked one up. A buck 89.

Hall had to release the pistol to move his hand from the plaid coat pocket and pull his change from the jeans pocket.

About $1.12.

He raised his eyes. The woman stood behind the cash register, arms folded, watching him. Hall looked back. She must have been about 45. Her black hair had been in a bun but strands had escaped. The cotton frock was frumpy. First Avenue life was beating the hell out of her. But she probably had a vivacious kid at Princeton. Behind her were racks of cigarettes. Before her a display of sandwiches and candy.

Hall replaced the Spam can and shuffled to the back of the store. That was where a plentiful supply of beer and high-octane wine was kept behind a series of thick glass doors. The beer and wine shelves were part of a refrigerated room.

A place where cops with shotguns could wait. Additionally, there was a closed wooden door at the back of the store. And what was behind it?

Scared, but without panic, Hall turned away from the shelves of beer and wine. If the cops were there, they had had a good enough look at the fugitive yuppie killer to come out firing.

As he ambled towards the Korean woman, he scanned the ceiling for cameras, fisheye mirrors, two-way mirrors, dark plastic bubbles protruding from the ceiling.

The little store was too poor for that security crap, although the woman could have her foot or hand on an alarm button. Certainly she could be no stranger to armed robbery.

It was now or never. Do it or get out!

Hall's hand returned to the K-54 and his thumb pulled back the hammer.

He approached the woman, still studying the feminine hygiene products, boxes of crackers and plastic bottles of Coke along the aisles.

"I help you?" the woman asked in a thick accent.

Hall stood before the sandwich display. Graying ham and baloney. Cheese that was too orange. Large slices of white bread. And nothing less than $1.50.

"You hongry?" asked the woman. "No money?"

Hall released the pistol and put his change on the counter.

The woman took two of the sandwiches from the very front of the rows and pushed them at him. They were the sandwiches with the grayest meat protruding from the edges of the bread.

"You take."

"I don't have enough money," replied Hall.

"They ol'. I throw them way you no take."

"Thank you," Hall said, taking the food. He turned, eager to get to the street to eat them in some dignity.

"Wait, you."

Hall turned, hand shooting to his gun pocket, expecting to see a weapon in the woman's hand. Instead, she was extending a fist towards him.

"Take money."

"No. Keep it for the sandwiches."

"You take," she insisted.

Hall retrieved the money with his free hand.

"Thank you. So very, very much."

He gobbled hungrily as he shuffled, another scruffy, unshaven man in a second-hand coat moving aimlessly among the yuppie stores and X-rated theaters of First Avenue.

So. He had some bad sandwiches. A charity buck ten or so left. And no prospects.

Except one. A woman whose career he had promoted. A woman who had moaned that she loved him. For whom he had risked his life to keep her from walking into a trap -- albeit still a playful trap Wozniak had set for the two of them -- no doubt to tell him he knew of their special relationship.

Shiloh Weeks owed him. Shiloh Weeks was going to pay him. What goes around, comes around.

Hall continued north towards Queen Anne Hill where Weeks lived in a renovated 50's apartment building with a nice foreground view of long, aging Piers 90 and 91 with their fish processing warehouses and auto import yards; then Elliott Bay and, to the left, the Dark Tower and the rest of Seattle's high-rise buildings; and then the background view of lights, gantry cranes, ships and stacks of shipping containers on Harbor Island.

It would be a long walk for a tired man clinging to waterfront shadows.

Hall arrived in the neighborhood of the five-story, white stucco building with small metal balconies trimmed in blue shortly after 3 a.m.

More out of habit than resolution, Hall approached the building in slow, ever-narrowing concentric circles. Because of their affair, and Beth's vindictiveness, Hall had always been cautious, semi-alert for private detectives and their vans, when he visited Shiloh's apartment.

Satisfied nothing was unusual about her apartment's immediate neighborhood, Hall moved in closer.

And then to the shadows of an apartment entrance across the street from Shiloh's place from which Hall made his final surveillance. Shiloh's windows were dark.

Hall reached for his key ring. He'd let himself in and pin

Shiloh to the bed and force her to listen and she would understand and pull his mouth to hers and. . . .

And after making love maybe he would tell her about Wozniak, how the killer had lured her to the dangerous Longbranch cabin as a deadly joke, endangered her life and why he had run from the cabin . . . .

Yes. Confide in her the way he had confided in Mary Kanawha.

And then get mocked, called Looney Tunes and dropped when the first corporate suit called for a date. That's what he had gotten for confiding in Mary Kanawha all those years ago.

No. Wozniak was his. Wozniak transcended it all. Nothing else mattered now.

Hall realized, as he stood looking stupidly at his key ring, that Shiloh had demanded the key's return months ago.

The apartment had a security door, complete with a surveillance camera and speaker system.

He couldn't get in through the front. Nor could he wait for Shiloh to emerge. He needed to talk to her alone. In a secure place.

Do something, even if it's wrong! That's what the drill instructors screamed in his face during basic training more than two decades ago. He'd do *something.*

Returning to the shadows, Hall shuffled up the alley and to the back of Shiloh's building.

Hall moved to the garage entrance off the narrow alley at the back of the building. A metal web gate controlled electronically by guests with remote controls in their cars protected the entrance.

And walls of metal bars protected the garage on either side of the electronic portcullis. The spear points at the bottom of the bars met the concrete foundations. But there was enough room for a slim man to squeeze across the spear points at the top of the bars.

And now, Hall was a much slimmer man.

He scrambled up awkwardly at the darkest section of the fence. The dull points of the metal bars pressed uncomfortably into his neck, sternum, gut and crotch as he worked his way across the top.

It hurt, but he was slim enough.

He dropped to a crouch and moved among the dark cars toward the well-lit garage entrance to the building. He paused amid the cars. A security camera with a tiny red light kept watch.

Entry into the building through the metal garage door required a numerical code, 3-5-9. At least that is what the code was when he and Shiloh would arrive, arms around each other.

Hall knew no guard monitored the security television screens. A resident had to tune his or her TV set to the building's closed circuit television channel to see the alternating views of the front and garage entrances.

Would anyone be watching at 3:30 a.m.? Shiloh woke up very early to put on her makeup. Did she rise that early? She didn't watch her security cameras when they were together. She painted herself and dressed to blues played on her CD player -- using earphones when he was there asleep. But these were different times.

Even if 3-5-9 got him in, then what? There was no place to go. Everything inside was locked, including the staircases and small rooms containing the garbage chutes. All he could do was ring Shiloh's doorbell.

And who would answer the door if anyone was home?

Shiloh was sleeping with a cop the night Mary Kanawha was killed. So there was no reason to think she was at home -- or was alone if she was.

The only solid evidence he had was that her white Acura was in its stall. Maybe someone else had driven on the date.

If she was at home, there was no reason to think she would open the door to him. She had called him a psycho at the Longbranch cabin. She saw him as a wanted murderer. She would call the police. He needed a chance where he had control to talk to her, to convince her.

So break in if he could?

What if a cop was in her bed?

Even if she was alone, she might be awake and watching the security camera. Wozniak was killing newspaper employees now.

Hall couldn't do it. He feared the camera and the light at the door.

He would have to wait until she came out -- or in -- and hold her in the garage until he could explain. Explain something. What? He was tired, hungry, desperate and innocent. Just let him rest and then he'd make sense. Then he would tell her about his hunt for Stephan Wozniak if he had to . . . .

Shiloh wouldn't take him on faith. And he couldn't tell her about Wozniak. No one could know what Wozniak had done. And

Shiloh would never believe such a man as Wozniak lived.

But he could tell her she owed him one for the Longbranch meth lab.

Hall couldn't think it out clearly. He looked around. A tarp covered one of the cars in the garage. That meant it probably wouldn't be moved.

Hall rolled under it. It provided a good view of Shiloh's white Acura. He backed up so he wouldn't be visible from the Acura, unless Shiloh knelt and looked.

And he folded his arms on the cement in front of him and laid down his head and closed his eyes . . . .

Shiloh's soft tones woke him. Instinctively, Hall reached out for her and felt only the rough, oily garage floor.

He turned his head carefully to avoid whacking it on the bottom of the car.

Shiloh's long, slim calves were by the driver's door of the white Acura, some 20 feet away. The legs were covered in white hose. Her pumps were flawlessly white. Hall could see as high as her knees but saw no sign of a skirt. So she must be wearing a short, tight, clinging one.

Only one pump rested securely on the ground with its foot and leg holding weight. The other foot was at a relaxed angle, the pump half off.

The beautiful woman's weight was being supported by the man in jeans whose legs were pressed against the front of Shiloh's white hose.

Hall inched forward. He could now see as high as the couple's waists. Shiloh's arms were not visible. Probably around the man's neck. The man's long fingers ranged freely over Shiloh's lovely, trim bottom.

The man whispered something that made her giggle.

Then silence. Apparently a long, lingering kiss. Shiloh's hands appeared at the man's waist and slowly pushed his body away from hers.

"I've got to get to work now, darling," she said softly, her hands still on the man's hips.

The man groaned in mock agony.

"Tonight. We'll meet at the Tower and have dinner and come back here and we'll . . . ."

But the man had pulled Shiloh back to him. Another long

203

kiss.

After a delay, Shiloh decisively pushed the man back and opened the driver's door of the Acura.

Hall finally saw Shiloh's lovely face as she sat behind the wheel. Her hair was in a bun. That must mean she had been too busy to work hard at the hair and war paint this morning.

She started the Acura, zapped the metal gate and then rolled down her window. The man backed up a step or two. She waved cutely with her fingers under her face.

The man apparently responded by blowing her a kiss. At least she caught at the air and placed her hand on her red mouth.

The car started to move and then it stopped. Shiloh leaned out her window and said to the man in the jeans, "I love you, Stephan."

Bitch From Hell, 1986

Hall didn't have a clear shot at either Weeks or Wozniak until he had scrambled from beneath the car.

By then the Acura was halfway through a right turn into the alley. The metal security door to the building's interior slammed shut behind Wozniak.

Hall raced to the door and punched the 3-5-9 buttons on the door's electronic lock.

He yanked on the handle. Locked. He punched 3-5-9 again. Nothing.

The code had been changed.

"Shit!" he exclaimed under his breath. He stood to one side, pistol ready, and knocked tenuously, as a woman or child might, on the steel door. Maybe Wozniak was waiting for an elevator on the other side of the door.

Nothing happened.

Would Wozniak have a car in the garage? Probably not. Months earlier Shiloh told Hall the management allowed only one car per apartment in the garage. He couldn't ambush him in the garage.

If Wozniak had a car, he'd have to park on the street. Maybe Wozniak left through the building's front door. Maybe he returned to Shiloh's apartment.

Hall hit the internal pedestrian button by the gate that opened the portcullis and raced to the street. No sign of Wozniak. He dropped his head and shifted to his slow wino's walk.

Wozniak must have returned to Shiloh's apartment.

That bitch. That bitch from hell.

Hall felt the fury rising. He wanted to shoot locks, break into the apartment and empty the pistol into Wozniak.

As much as he wanted to run to the paper and blow away Shiloh Weeks.

Hold on!

He continued the eyes-down, shoulders-hunched shuffle.

Think it through. And move one jump ahead!

205

He couldn't think. If Shiloh had been there he would have killed her on the spot.

How could she?

Was it intentional? An extra ladle of punishment, added to the penalty she inflicted when she furiously ended their affair after he gave the city editor's job to Anne Fisher? Was she trying to hurt him? Mock him? Like Mary Kanawha did so many years ago?

How could Shiloh know? Had he ever, ever mentioned Wozniak by name or by description when they were lovers?

No.

Ever put anything about him in writing that she could find? That she shouldn't be able to find?

No. He'd never put anything about Wozniak in writing anywhere, anytime, anyplace. Never told anyone except Mary Kanawha. Who didn't know Shiloh. Didn't even talk to the press since she went on the bench.

Shiloh might know he had the Gerber stabbing knife. The old VC pistol as well.

So what? She wouldn't know why. It was just a knife. An ugly, wicked knife. And the gun? Lots of people had guns. Shiloh didn't know anything about guns, wouldn't know it was a Chinese model used by the VC. And so what if she did?

Hall had come to a long metal fence with a brick foundation. He sat on the brick. The front entrance to Shiloh's apartment was well within view half a block to his left.

He pulled the bag containing the Thunderbird from the coat's left pocket and took a long draw, swishing the strong wine around his mouth. He had to smell and look like a drunk if the cops checked. They might check carefully in this neighborhood.

At least he was shaking like a drunk. And the shaking was genuine.

How could she?

His mind searched frantically for some explanation for the scene he had just witnessed. There were only two: he had dreamed it or it was real. It was no dream that he was sitting outside Shiloh's apartment.

There was only one explanation: Shiloh and Stephan Wozniak were lovers.

"I love you, Stephan." That's what she had said. There was no way around it.

206

So why Wozniak? How Wozniak? How had she found him of all the men in the world?

Move another jump ahead. Ambush the ambush.

Because Wozniak had found her. Subtly, of course. Who was Hall's closest colleague? His wife? His girlfriend? His weakest point? Wozniak would have asked Ed Caldwell those questions, probably dangling a baggie of heroin in his face.

Caldwell would have told him about the rumors about Hall and the beautiful Shiloh Weeks. And then Wozniak would have moved in slowly, inconspicuously, slyly, probably positioning himself so Shiloh would find him. A chameleon. Becoming whatever he perceived Shiloh wanted most.

That wouldn't be a murdering felon from a prison. To Shiloh, Wozniak was someone else.

Why Shiloh?

For the Backatya Boy Buu.

That's why Wozniak was staying at Shiloh's apartment. Wozniak wanted him to know Shiloh had betrayed him.

Wozniak wanted him to kill Shiloh. Just as Wozniak had been tricked into killing Buu.

Move another jump ahead.

Kill Wozniak.

That's the mission. And nothing can interfere with the mission.

"Mission is everything." That's what Wozniak had said at Ap Thuy Tu. And nothing was going to interfere with this one.

Move another jump ahead.

Use Shiloh to kill Wozniak.

Now it all made sense.

The shaking stopped.

Hall glanced at his watch. He had been sitting on the wall for almost an hour.

Too long.

There had been no sign of Wozniak. But he had to move. The mission was everything but he'd been in the open too long. Wozniak may have slipped out the back of Shiloh's building, or come down the fire escape, and was closing in to blindside him. . . .

If he figured it right, it wasn't his turn quite yet. But he was too easy a target. And the last thing he wanted to do was make any assumptions about Wozniak's intentions.

The arrival of a slow-moving patrol car clinched it. Hall rose and pushed his bag into his pocket like a drunk who knew the-move-it-along police drill well enough and was avoiding another hassle.

The cops seemed satisfied the bum was shuffling along.

As soon as he was out of sight of the cops and the apartment building Hall stopped at a phone booth and dialed Shiloh's home number. Maybe Wozniak was still there. Maybe he would answer the phone. Then what? Hall wasn't sure.

"This is 522-4022. Leave a message," said a man's voice. Hall knew the recording for the answering machine was made by one of Shiloh's male neighbors to discourage obscene or annoying calls. Hall hung up.

At least he had found Wozniak's lair.

And Shiloh was still alive -- only because she had not called her lover by name until she was on her way out of the garage.

Lamb Chop, 1986

Shiloh Weeks left the paper furious. She would have no story in tomorrow's editions although one of the best stories in years was poised and primed to write itself.

She had spent most of the day arguing that it was legit, even compelling, to write a story suggesting Van Gelder's death was another murder. And she wanted to publicly link Jeremy Hall to it. Officially the cops and FBI were only saying they wanted to question an unnamed former city newsman in connection with the string of murders.

The newsroom knew better. It knew Hall was a prime suspect on the run. But the newsroom was leaderless and in turmoil. A reluctant business editor had been drafted by the publisher to act as editor.

Under most circumstances, vacancies in three top newsroom jobs would have ignited a savage scramble for promotion. But everyone feared Hall because of what he had done to Caldwell, Fisher and Van Gelder. No one wanted to become his next victim by accepting a promotion to the top editor ranks.

Certainly the pro tem editor wanted to do nothing that would incite Hall.

So he refused to print any story linking Hall in any way to the murders.

But Jeremy was a murderer. He had to be.

Buck had given her a copy of his notes of Van Gelder's frantic allegations on the FAA tape as his plane plunged into the Cascades' clear cut.

To Shiloh, it was clear deathbed testimony. Good as gold.

But the chicken shit business editor, and for other reasons, the publisher, had claimed it wasn't good enough.

First they wanted a copy of the FAA tape.

Buck and the FAA refused.

A Freedom of Information request had been filed hastily. But it would take days to resolve, longer if it got into the courts.

And the paper's lawyers predicted the paper was going to

209

lose. Clearly the tape was part of an on-going investigation and therefore exempt from the Freedom of Information Act.

There was worse news from the paper's own lawyers. One had flat-out told her she had "displayed a colossal ignorance" by asserting Van Gelder's angry accusations from the plane "rose to the level" of a deathbed confession. Those were the lawyer's exact words.

God! What bullshit! It was all so clear.

Of course the National Transportation Safety Board was no help. Their preliminary investigation had indicated the oil hose apparently had disconnected from the engine block prior to impact. Maybe someone had loosened it. But engine vibration easily could have caused it to disconnect if the connection had been allowed to loosen over time. There also were reports from climbing guides on Mount Rainier that Van Gelder had been flying like a crazy man before the strange distress call. The guides had taken the plane's number so there was no mistake. So alcohol, drugs and even insanity were possible factors in the crash, as well as the radio call implicating Hall, according to the crash investigators. If alcohol, drugs or insanity turned out to be a contributing factor, it would not be surprising if Van Gelder had performed an incomplete pre-flight check of the Beechcraft. At least that was Buck's reading of the NTSB's first pass.

The upshot was that nothing got into the paper except a couple of paragraphs -- with no byline -- saying the investigation into Executive Editor Francis Van Gelder's death was continuing.

Weeks almost wished Stephan hadn't come into her life in Seattle. If only he had waited a couple of months until she made the New York move. She couldn't remember a time when she had wanted so badly to tell a bunch of bosses to shove it. The New York papers still had balls.

Still, Stephan was such a delightful, dependent complication. So naive. Just interested in her and his calculus. And nailing Jeremy Hall. She had to admit she had noticed a harder edge at times. Like all that crap about lambs and lamb chops. And calling her his "little pussy." He probably didn't even realize that could be taken the wrong way.

Weeks was in the enclosed lot where she paid $120 per month to park the Acura. She'd shoot home, clean up and change and meet Stephan downtown. What an earful she had for him!

She pushed the small gray button on her Ungo car alarm. The alarm in the car responded with a double squeak.

As she unlocked the car door she remembered she hadn't checked the lot for weirdos. She turned her head as she opened the door when . . .

A hand clamped around her mouth and another seized the hand that held the key ring. Her fingers could not smash the Ungo button to set off the panic alarm.

A shoulder pushed her across the Acura's front seats and a man with a rough but familiar voice was on top of her hissing "Shut up!" into her ear. She felt the pearl earring in her left ear pull against its hole. The man's whiskers were beyond stubble so they didn't scrape badly. But the short beard was stiff because it was unwashed and it smelled of cheap wine. So did the man's breath.

"Please don't hurt me," Weeks whispered into the car seat. "I'll do what you want. Take my purse." She was trying to sound weak and scared. If the man loosened his grip she'd go for the eyes with her nails.

"I want to talk to you, Shiloh. Listen carefully. You may even get a story out of it. First, hand me your car keys."

Jeremy allowed her to raise the hand with the key ring. He suddenly released her hand and his fingers wrapped around the car alarm's remote control device. She watched his hand tighten and then relax. The alarm device was crushed and broken. There would be no panic alarm.

"Now," said Jeremy. "We are going to hold each other, just like old times. I am going to talk and you are going to listen."

"Whatever you say, Jeremy."

He sat up and pulled her to him. As he did she saw his face and was shocked.

He looked more like an animal than he had at Longbranch. His eyes were dark and sunken. The double chin was gone and his cheek bones protruded. A big cut was not healing well. His shaggy long brown hair and short, salt and pepper beard were matted and dirty.

Her face was pressed against his mean head as he held her to him. She moved her hands along his sides. The fat, the incipient love handles were gone. He was hard and bony. Jeremy's body felt much like Stephan's.

"Shiloh . . . ." began the specter. He stopped. Was he

211

caressing her? She could feel her short, white skirt was hiked up. She was wearing Poison. She pressed her face against his and breathed softly against his ear.

If he would release her for just long enough for a clean shot at the eyes . . . .

There. He was relaxing his hold a bit . . . .

Fingers bent into a claw, Weeks's right hand shot at Jeremy's forehead. But there was no face to rake.

With perfect timing, Jeremy had drawn back his head just out of range.

And then pain shot through her solar plexus and she fell helpless against him, gasping for air. Nothing ever had hurt so much . . . .

Through the pain she heard him saying, "You're lucky. Nine hours ago I would have killed you on the spot. Don't try anything like that again or I still may."

Weeks could only cling helplessly to him. She felt the nausea rising, her head rolling.

Jeremy held her steady. "You'll be all right."

Weeks doubted that. She had never been in so much pain or felt so helpless.

"What are you going to do to me?" she asked weakly into the side of Jeremy's head.

"You're going to disappear," he replied softly.

Fear fused with nausea.

"Please Jeremy . . . I'm sorry for what I've done."

"No groveling. It doesn't become hotshot big-time reporters."

"Please . . ." she whispered, remembering how Jeremy had hurt Anne Fisher with his first bomb before killing her with the second at Joan's house.

"Are you ready to travel?"

"Please don't kill me."

Jeremy released her. Near vomiting, she pulled herself into the passenger's seat and folded her arms across her belly in a futile effort to contain the pain. She was as doubled over as the car's cockpit would allow. The nausea grew worse.

"Please don't kill me," she said again.

"Please do as I say then," he replied. He was driving the Acura into the street.

"Is your friend at your place? Does he have a key?" Jeremy

was on Alaskan Way heading towards Queen Anne.

"Stephan?"

"Yes, Stephan."

"No," she said. Probably too quickly.

Jeremy pulled his pistol part way out of the pocket of his strange plaid coat.

"The games are over, Shiloh. This is for keeps."

"No. He isn't there. Yes, he has a key."

"Where is he?"

"I don't know. I swear."

Weeks sensed Jeremy was looking at her and she turned her face towards him. His eyes were cold. Lifeless. The eyes of a murderer. One hundred and eighty degrees from Stephan's gleaming, life-affirming eyes.

"Is this about jealousy? Please leave Stephan out of this. He's harmless. He's a mathematician."

"Is that what he told you?" At last some emotion from him. Jeremy sounded amazed. And amused.

"Yes."

"Shiloh, I thought you were one of journalism's best. But you are one of the biggest chumps I have ever met. Maybe the two aren't mutually exclusive."

"Screw you!" she replied. But quickly added, "I'm sorry."

"Where does your Stephan live?"

"I won't tell you."

Weeks saw Jeremy's right hand cock back and his hand close into a fist.

"I don't know. And that's the truth."

"I don't believe you," he replied. His arm still was cocked to punch her.

"He has a small apartment somewhere in the University District."

"The address?"

"I don't know. I've never been there. Stephan says it is unfit for a lady."

Jeremy erupted in genuine laughter and his hand relaxed. Then he asked, "What is his phone number?"

"I don't know. He calls me or we . . . "

"We what?"

"We usually meet in the evening after work."

"What does he do?"

"Teaches at the U.W."

"How do you contact him there?"

"I've never tried," Weeks admitted, feeling a mounting unease.

"Shiloh, have you ever confirmed he teaches at the university?"

She didn't like the direction the conversation was going. So she replied, "I've been very busy, Jeremy. You've been. . . there is a mass killer loose in this city. It's a damn big story, especially since he is after people at the paper."

But Jeremy wouldn't let go.

"So you don't know for sure. Where do you meet?" he asked.

Weeks hesitated. "At the . . . various places. We make plans each . . . ."

"Each morning?" he asked.

"Fuck you."

They were at her metal garage door. Jeremy reached for the electronic door opener she kept over the passenger side sun-visor. He aimed it at the electric eye and opened the portcullis.

Jeremy parked and held her arm, his right hand in his pocket, as they went upstairs in silence. He seemed worried and cautious.

In response to Jeremy's whispered order, Weeks announced loudly, "Hi, it's me," as she pushed open the apartment's door. There was no answer and Jeremy pushed her along in front of him as he made a methodical search of the place. His gun was out. Then he double locked the doors and braced them with chairs.

Apparently satisfied Stephan couldn't get in with his key without raising a terrible racket, Jeremy made an even more systematic search of the place.

"Stephan's?" he asked when he opened a bureau drawer and saw a couple pairs of men's briefs, socks, folded jeans and a couple of clean shirts.

"Yes," she admitted sullenly.

"When and where are you meeting him tonight?"

"I forget," she replied. She was feeling better now.

Jeremy pushed her roughly towards her desk.

"Write," ordered Hall.

Weeks removed a piece of delicate pink personalized stationary from her drawer and screwed up the point of her gold

Cross pen.

Jeremy dictated: "Stephan, there's been a big break in the Hall story. I'll be out of town for a couple of days. I'll meet you at the Tower when I get back."

"How did you know about the Columbia Center?" she demanded, looking up.

"I figured that was the Tower you two were talking about. Keep writing."

Weeks looked into his face. His eyes. But saw nothing.

"Write," he ordered, again.

She finished the note.

"Now sign it so he will suspect something is wrong."

"What?"

"Sign it 'Weeks' or your middle name or something unexpected. Does he have a nickname for you that you don't like?"

"If you know about the Dark Tower . . . ."

"Sign it!"

"All right." Weeks wrote "Lamb Chop" and underlined it twice.

"Will he find it on the desk?

"Probably."

"Let's make sure," replied Jeremy. He removed his soiled Goodwill coat and put it on the spotless desk. Then he examined the note and placed it on the coat.

Jeremy seized her wrist and hauled her to the bathroom. He pushed her against the wall. Then he washed his face and shaved with her Lady Gillette razor.

"Strip," he said as he wiped his face.

"Go to hell."

"Strip and get into the shower." It was an unmistakable order.

"This adds rape to kidnapping and battery," she said defiantly.

His strong hand grabbed her forearm and held her while he adjusted the temperature of the rushing water in the tub with the other.

"Do it."

She unbuttoned her blouse and pulled the zipper on her short skirt. But she couldn't wiggle out of the skin-tight garment with only one hand.

"I can't," she said.

Jeremy released her arm. Placing himself between her and the door, he removed his filthy rags. He put his pistol on his pile of clothes. She noticed he had his thin, nasty knife from his drawer at home in his sock and strapped along his leg with a multi-colored strap. Jeremy took off his sock but he didn't remove the strap or his knife from his leg.

Weeks removed the skirt, blouse, French bra, white panty hose and white bikini panties.

"Get in," the naked man ordered.

As a sign of defiance she made no effort to cover herself but stood against the far wall as Jeremy luxuriated under the steaming water.

It was the soap and hot water he wanted. Not her.

As he washed she noticed how much Jeremy had changed. With his slim body and long hair and, without the grayish beard, he looked years younger.

Weeks felt the uneasiness flitting back as she watched her former lover wash.

She examined the developing bruise on her belly to distract herself but found herself really examining what she knew for sure about Stephan Wozniak.

She had to admit she didn't like what Jeremy had made too obvious.

She had dropped her guard where Stephan was concerned. She couldn't believe she didn't have a phone number for him. But he always seemed to be around when she wasn't working. She hadn't ever had the occasion to call the university's operator and ask for his office. She simply was working too hard. She wished she had a number, if only to dispel the uneasy feeling, and put Jeremy in his place.

She also couldn't be sure Stephan really knew calculus or other esoteric math. He always deflected her inquiries. If only he read math books. Or worked with figures on paper or on a computer at her place. Or introduced her to colleagues.

Hall's lanky naked body reminded her of Stephan's. But Jeremy's didn't have the scars that defiled Stephan's body. What kind of holes could a combine make in a person? What the hell was a combine?

"Jeremy," she said.

He was scrubbing his head for the third time.

"Yeah?"

"Tell me about Stephan."

"You're the hotshot reporter. You find out."

"He says he knows you. From Vietnam. He says you were a blood-thirsty killer then and you are now."

Weeks braced for a slap or punch.

But Jeremy just said, "Right you are if you think you are, hotshot."

Weeks had never before seen this side of Jeremy Hall. She had seen him ache for her and seen him as a fine editor, enlightened liberal, friend and adventurer. But she had never seen him indifferent to her. Or her body.

He just didn't care what she said, even if she called him a murderer.

"I want to talk, Jeremy," she said.

"Too late for that, Lamb Chop," he replied, turning off the shower. He stepped out and took a towel for himself and tossed one to her.

"What time were you meeting your friend Stephan?"

"Were?"

"Yes. Were."

"What are you going to do to me?"

"Just answer my question." Another order.

"Eight."

He looked at his watch. "We've got almost two hours in all this luxury. How about a drink?"

"No."

"Is it still in the same place?"

"Yes."

Hall wrapped his towel around his waist and waited for her to wrap herself. He picked up his gun and towed her to the liquor cabinet.

"I've always had a weakness for the good stuff," he admitted, removing a bottle of Chivas Regal.

"So does Stephan," Weeks said.

Jeremy ignored her. He stuck his gun into his arm pit, picked up the bottle and glass with one hand and grabbed her wrist with the other hand and took her to the refrigerator. After a brief hesitation and inspection of its back, he opened the freezer for ice. He dropped in a couple of ice cubes and poured three fingers of the amber liquid into the glass. He took a long drink.

Then he towed her to the bureau where Stephan's clothing was kept. He pulled on a pair of Stephan's underwear then socks, jeans and shirt. Then he towed her back to the bathroom where he handed her a hairbrush and ordered, "Brush it."

"Jeremy, don't be silly . . . ."

"Fix my hair, damn it," he ordered.

Weeks stood behind him and brushed. She caught herself doing it slowly, carefully, as though they were playing when they were together in a San Juan Islands hideaways . . . .

She watched his reflection in the mirror. Jeremy sipped his drink and studied his face.

Finally she slipped a rubber band around his hair, giving him a short ponytail in the back.

The transformation was amazing. A hip, upscale Microsoft programmer stood before her. If the police were looking for a chubby, Tory politician -- which was how Jeremy used to look -- or a killer disguised as an old drunk, they'd never take a second look at this Jeremy Hall.

He put on his hiking boots and stuck the pistol in his pants.

"Do you have any clothes line or rope?" he asked.

Weeks held out her arm. Hall took it and she led him to her utility closet.

Hall cut a length of her light, strong rope with his knife and pushed her towards the bedroom.

"Set the alarm for 7:45 p.m.," he ordered. She complied. Hall picked up the clock to check.

He threw the piece of the rope on the bed. "Come here."

"You've gotten kinky on the run. Something you learned on the streets?" she asked.

He replied by tying a piece of rope to her left wrist. He tied the other end to his right wrist.

"Lie down," he ordered, yanking the phone cord from the wall.

They lay down beside each other. He held his gun ready in his left hand, on the other side of his body from her.

Weeks tried to relax. And she wondered how she would react if he reached for her towel concealing her body.

Jeremy's Back, 1986

The harsh red digital numbers on the clock said 7:40. Shiloh Weeks had been lying on the bed watching each minute flash by for almost an hour and a half.

Jeremy said she was going to disappear. If he was going to kill her, why had he tied her to him? To torment her? The cops thought Jeremy had tormented Ed Caldwell with drugs. Then he had used a big firecracker to scare Anne Fisher before killing her with a real bomb.

She was going to become the next victim if she wasn't careful. It made a lot of sense. She had dropped him when he hadn't promoted her. She had wanted him to be the killer so she could get her big story. She had pushed the cops and Van Gelder to arrive at the same conclusion. If Jeremy was going to kill someone else, she made an excellent candidate.

But she had the uneasy sense that there was more going on than just mad serial killings. Something about the 303rd that Jeremy and Stephan shared and it wasn't exactly the way Stephan had told it. Stephan's scars and the tattoo worried her, she had to admit.

Neither man seemed willing to confide anything real in her. And she wasn't going to wait around and find out if Jeremy was going to tell her more or kill her.

It was now or never.

She looked at the man sleeping tied to her. He must have been very tired. He had said he was just lying down on the bed for a few minutes. The first bed he had seen in many days, he said as his head sank on the pillow which only hours before supported Stephan's head.

Instead of just resting for a few minutes, Jeremy had fallen into a deep sleep and turned towards her. He was on his right side in a modified fetal position, one he often assumed when he slept after a long day.

He had turned without his gun.

So it had to be behind him.

7:41.

The alarm would go off in four minutes.

She hadn't dared move. But if Jeremy was in a deep sleep and the gun was still on the bed, maybe she could reach it without waking him. When they were lovers he would get restless and often woke if she left the bed for the bathroom or refrigerator. He clearly was exhausted now. Would he remain asleep if she reached across him?

7:42.

Do it!

Weeks lifted her head from the pillow. Jeremy did not move. Higher. No sign Jeremy was stirring. She lifted herself on her left elbow and raised her right arm over him. Her hand inched across his body.

There. Her hand closed around the pistol. She was so close she could feel his breath on her face. She detected no change in his breathing. She picked up the pistol and pulled it back towards her and her elbow brushed Jeremy's side.

She paused. Jeremy still seemed asleep.

She had continued to slowly draw the pistol to her when suddenly he hooked his left arm over her arm with the gun. His right hand pulled down the piece of rope so her left hand was pinned to the bed. He spun over, pulling her body across his and she flew from the bed. She was surprised to find the pistol was still in her hand when she hit the carpet. Jeremy followed right behind her.

Jeremy was yanking on her tied hand and rode her back while grabbing below her for the gun.

How did the damn thing work? Did she have to pull the sliding thing on the top back? Pull back the hammer? Did it have a safety? She rolled on the floor trying to keep her body between the pistol and Jeremy while she fumbled with it.

Pandemonium broke lose. The towel sprung free from her body. The alarm exploded in a loud, shrill EEEEEEEEEEEEEEEEE. And they crashed into the bed table, knocking the phone, a lamp, glass, small pitcher, book and who knew what else into the melee on the floor.

Jeremy was forcing her to her stomach. She struggled to keep the barrel pointed away from her and to figure out the gun while she bucked and elbowed him. Her fingers found a small button on the left side of the pistol just behind the trigger and trigger guard. The safety? She pushed quickly. She might have only one shot.

There was something at the bottom of the handle. She pushed and shoved at it. Something happened: something from the gun fell and hit the thick carpet amid the debris in which they were rolling.

Jeremy got a hand on the weapon. His other arm tightened around her neck.

She pulled the gun from beneath her and pulled the trigger.

The gun kicked back into her breasts in a burst of noise and flash. The explosion must have startled Jeremy because he loosed his grip briefly.

Weeks had seen people pull the top back when shooting automatic pistols. Was this the time? Weeks ripped hard on her tied hand to gain some slack. She pulled the top of the gun back. Something -- the empty cartridge maybe -- flew into her stomach.

Then Jeremy had a solid hold on the gun and ripped the weapon from her hands. He shoved her roughly into the debris on the thick rug.

She turned, expecting to see him aiming at her. But he had stuck the pistol into his jeans. He rose and used the rope on her wrist to haul her to her feet.

Still using the rope, Jeremy dragged her to the utility closet where he picked up the rest of her rope. He cut several long pieces and stuffed them into the back pocket of the jeans. He pulled her to the front door and pinned her to the wall. With his free hand, he opened the closet door and yanked her beige London Fog raincoat with the lining from its hanger. He found her snakeskin cowboy boots on the closet floor.

"Put these on," he ordered.

"Don't hurt me," she blurted.

"Do it."

Jeremy untied their hands as she wrestled with the coat. She pulled it around her and buttoned it closed. She pulled the boots over bare legs. Jeremy thrust her heaviest winter coat and purse into her arms.

Weeks felt tears come as Jeremy pulled her into the hallway, an arm around her shoulder, another at her elbow. He hurried her towards the staircase.

"Television blew up," he said.

Weeks looked up. An elderly woman in curlers peered over the short chain connecting the door with the frame. Her eyes were wide. She seemed unable to move.

Weeks looked back, sure her own eyes were equally wide. She was too terrified to scream.

In the garage, Jeremy unlocked the passenger door on the Acura and pushed her into the car.

He went around to the other side and got in beside her.

"If I have to I'll bat you with this gun. Don't make a single mistake." The words were cold. A statement of fact.

She nodded, sobbing.

What was going wrong? She was a reporter. She was used to exercising power, not being pushed roughly down stairs. She could write a story or not. Slant it or not. Mention a powerful name in an uncomplimentary way or not. Here she was in the middle of something she did not understand at all and no one cared. She sat feeling dull, impotent, watching Jeremy's route out of the city.

She turned to her former editor and lover. He drove, but he was elsewhere. She had become a nuisance. An impediment. She was powerless. And there was a new person beside her. His eyes were narrowed, he apparently was deep in thought. But the muscles of the face and the neck were relaxed. Jeremy, her liberal editor, seemed to have found some kind of peace in murder and kidnapping and guns and whatever else? What was he going to do to her? What did Stephan have to do with this? Jeremy knew something about Stephan. Stephan knew something about Jeremy. And she needed to know their secrets. If she hadn't lost the power, she would have asked. He would laugh at her questions now.

He drove up Mercer to Interstate 5 and headed south. Then east on Interstate 90.

Across Lake Washington and through the lights of Bellevue and Issaquah on the interstate. Soon the highway took wide, long sweeps as the Acura climbed the foothills of the Cascades.

They passed the dark shape of Mount Si on the left. Other, higher peaks formed a dark mass before them.

Jeremy left the interstate east of North Bend. Soon Jeremy was lost in a maze of logging roads marked only by little signs with numbers like "2356" and "459".

Then Jeremy turned off the lights and stopped. He just sat looking into the dark, studying the rear view mirror. After a few minutes he started the car again and resumed the uphill climb. But he did not turn on the headlights.

He found a small cut in the brush and turned into a side trail.

Weeks listened to the branches scrape the sides of her Acura. He stopped when he found enough room to take a U-turn.

Finally, he turned to her. "Get out."

"Jeremy, please . . . we loved each other, please." She felt so helpless.

Jeremy got out of the car and walked around to the passenger side. He opened the door and pulled her from the car.

She had been gripping her purse tightly to her on the trip. He ripped it from her hands and took out the wallet. He removed all the bills and stuffed them in his jeans.

"Now walk," he said pointing to the woods.

"I'm cold."

"I warned you to run for your life. You wanted to stay and play. Now you are." he replied, cryptically. "You better put on your heavy coat. Then walk."

"Killing people isn't a game, Jeremy. Maybe it was in Vietnam but . . . ."

"Walk," he ordered, pushing her roughly into the heavy underbrush as she struggled with the coat. Stumbling, she saw they were in a clear-cut, at the edge of a forested area the loggers had spared.

She walked carefully, but branches and brush ripped at the expensive boots. There were hidden dips and depressions where she stumbled. The walking was easier when she got to the trees. She paused and looked back. Jeremy was behind her, one hand holding the pieces of rope. She was surprised how well she could see in the dark. Jeremy nodded towards the forest.

"Jeremy, what do you want? Sex? I'll do anything you want."

"I want you to keep moving."

Finally, about 30 yards into the forest, Jeremy ordered her to stop. He motioned toward a large fir. It had to have a diameter of four feet at the base. There was room for her to stand below the tree's thick branches.

Weeks faced against the tree.

"Turn around," he said.

She turned so her back was against the tree.

"Please kill me quickly," she pleaded.

"Shut up."

Jeremy tied a piece of rope around one wrist and pulled her arm uncomfortably behind the tree. Then he tied the second wrist.

Her arms were tied around the tree. She realized what he was doing. Tying her arms around the big tree meant her hands would not be close enough to work together on the knots he was tying so tightly.

Jeremy walked behind the tree and tied her hands with two more ropes. If Jeremy left her like this, she would never be able to work her way free. And no one would ever hear her calls. . . .

Then Jeremy was standing in front of her.

"I'm only going to say this once. It is very important. So no bullshit, okay?"

"I promise. Please don't hurt me."

"I am not going to hurt you if I don't have to. But your friend Stephan must be convinced I have killed you. The note at your apartment should do that. Stephan expects me to kill you for betraying me with him. That is why he is fucking you. So it must appear that I have killed you. There cannot be any chance you will get to a phone or interfere with me in any way. When all this is over I will return for you if I can. Before your friend and I meet I will send an anonymous letter to the police telling them where you are in case he kills me. So you are going to be here a day or so. It will be uncomfortable. But you will be all right. Do you understand so far?"

Weeks nodded. Her head reeled. If only that company lawyer knew how much colossal ignorance she had been displaying.

"Now, it is clear to me you and Wozniak frequently met at the Columbia Center. Why?"

"It was near our . . . my . . . office. And he liked it. Liked how big and black it is. He said he liked the symbolism or architecture or something. And he, he liked all the shops on the lower floors. It was our place, in a teenage kind of way." Weeks whimpered.

"Where did you meet?"

"At the fountain on the bottom floor."

"Where else did you meet?"

"Only by that fountain."

"Did Wozniak make any secret of the fact that he was seeing you?"

"No. He liked to be seen with me," Weeks replied.

"So Stephan Wozniak flaunted the fact that he was screwing you and that you always met at the Columbia Center's indoor fountain?"

She heard herself saying, "We were in love, Jeremy." But she didn't believe it.

"You always met at the Columbia Center, is that right?"

"Yes. Jeremy?"

"Yes?"

"Don't hurt him, please?" Her mouth said it, but she wasn't sure how concerned she really was about Stephan's well-being.

Jeremy laughed and replied, "Shiloh, darling, I am going to kill him."

"Jesus, Jeremy. What did he do to you?"

"You lack the standing to ask the question," he replied.

"What?"

"It's something Mary Kanawha used to say to me. Judge shit."

"Did you kill her?"

"No. Wozniak did."

"And the others?"

"Wozniak."

"Jeremy. Let me go. I'll help you."

"I'm sorry, Shiloh. I have a mission to accomplish. Your disappearance is part of the mission. Security is everything. Surprise is everything."

Weeks was surprised. Even though Jeremy had just tied her to a tree in the middle of nowhere she felt oddly relieved. It wasn't just that she believed Jeremy really was going to spare her. Maybe it was the scars and tattoo on Stephan and the way he had called her a lamb.

Maybe Jeremy was tying her in the middle of the forest, but she had the feeling it had been Stephan who had staked her out like a hunter using a lamb for bait.

"I'll be all right," she said.

"You will be."

"What are you going to do now?"

"I've got to pick up a couple of things. And then find an ace in the hole."

Jeremy walked up to her and pulled her face to his. His mouth was on hers. She hesitated and then closed her eyes to press her lips to his.

But Jeremy had disappeared in the dark.

The Dark Tower, 1986

The trash can in the Dark Tower's small basement utility room contained: the stolen green florist jacket Jeremy Hall had worn; a watering can; spray bottle; a cleaning rag; most of the elements of the Martin M1 Tiger compound bow newly purchased with Shiloh's money. And his prize—six bullets from a .38 Police Special pistol he had found in the tower's ornamental shrubbery. Finding the pistol had taken several hours of fumbling work as a pretend florist. He stuffed his latex surgical gloves into his pocket.

Then he gathered his long, loose hair back into a tiny pony tail and placed the Wall Street Journal under his arm. He slipped into the hallway, climbed the stairs and strode out among the shops and food stands on the Dark Tower's first public floor. He assumed the persona of a successful artist or programmer from the San Juan Islands or Redmond in town for a visit to his accountant and then perhaps a dinner date with a beautiful woman.

It was just after 8 p.m. and the crowds were gone. A few driven lawyers, bankers and insurance executives in fine suits raced by on their way to the next appointment over drinks at FX McRory's Sea Food Bar or at the posh Olympic Four Seasons Hotel.

Hall kept a wary eye on the scampering suits. Wozniak was coming. He might appear in one.

But Hall's eyes continually were drawn to the middle of the floor.

For there stood a large dark stone, perhaps 30 feet high. A soothing flow of water washed its sides, an automated version of the workmen who seemed to continually wash the outside walls of the 76-story Dark Tower.

The water collected in a pool at the base of the large black stone. Recessed lights outside the base of the fountain cast an eerie red glow on the rug around it.

An Aztec killing place produced by the subconscious mind of a tony 20th century decorator.

There was more. Nine large pillars covered in reflective black glass formed a triangle surrounding the pit in which the black stone fountain with its blood-reddish base waited. Visitors might not like what they saw in the ubiquitous black glass. But they had to look. Certainly Hall did.

Forty-two enormous, waist-high ceramic pots containing a variety of light-shy jungle plants were placed among the black columns. The jungle foliage buttressed the effect that the place was a modern pagan killing zone.

Heavy, stuffed chairs covered in fake leather beside coffee tables had been placed in the pit surrounding the black fountain. Four brick steps on each side provided exits from the pit. The large pots and jungle plants blocked escape between the black pillars.

Hall scanned the area around the pit. Along one side of the triangle were red metal tables and chairs; matching white tables and chairs along another and black ones on the third.

Along the walls were the small food stands, espresso bars and shops.

Some food stand operators still were there, feverishly cleaning their grills, latte-makers and floor space.

Hall checked the ceiling for the locations of the surveillance cameras. His earlier reconnaissance as a florist's assistant revealed a single guard sat in a high-tech information booth on the third floor. The guard had banks of television screens to which the cameras reported.

He found a dead zone uncovered by the electronic eyes among the white chairs and tables near a Mexican food stand. That's where he sat and spread the stock tables in the Wall Street Journal's third section before him. Behind him, an old oriental man vacuumed a taco stall's floor.

Then a cleaning woman appeared and added the din of her vacuum in the common area amid the metal tables and chairs to that of the old Japanese man. Clearly, the operators of the espresso bars and eateries were responsible for cleaning their own spaces.

Hall studied his stock tables.

A man in a red jacket with writing on the breast pocket appeared and hovered. The guard checked his watch frequently. The message was that it was closing time. First the Japanese man and then the cleaning woman left. The guard went on a brief patrol. Hall knew the guard would be back.

He left his paper on the table and vaulted the taco joint's counter.

He dropped to his knees. And waited.

He heard noises. Someone was shuffling paper. The guard was collecting the newspaper.

In minutes, the overhead lights dimmed. The escalators, which also were supported by black glass columns, stopped moving.

The only sound in the belly of the Dark Tower was the soothing sound of water cascading across the faces of the black stone fountain in the pit.

Hall pulled the pistol from Wozniak's jeans. Shiloh had fired one round. But he had loaded the K-54 magazine with a full load-- eight rounds. Seven rounds should be plenty. He would fire only when he was close and could not miss.

But something was wrong. The gun felt too light.

Hall's fingers jabbed for the base of the gun's handle.

The magazine was gone! It must have dropped out in the fight with Shiloh. He had no ammo -- wait. There had to be a fresh round in the chamber. He covered the gun with his body and pulled back the slide. Nothing was ejected.

Shit! The pistol was empty.

All right then. Get out of here. This is the place Wozniak wants the showdown. Leave. Get more ammo. If you're not here tonight, he'll be back. He will be back again and again and again until it is over.

But the doors will be locked. The eyes of the cameras searching. Surely the guard on the third floor, alone in an empty 76-story building, had a finger on the alarm that would bring the police. They would come en masse for a prowler in the Dark Tower. Too many paintings and vases and lawyer's files and commercial secrets at risk.

The alternative was to remain hidden. Postpone Wozniak's show-down. Stay in a position of strength. Wozniak surely will have a weapon with him -- he'd already found Wozniak's ace in the hole.

So get HIS ace in the hole! Get the .38 from Wozniak's hiding place and the bullets you left in the utility room!

No good. The guard could see him move. Besides that, he dare not now. Wozniak had to be somewhere in the building.

Hall forced his body tightly against the base of the taco stand. The counter gave him overhead cover. He could wait here until the building opened in the morning.

He waited in silence, moving only occasionally to glance at

his watch.

And then it was 2:20 a.m. -- 0220 in army time. About the time at Ap Thuy Tu that the shy figure exited the hootch at the belly of the Black Virgin. . . .

But in Seattle the Dark Tower was silent except for the water washing the sides of the black stone in its belly . . . .

And then it was 2:22 a.m.

That is when the common area beyond the taco counter erupted in light.

And a loud humming noise commenced. The escalators started.

And a voice announced, "Its 0222 hours, lootenant. D-Day. H-Hour. M-Minute. Game time."

Hall crawled forward so he could peek around the taco counter.

There!

On the escalator. Like a cocky, successful insurance salesman making an entrance as he descended to a lunch break.

Wozniak said, "Come on out, lootenant. I know you are here. I watched you enter the building."

Did Wozniak see what he did when he came in the building? Does Wozniak know about his ace in the hole?

Hall crowded against the counter, quietly cursing the Chinese pistol. With ammunition, he could have run out and fired several quick rounds while Wozniak was exposed on the escalator.

"I saw the note at Shiloh's place. Poor Shiloh. Hell of a piece of ass. I really enjoyed your young Shiloh. So young. So prime. So naive. You journalists have to pass some kind of dumb shit test to get your jobs? Anyway, she did anything I asked. And some things I didn't ask. Some sex machine, huh? I was thinking of marrying her before we played out this little scene. Bet that would really have pissed you off, huh? Tell me how you killed your deceiving little tramp? Like you did Hau? A bomb? Or did you just kick her sweet ass out of a chopper, like you did Ky? Maybe you're smarter than I think and didn't kill her at all. No matter. It's just you and me now."

Wozniak was at the base of the escalator, looking around like a bewildered tourist. But his eyes gleamed, unlike those of any tourist.

"Come on out. Let's chat. A couple of old comrades in arms can talk about old times and savor the new, can't we? How do you

229

like the place? This big black building reminded me of something. Maybe Nui Ba Den. Just like old times, huh? Had a lot of missions around that old black mountain. Remember? You must. Shiloh told me you didn't like this building. She said it got to ya. That's why I picked the place. But you know that. Man, to just the two of us it is just like Nui Ba Den. We should have nuked that old black hill. Course we should have nuked a lot of things. But then how would old grunts like you and me have had our fun?"

Wozniak was still at the base of the escalator, peering around the area.

"I know why the building bugged you. Made you think of depressing things. Like that kid you offed. I know how you feel. Just can't shake them 20 years. If it was just Buu and the boys -- well, I might just give you a pat on the back for the way you pulled it off, lootenant. Old Wozniak ain't fooled for so long like that."

Hall looked for a weapon. Wozniak's hands were curled, ready for action, but empty. Maybe a gun stuck in his jeans in the small of his back. Or strapped to a leg?

"What are you worried about?" Wozniak asked. "That dude in the red jacket? No sweat. He's out. No one watching all them televisions. No one to call the cops. We've got this whole place to ourselves. Ready to rock that croc cortex?"

Wozniak's twinkling eyes scanned the tables and chairs and black fountain again.

"Well, lootenant, if you won't come out, I'll guess I'll just have to come find you. By the way, I found this magazine and a live round." Wozniak held up the K-54's clip. "Yours? Found them in Shiloh's bedroom. Sloppy, lootenant." Wozniak waited, holding the clip and bullet over his head.

Wozniak strolled towards the fountain as though he was taking his sandwich to one of the false leather chairs to enjoy the soft flow of the water during a noontime lunch.

More importantly, his feet did not make a sound.

Then Wozniak was gone. The monologue ended.

Hall watched and waited. From his position under the counter he would never know if Wozniak found his hiding place until the killer leaped over the counter and grabbed for his throat.

Hall rose to a crouch and held the gun like he could fire it. Wozniak couldn't know for sure it was empty. Wozniak wouldn't believe he was that dumb.

Nothing is useless. Everything is a weapon. That's what the army said.

God damn Shiloh. For everything.

Hall peered around the corner. Wozniak was nowhere in sight. Maybe he could take Wozniak from behind. One smack from the pistol . . . .

Moving was better than remaining still and sweating until Wozniak found him through a slow process of elimination.

Still no sign of Wozniak. Hall crept low and slow through the tables towards the shelter of one of the black columns. He moved among the large pots of jungle plants and the columns arrayed around the fountain's pool of red light.

No sound, except the gentle flow of water down the dark stone. No movement, no flash. Wozniak, who had smoked while he lurked in the rice fields of Vietnam and followed Backatya Boys who violated all of the laws of stealth, clearly could be a phantom when he wanted to be.

There were so many places to hide. Behind one of the food counters. Maybe the hotdog place. The Japanese takeout. The chili joint.

Or the florists cart. Or even behind one of the fake leather chairs. Or behind one of the large reddish vases, Wozniak's reptile head could be peering through the heavy green foliage and large orange flowers.

Hall kept moving, using the dark mirrors of the black columns to watch his rear, striving to avoid looking into his own thin face that looked so much as it had in Ap Thuy Tu. Except for the strain and worry.

If he could crush Wozniak's head with the empty Chinese pistol . . . would he finally make peace with the little girl who had come out in the lustrous Vietnamese night to pee in the shadow of the Black Virgin?

Hall moved into the pit and crawled among the fake leather chairs and coffee tables, moving ever closer to the fountain.

Then he was at the rim of the fountain's pool. The recessed lights bathed his right shoulder and arm and the Chinese pistol in their reddish glow.

Hall paused. An idea occurred to him. Could Wozniak be in the fountain, behind the tall black stone, watching silently as Hall moved around the pit? Moving slowly around the black stone to

231

keep it between him and his quarry? Hall listened for a disturbance in the pool. There was nothing except the fountain's flowing waters.

Until the explosive splash like the sudden eruption of a lurking crocodile whose unfortunate prey finally had edged close enough to the bank of a veldt's drinking hole.

Wozniak, who had pressed against the pool's edge in the water to set up his ambush, had had to guess at where Hall would be. Because of the pause Wozniak guessed wrong. He leapt out just ahead of Hall. Hall drove the pistol into Wozniak's rib cage as the killer's elbow jabbed harmlessly into the floor.

If the blow hurt Wozniak, he didn't show it. Spewing water, he spun away from Hall, faked to the right and then sprang back into the water.

Hall followed, chopping the air hard with the pistol. Wozniak was too fast and agile for him to connect.

Then Wozniak danced in the fountain, beckoning for Hall to pursue him.

Wozniak was in action. His eyes twinkled. His mouth grinned. He did nothing to indicate he had a weapon. Or that he feared Hall's pistol. Wozniak was quick to sense Hall's weakness.

"Go ahead. Shoot," Wozniak said. "Or did the lootenant forget his ammo? Piss poor planning makes for piss poor performance. You remember that one?"

Hall shifted the pistol to a throwing position.

"You're going to throw that gun at me? You do have your troubles, don't you, lootenant?"

Wozniak relaxed. His feet were about a foot apart. His arms hung loosely at his sides. He was about eight feet away when Hall threw the pistol at the center of Wozniak's chest. He followed, leaping at Wozniak from the side of the fountain's pool.

Wozniak simply turned sideways to let the pistol pass within a few inches of his chest. Hall saw but could do nothing as the pistol struck the fountain's black column. Wozniak continued his turn, Hall saw him spin, his torso and head leaning backwards. The heel of Wozniak's right foot arrived precisely at the same time Hall's flying body reached the spot where Wozniak's head should have been.

Hall felt his head jerk to the left as the karate kick landed on his temple.

Then he was in the water struggling to get up. Wozniak waited at the base of the black rock.

232

Hall's head was spinning. But he was able to stand. Wozniak grinned a few feet away.

"Don't worry, lootenant. I didn't bring a gun. I'd violate my probation if I possessed a piece. Besides," Wozniak grinned, "There are some things better done by hand. Don't you think, lootenant?"

Wozniak held his two hands at chest level as he spoke.

But it was his heel that would have shattered Hall's face if he had not jerked back from a second spinning karate kick.

Wozniak recovered easily. He was on his toes, dancing lightly back and forth in the shallow water. His open hands were before him in a relaxed fighting stance.

Hall would have to land a good punch or kick. He wouldn't have long. He couldn't let Wozniak set the rules. So he faked a high punch at Wozniak's face and kicked for keeps at his crotch.

Wozniak stepped away from the feint and struck Hall's leg with a stinging blocking cut with the edge of his hand.

Hall backed away. Wozniak danced in pursuit.

Until he got close enough to kick at Hall's knees.

Despite the water's drag, Hall pulled back in time, but Wozniak now was in close. Hall felt two painful punches in the chest and then Wozniak was spinning again. His elbow smashed into Hall's ear and he dropped into the water.

Hall flailed with his elbows, fists, knees and feet and rolled away through the fountain's shallow water.

Wozniak again was standing, dripping, grinning.

His mouth went into a pout, his eyes still twinkled.

"Lootenant, you're still disappointing me. Maybe a little boxing? Queensberry rules? Maybe you'd like to get your gun and throw it again?"

Saying nothing, Hall moved towards the black rock. Somewhere in the water was the pistol. There! His foot felt something.

"Be my guest," grinned Wozniak.

Everything is a weapon. Even an empty gun.

Wozniak exploded through the water as soon as Hall had the pistol in his hand.

Wozniak was close, kicking straight ahead this time. It was like a two-legged ballet kick, one foot high, the other low. Hall swung the gun at the high leg. Felt Wozniak's other kick sting a thigh.

233

Neither was intended to do any damage. Wozniak splashed away, taunting, "Come on, throw it, lootenant. Give me your best shot."

Hall circled in the water, holding the pistol like a hammer. "Show me . . . " began Wozniak. The chatter was the signal for Hall to awkwardly simulate Wozniak's spinning back kick. While Wozniak was able to kick at Hall's head, Hall would be lucky if he connected with Wozniak's knee . . . .

Wozniak drew back expertly from the kick and then moved in with a short punch that began at his waist. It was aimed at Hall's stomach. But the fist crashed into Hall's kidney because he had continued his spin. Hall was able to slash hard with the pistol as the pain began radiating up his back from his kidney.

Wozniak apparently had not expected him to slash with the gun. He had brought up a forearm in some automatic blocking kata. Hall missed Wozniak's head but caught the arm. Very hard. Wozniak grimaced and pulled his arm into his body. But not fast enough. Hall smashed it again with the pistol butt.

The gleam left Wozniak's eyes. Fool around time was over.

One foot suddenly and effortlessly kicked the pistol from Hall's hand. A low kick from nowhere caught Hall's right knee. Hall dropped helplessly into the water, unable to make his right knee hold his weight. The pain from the kidney punch now radiated throughout his back and down his legs.

And he was in the water. Wozniak's knee pinned him to the bottom. Hall's mouth and nose barely could suck in air.

That didn't matter anymore as he felt Wozniak's hand grab the shoulder of his shirt and then the hard bone in Wozniak's forearm drive into his neck to the left of his windpipe. More of Wozniak's Japanese martial art's games. On a more primitive level, Wozniak also was pushing his head beneath the water.

The pain was intense but final relief was coming rapidly.

Darkness descended. Hall saw the fountain's black rock shimmer through the water.

But then he was able to breathe again. Someone was slapping his face.

Hall opened his eyes as an open hand knocked his head sideways.

"This is it, you little fuck. I could kill you fast. But I want you to suffer. Wake up," hissed Wozniak through clenched teeth.

234

THWAAAAK!

The next blow from Wozniak's open hand made Hall's ears ring.

Then Wozniak's hands were on his neck and his thumbs pressed into his windpipe.

Hall swung a haymaker, which Wozniak ducked. The thumbs pushed harder. Hall felt his head being pushed beneath the water again.

He thrashed for his life but could not budge Wozniak.

And then it was as if he was drifting back into the muck of Ap Thuy Tu's wet rice paddies where he had choked after jumping from the APC. When he had begun to die. Where he had gone limp and where Wozniak had ceased shoving his face into the wet goo.

Another image returned from the descending blackness of the Vietnamese mud.

. . . . *The enduring coyote stalked closer, black lips curled up to black nose, canine teeth fully exposed, the crushing teeth visible. . . .*

Hall ceased struggling. How resourceful could the coyote be? How long could it hold on? The fingers pushed into his neck. The water covered his head.

Wozniak wasn't going for the ruse. His thumbs pushed harder. His arms held Hall's head against the fountain's bottom. Hall had milli-seconds of consciousness left . . . and no ability to roll, punch or kick.

Suddenly, Wozniak's fingers relaxed, perhaps as a test. Hall did nothing, the coyote ruled now in the mist of his remaining consciousness. Only the coyote could help now. . . . He could not move, not yet . . . . His head was pulled from the water.

"Jesus!" said a voice.

St. Peter? An angel? God? Wozniak?

"What a fucking wimp. You were a wimp in Nam and you still are," said the voice. "But now you're a dead wimp."

Hall felt the strong fingers loosen and his head was descending back into the water which distorted Wozniak's gleaming eyes . . . .

Wozniak had leaned forward for better leverage on his neck . . . .

The coyote moved suddenly and hard and fast. It was its last chance. Hall erupted from the water, his mouth open. His mouth felt

235

taut flesh.

Wozniak's neck.

Hall bit deep. The fingers released his neck. But fingers were pushing at his eyes and pulling at his hair. Hall punched hard. The distraction gave him a chance to loosen his teeth's grip on Wozniak's neck and take a deep draft of air. And the chance to take a harder, deeper bite.

Wozniak spun wildly in the reddening water.

Hall felt punches land. He bit deeper, using his arms to hold on and to protect his head and his grip on Wozniak's neck.

With the air rushing into his lungs, Hall felt clarity return. He had a solid hold on Wozniak's neck. But did he have the wind pipe? Could he tear it out? Did he have a death hold?

No. He had the side of Wozniak's neck. Somewhere nearby there would be a key artery -- like the one Wozniak's forearm pressed in his own neck only seconds before and nearly caused him to black out -- but Hall could not be sure he had it. Hall shook his victim like a pit bull that had seized a bigger, dangerous dog in a non-lethal throat hold.

Wozniak responded with a shriek. Not in pain. It was some kind of war or karate whoop. The lean coyote within Hall began a growl deep in his chest that rose to his throat.

In defiance, Wozniak emitted his whoop again, and flipped so that his feet were beneath him in the pool. Slowly he rose, his neck dragging Hall's weight from the water. Hall chewed at sinew and cartilage and skin, hanging by his teeth and using his arms to protect his canine hold.

Clearly indifferent to the damage it would cause his throat, Wozniak lowered his head and then suddenly jerked it upwards -- hard.

Wozniak's move worked. Hall felt his head and body fall back into the shallow water. He tumbled and spun away, rolling in the reddish water, waiting for the pain of Wozniak's knee smashing in his gut.

Hall darted through the water and rolled around, legs kicking and fists flying. They connected with nothing.

So he risked a fast look around.

Wozniak had leapt from the water, both hands at his neck. Hall scanned the reddish water of the shallow pool. He spotted the K-54, picked it up and, dragging his injured right leg, followed

236

Wozniak.

Despite his wound, Wozniak was moving quickly away from the pool. Hall followed as fast as he could. Could Wozniak still turn and attack with another array of sudden, bone-shattering kicks and punches?

At least he remained the pro in one respect. Wozniak pressed his hands against his neck to stanch bleeding as he retreated. To what?

Was he going for his ace in the hole?

He was. Wozniak reached into one of the large pots of jungle plants that separated the black columns at the border of the fountain pit. The one which Hall had laid his booby trap over the .38 pistol— whose bullets were in the basement utility room.

Hall splashed through the pool at Wozniak, raised K-54 held like a hammer.

Bring home the pressure. Now!

Wozniak's right hand reached deeper into the jungle leaves.

He was literally over the pot, his bloody fist deep into the thick jungle foliage.

Then Wozniak's head jerked back, violently. Another shriek. But it wasn't a warrior's shriek this time. It was fear.

The shriek meant Wozniak's plunging hand had struck the thin, transparent fishing line concealed in the plants. Wozniak would be feeling the terror any war veteran knows when a string goes slack.

Wozniak turned back to Hall because he knew. In an instant, free of the restraining jaws of the clothes-pin, the fish line released the powerful bent fiberglass portion of the Martin M1 Tiger bow and the thin-bladed, sharp Gerber stabbing knife lashed tightly to the released end.

Hall stopped, watching as the power of the fiberglass bow drove the knife upwards.

Through Wozniak's hand and into the bite wound on his neck. Hand pinned to his neck, Wozniak turned, staggered towards Hall at the fountain.

Wozniak's free hand joined his pinned hand. Together they tugged at the knife.

But Wozniak was mortally wounded and bleeding badly. His free hand could not free his wounded hand that was pinned deep into his neck by the Gerber blade. Blood flowed heavily.

Wozniak was at the fountain. Swaying. He gave up.

His free hand fell helpless from his neck. Hall watched Wozniak relax.

But Wozniak looked up and their eyes met. The luster and twinkle left forever as Wozniak's eyes dilated.

Enough life remained for Wozniak to see that Hall was watching him die. Wozniak used the last of his strength to turn abruptly away as he fell into the fountain's pool.

Wozniak was face down. The blood from his neck formed a fast flowing plume that moved with the gentle current toward the black stone at the center.

Hall remembered how he had used his weight and the flak jacket to push the Gerber stabbing knife into the little girl at Ap Thuy Tu and how he had stumbled away, refusing to look.

Hall sat near Wozniak at the base of the fountain, rubbing his knee. He watched the red plume flow, dissipate, disappear.

Shiloh, 1986

"Jeremy. It's good to have you back. Whatever you've been up to certainly seems to agree with you. You look great."

Hall looked up from his cup of foul tea with a coffee after-taste. It was Van Gelder's protégé from the Washington D.C. bureau talking. Van Gelder had brought him back to the city desk shortly before his death, probably to help set the stage for a newsroom slaughter.

The protégé had been the first to arrive at Hall's office when he returned to the paper and was reinstated as executive editor. The man desperately wanted to escape to Washington D.C. Hall planned to keep him close for slow execution.

"Thanks," smiled Hall. "I haven't had a long hike like that in years. It was good to get away and take a walk on the wild side."

"Have you given any more thought to my request to return to Washington D.C.?" asked the protégé, almost pleading. Other editors around the table looked at their notes or out the window as they awaited Hall's answer to the pathetic question.

"Can't spare you. I need your political savvy here now. Maybe we'll come up with something soon. Stand by," Hall responded, making no effort to conceal the menacing sarcasm in his tone.

He looked around the room at the new faces at the table for the daily story conference. It seemed a strange and alien place.

He had hired a new editorial page editor. She was a black woman who had been one of the top assistant editorial writers at the Atlanta Constitution. Instead of lurking behind his back with awful cigarettes as Van Gelder had, the woman sat at the conference table with the rest of the editors. She was intelligent and seemed intent on making the editorial page lively, interesting and relevant. The same promise Van Gelder had showed as a young man. Hall would wait to see if the Atlanta woman was as good as she seemed after she'd had time to burrow in.

Meanwhile, she seemed to be working out well with the staff, although many of the in-house candidates had expected to move up.

239

Hall had sent out the word that he wanted the woman to feel welcome. No one was giving him any lip. Hall wanted to bring in more new blood but the publisher had drawn the line at one. But because the publisher had wrongly dismissed him in absentia, Hall had the moral high ground, and planned to exploit it. Change would come—slowly.

Fisher's death also had required some shuffling of the in-bred crowd.

Overall, though, Hall thought he had a well-qualified group. He'd know better who needed to be whipped into shape at the end of the story conference, his first since his return to the paper.

"Everyone here? Fine, let's get started. What's good today?" Hall asked.

"Nothing much except the usual starvation, wars and ecological disasters," said the foreign editor, shaking his head.

Hall shook his head as well. "Anything good from anywhere else?"

He drew only blank looks.

"Persons. I've got a fucking paper to fill!"

The glances around the table were furtive and intimidated.

"All right. I've got some ideas. First, let's get someone started on a real takeout on homelessness," stated Hall.

The suggestion drew several tentative groans but no comment.

"What's the problem now?" asked Hall.

One of the assistant city editors finally volunteered, "That's been done up the ying yang. By us and everyone else."

Hall felt the menace return to his voice. "I still think it is a serious issue. We'll do it different and better. Rather than just interviewing the usual suspects, take the wallet, credit cards and car keys from one of the reporters and kick his -- or her -- ass out on the street for a few days. Take my word for it. The fight for a single meal, a dry place to sleep -- there's some real drama in that. Done right, it would make a hell of a yarn. And it better be done right," Hall said. Then he waited for the assistant city editor to groan again.

The subeditor just nodded.

Hall turned to the assistant city editor who rode herd on the cop and courts reporters.

"What do you have?"

"We've developed some more on this guy Wozniak," said the

ACE, Roscoe Levinthall.

Hall faced him squarely. "Let's have it."

"Well, you know he was apparently setting some kind of booby trap that misfired. It featured a knife set in a spring made from a piece of a hunting bow. He was rigging up an elaborate arrangement with a trip wire that ultimately was just barely held by a clothes-pin. One slight touch was all it took to release the string. Wozniak had been in Nam and I guess clothes-pins were used like that and, with a little wire and metal, as detonators of various types over there. A nice, homey touch. Anyway, he died when the knife cut right through his neck, severing nerves, veins, arteries -- you name it."

Levinthall waited, apparently to see if anyone would challenge his description of the damage inflicted by a sharp knife driven through a neck.

Hall gave Levinthall a "round'em up and move'em out" gesture.

"Lieutenant Buck is not sure who Wozniak was after. There were lots of lawyers, professionals of all types with offices in the Columbia Center. But that booby trap was nothing to fool with. That clothes-pin was restraining a hell of a lot of power."

"Go on," urged Hall.

"Buck checked his records. Wozniak had just gotten out of the pen in Kansas. Twenty-odd years before the penitentiary he had been some kind of dirty tricks specialist in Nam. Buck also found a .38 pistol in the pot with the trap. Wozniak's fingerprints all over it. No one else's. It gave Buck an idea."

Levinthall was warming to his task, clearly trying to let the suspense build. He paused and took a drink of his coffee.

"The idea?" demanded Hall.

"Buck went back to the earlier crime scenes -- Anne's, Ed's, the courthouse, Harry's apartment and the Vietnamese's folks' house and really searched the neighborhoods. In the vicinity of most of the murder scenes there was a hidden weapon, some with Wozniak's prints. Same with the hanger where Francis kept his plane. It appears this guy Wozniak's M.O. was to give himself an extra edge. A little surprise hidden in each place. He would apparently scout -- Buck calls it 'recon' -- in advance each place he planned to commit a crime and hide a weapon of some kind. They link him conclusively him to most murder scenes. Buck is still looking at a couple where they didn't find anything on the first pass. There is absolutely no doubt that he broke the neck of a guard at the Dark Tow . . . Columbia Center," said Levinthall.

"So it's all wrapped up -- Kanawha, Anne, Francis -- everyone?" asked Hall.

"Well, not tidily. But the cops are happy. They say every murder investigation leaves a few ragged ends. But Buck thinks this is cleaner than most. By the way, Buck sends his apologies for the all-points-bulletin he sent out on you. He says you should have called in occasionally while you were backpacking."

Hall nodded and began, "Let's move on . . . ."

But Van Gelder's D.C. protégé, apparently understanding he was doomed anyway, persisted, "What are the ragged ends? Any in Francis' murder?"

"Let's see," said Levinthall, consulting a paper before him. "Nothing striking about Van Gelder. I guess the loosest end was the fact that Wozniak's pistol was in the big pot. But the bullets for it were in a utility room with the rest of the bow and some props that Wozniak apparently used to look like a building employee so he could move freely around the Tower, recon the place, move the pot to bobby-trap it and so on. His fingerprints weren't on any of the stuff in the utility room except the bullets. So why was he making a booby trap over his own empty gun?"

"Why?" demanded Van Gelder's protégé.

"Buck thinks his intended victim was expecting a gun to be hidden in the pot. So he put an empty one in there, under the booby trap. Then the clothes-pin let fly a little prematurely," said Levinthall.

"What else?" demanded the protégé.

"He had a horrible wound on his neck."

"You said there was a knife in his neck," noted the woman from Atlanta.

"This was something else. The neck was too ripped to tell for sure. It was inflicted at the same time and place as the knife wound. But the pathologist said it was very ragged and torn. The wound was not very deep and certainly not fatal. It may have been part of the knife wound, like maybe Wozniak clawed his neck after he was stabbed. He did have fairly long nails and bits of his skin were under them. Maybe something or someone ripped his neck with teeth. It just isn't clear."

"Bitten? He was bitten?" Van Gelder's damn protégé again. "Why can't Lieutenant Buck find out if Wozniak was bitten? Bitten means someone else -- some kind of animal was there."

"Because," said Levinthall, "There was a lot of blood from the pot to the fountain. But nowhere else. Wozniak was in the water all night. The cops don't know why he staggered to the fountain after the knife stabbed him. But the water had changed and been filtered many times by the time the cops got there. The wound had been in moving water for hours. They didn't find anything. Something might have happened in the fountain but they don't know what."

"If he is a mass killer who just got out of the penitentiary, it seems very possible he could have had some nasty friends," suggested the Atlanta woman.

"No doubt about it," agreed Levinthall. "And it appears that since prison, Wozniak was supporting himself by ripping off drug dealers. Mr. Wozniak couldn't have had many friends in this city. In fact, I couldn't imagine anyone wanting anything to do with the man. He was an evil, cold-blooded murderer."

"Let's cut to the chase. Have the cops wrapped up the case or are they still looking for someone else?" The question came from the newspaper's new city editor, Shiloh Weeks.

Hall looked at her at the opposite end of the table. She directed the question at Levinthall. But she was looking right at him.

"Buck wishes all his murder cases fit so well into a box. The backtracking linked Wozniak's to this pile of bodies. They're moving on to other things. And there are plenty of other cases to work on. For example . . . . "

"Good," interrupted Hall. "Give us a story with all that in it. I'll put in on the front page, even though it is a crime story.

"Now. Let's talk about what's been going on around here? You people been doing any work at all? I go on vacation and come back and you tell me you don't have any enterprise work. If it wasn't for this Wozniak we wouldn't have anything local on the front page. What the hell is the matter with you people?"

Everyone again was staring at notes or out the window.

"I want answers or maybe I'll get myself editors who can give me some." Hall felt himself snarling.

Levinthall began, "Jeremy, it's been a tough time. Wozniak was murdering our colleagues . . . ."

Before Hall could respond Weeks interrupted.

243

"You're right, Jeremy. You've got a good staff here and we'll get the stories. Let's all get to work now. Thank you everyone."

The editors scurried for the door.

Weeks remained at the table, eyes locked on Hall.

When they were alone, she shut the door and walked behind him.

Hall felt her arms wrap around his neck, her face against his ear, the sweet scent of Poison . . . .

"What happened? That wasn't you," she whispered.

Hall buried his face in his hands.

"I don't know. I was so jazzed. Like this power, this animal was . . . just there. Had to be used. If I can take Wozniak, I wasn't taking shit from anyone. Not anyone. I couldn't help myself."

She rocked his body gently.

"It's all over now. It's all over forever, darling," whispered Shiloh.

Made in the USA
Charleston, SC
12 October 2013